JONAH

THE STYCLAR SAGA

JONAH

Nikki Kelly

FEIWEL AND FRIENDS

NEW YORK

For my mom—
without whom this story would never have been told

A Feiwel and Friends Book
An Imprint of Macmillan Publishing Group, LLC

Jonah. Copyright © 2017 by Nikki Kelly. All rights reserved.
Printed in the United States of America by LSC Communications US,
LLC (Lakeside Classic), Harrisonburg, Virginia.
For information, address Feiwel and Friends,
175 Fifth Avenue, New York, N.Y. 10010.

Our books may be purchased in bulk for promotional, educational, or
business use. Please contact your local bookseller or the Macmillan Corporate
and Premium Sales Department at (800) 221-7945 ext. 5442 or by e-mail
at MacmillanSpecialMarkets@macmillan.com.

Library of Congress Cataloging-in-Publication Data is available.

ISBN 978-1-250-05154-7 (hardcover) / ISBN 978-1-250-13189-8 (ebook)

Feiwel and Friends logo designed by Filomena Tuosto

First Edition—2017

1 3 5 7 9 10 8 6 4 2

fiercereads.com

Sometimes people deserve more.
Sometimes people deserve to have their faith rewarded.

—Batman
in *The Dark Knight*

PROLOGUE

IN THE BEGINNING, there were two.

The shimmering silver spilled as the Arch Angels passed through the fixed gateway. Eden took a deep breath, inhaling the scent of Earth's warm summer day as his bare feet patted down the fresh planes of green grass. He stepped from the apple tree's shade, and his white feathered wings rose up and out, fluttering against the gentle breeze.

Orifiel followed behind, turning up his nose as he entered the second dimension's atmosphere. The land underfoot was damp. Sometime before their arrival, water had fallen from above.

Mortals called it rain.

Cold, wet drops that came down from the sky.

And they drank it.

Water and food—mankind required both of these things to keep their fragile forms functioning. It was an unfamiliar concept to Orifiel. In Styclar-Plena, the crystal had not only created his world and the beings that inhabited it, but it sustained their immortal lives, too. The crystal's light was all he and his kind needed to survive and flourish.

Unlike humans, the Arch Angels' forms were not weak. Created in the crystal's image, their bodies were hard-wearing. Here, in the second dimension, Orifiel had yet to find anything that could scratch, mark, or damage him in any way.

There was only one thing that could penetrate an Arch Angel's suit of white armor.

Darkness.

True darkness.

The same that had fallen upon Styclar-Plena the day the crystal began to fail.

That day, a rift had appeared in his world—in the first dimension—and Orifiel had traveled through alone, finding himself in the second dimension—Earth. It was in this second dimension that Orifiel learned of a way to quell the darkness and to keep his world alive. By moving the clean, light souls of mortals that were released in death across the planes, he was able to refuel the crystal and keep the darkness at bay.

That was the day Orifiel saved Styclar-Plena.

The first of the last of days.

"Is it far from here?" Eden asked.

"No." Using the power of thought, Orifiel concentrated on the dipping branches and willed them to part. Here in the second, he preferred to touch as little as possible with his bare skin. The branches abided, and Orifiel pointed ahead, directing Eden away from the aging tree to a small clearing.

Eden hesitated, marveling at the red apples blossoming. He reached up and picked one. Taking a step forward, Eden, in quiet contemplation, pressed his thumb to the smooth, waxy coat of the sumptuous piece of fruit.

Hurried whispers came from the young of the land hiding behind the nearby bushes. The boy and the girl were well camouflaged, wearing fig leaves that covered the delicate parts of their naked bodies. They blended seamlessly into the setting as they spied.

Side by side, the Arch Angels continued on, the wind delivering the sweet scent of the roses growing from the ground.

"You like it here?" Orifiel asked.

"I do. What do you call this place?" Eden said.

"A garden." Orifiel cast his gaze all around. The rose stems here had no thorns, and he thought then that they were like the friend beside him. "Then I shall name this the Garden of Eden. A tribute to you, my dear brother, for all that you have done."

The children raced from tree to tree, following the winged beings, observing and listening to them with curiosity.

Eden smiled and, extending his hand, called out, "Come . . . tell me your names."

The children froze and then ducked down low, nervous and unsure.

"The boy goes by Adam. The girl, by Eve." Orifiel answered on the children's behalf, taking a moment to smile reassuringly at the pair in the shrubbery.

"You know them, and they you?" Eden asked.

"They are harmless. Same as the elder mortals, the young are ignorant. Mankind's understanding of things appears to be . . . *limited*." Orifiel waved his hand dismissively. "The first time I came to this second dimension, the boy saw me enter through the gateway, having taken shelter from the rain under the branches of the apple tree. He did not try to run and so I asked his name, and he gave it. He thought me to be a servant of the God of light and so referred to me as an Arch Angel. I did not correct his belief."

"A God of light?"

"Yes. Mankind worships the day and a God who commands their sun, for the light grows their crops. They fear the night and a Demon God they call Zherneboh, whom they believe wields the darkness."

"*Zherneboh . . .*" Eden repeated curiously. "And *Arch Angel*? You took the name Adam gave you and bestowed it upon us?"

"Yes, I rather liked it. The mortals here call their offspring 'descendants.' Fitting, it also seemed, to adopt that terminology for the Angels we are creating ourselves, given the human race inspired the solution to our population problem."

Eden nodded thoughtfully. "I am surprised the boy did not try to follow you through the gateway."

"I told Adam that this tree holds the knowledge of good and evil and that what glistens within its branches must go untouched by man and remain concealed by the apples that grow and hang low. I forbid the fruit from being picked so that the gateway would remain hidden from view. To make quite sure he listened, I explained that should any man or woman disobey my will, their God of night would be given a physical form and would deliver a terrible darkness, bringing about the beginning of the end of this world." Orifiel paused, searching Eden's expression. As he anticipated, Eden's lips turned down at the corners as he struggled to understand the concept of deceit.

"Hmmm . . ." Eden mumbled as he stroked the apple's skin. He was about to ask more on the subject when something unfamiliar caught his attention. Eden tipped his chin and focused intently. The nearby river whooshed and spat as it collided with a rock formation.

"They call that a river—a natural stream of water. There are objects—rocks—that block the water's passing, and the fight between the two causes that sound," Orifiel explained.

"The *fight*?" Eden said.

"To fight, to *battle*, is to try to *defeat* something. The river is one force and it runs, hitting the opposing force—the rocks. For the water to get past, it will try to go under, to go over, and to find holes and cracks within the object. The water is clever;

it seeks a path to get beyond what stands in its way. *To win the fight.*"

Words such as *fight*, *battle*, and *win* were new to Eden, and he sighed heavily. "We have so much to learn about this world; we must do so quickly when we relocate here."

Orifiel nodded, slowing his pace. He gradually fell behind Eden. Holding his hands behind his back, he rubbed his fingertips into his palms.

Searching the scenery, Eden paused. "Where is Malachi to greet us? I wish to see the structures he's created, to see our new home." Eden had no desire to leave Styclar-Plena, but he knew they must. It was not right to stay and continue as things were.

"He is not far. Come, walk with me a little longer." Orifiel didn't have to persuade his fellow Arch Angel to abide by his request.

Born into a perfect, peaceful world, the inhabitants of Styclar-Plena had never been exposed to things such as deceit. But unlike the other Arch Angels, Orifiel had frequented and explored Earth. He had seen the horrors this world had to offer firsthand. Horrors he had no intention of sharing with his kind, whom he wished to remain untouched and pure, just like their world.

Ahead, Eden came to an abrupt halt, startled by what appeared in front of him.

"Orifiel?" he said quietly. His wings fluttered as he observed the black fissure slicing through the air.

Orifiel stopped, too, and began to speak. "When I first traveled through the rift from Styclar-Plena, the gateway, as you know, became fixed. It seems the very moment I stepped across, another gateway opened and has also remained. But as you can see, it's somewhat different in its nature."

A cold chill crept up Eden's neck as he studied the dripping ink. "Where do you think it leads?"

"I don't think it leads anywhere." Orifiel paused. "The light from the crystal creates life on Styclar-Plena, and we now know that in our world, without the light, the true darkness takes its place, erasing that life. That gateway is black, nothing more than a void. I believe it to be death."

Eden glanced from the dark gateway to where Orifiel stood behind him, trying to comprehend what his leader was telling him. "Why has Malachi built our structures so close to something so *dangerous*?"

Orifiel's answer came swiftly: "Malachi hasn't."

"I don't understand." Eden turned around fully now, his back to the rift.

"I am sure that you don't. I am sad to say that today I am the river, and you, my friend, are the rock."

Eden shifted his weight from side to side. "You do not mean for us to leave Styclar-Plena, then? We are not relocating to Earth?"

"No, Styclar-Plena is our home. Our only home." Orifiel brought his hands forward, his knuckles cracking as he flexed them in readiness.

"But we cannot remain there. . . . The cry, it was so, so . . ." A tear formed and splashed down Eden's cheek. "We cannot continue. You heard it—"

"Yes, I heard it. And, like you, I know what it means. But it changes nothing."

"It does. It must. I will tell the others—" Eden retaliated.

"No. You won't. The Arch Angels are my people. Styclar-Plena is my world. You will not take them from me because you heard it *cry*." Orifiel brought his hands to his chest and willed a spark of light to form within his palms. "But I will bestow upon you something else you do not understand. *My mercy.* I will spare you from having to hear another second of that sound."

A white flame ignited, twisting between Orifiel's fingers as he entwined them together. Still, Eden remained fixed where he stood, unable to grasp Orifiel's intention.

Orifiel blew into the center of his palms, feeding the white flame so that it projected the energy forward. Parting his hands and flexing his fingers, Orifiel commanded the countless dazzling crystal spheres to form into a set of slender, spiral curves. "I don't suspect you have ever seen a serpent before." Orifiel's words were easy, and he willed the crystals to create a cluster at the end of the coils, manifesting into the shape of an arrowhead. Meeting Eden's eye, he finally said, "Good-bye, dear friend."

Orifiel clapped his hands together, and the crystal snake darted forward.

Startled, Eden stretched his wings and bent his knees,

preparing to jump, but he was too slow. The white inferno struck him above the eye, propelling his solid body backward, and the apple fell from his grasp, tumbling to the ground. Eden's wings wrapped around his form, covering his face and neck, as he flew through the air. His light rose to the surface, electrifying each feather and acting as a shield. But Orifiel did not need to strike Eden twice; the force of the first blow had catapulted him to the center of the dark gateway.

Eden whimpered, but as his dovelike feathers melted, stripping back to their liquid keratin base, the sound transformed into a shrill shriek. As his face, neck, and shoulders were pulled into the dark gateway, ink overspread his form, shaping black quills, which tattooed his skin. His body lurched backward, and his white cloak darkened to soot.

The twinkling serpent broke apart, dispersed into millions of microscopic crystals, and faded away.

The dark gateway rippled and then pulsed inward, swallowing Eden whole, before returning to the stagnant state it was in before Orifiel and Eden arrived.

Orifiel headed back the way he came, and the whispers from the children still hiding in the bushes fell quiet. Approaching the apple tree, he willed the branches to part and stepped toward the sparkling gateway. He took a moment to stretch his magnificent feathered wings, and a triumphant smirk crept up the left side of his face, as he believed that he had once again saved Styclar-Plena.

In fact, unbeknownst to Orifiel, he had sealed its doom.

Dipping his toe into the rift through which he'd arrived, Orifiel allowed the coolness to rush over his foot. Moments before the gateway took him, a quaking roar tore across the land. Orifiel twisted his neck in surprise. Through the foliage, a cloaked beast pointed its talons at him from the depths of the Garden of Eden.

The river and the rock.

In the end, there would be only one.

ONE

I WAS WEIGHTLESS IN THE WATER. There was nothing to be done now but wait for the tide to take me to shore.

Nothing happened.

Perhaps I had already washed up.

Perhaps I hadn't survived the journey to the third.

Perhaps I was dead.

As quickly as my thoughts turned over, so too did the realization that the word *I* had formed in my mind, and I knew then that I was still alive. In the nowhere, that empty space where I was trapped between life and death not long ago, I'd had to fight to comprehend the "I" that referred to my existence.

But I still knew my name.

Lailah.

I knew his name, too.

Jonah.

I struggled to see, but there was nothing *to be seen*.

Malachi had said that the third dimension existed in a state of cold, dark matter, which was nothing more than a void, just another version of nothingness. . . . But then, the Purebloods existed here as did their scavengers, so nothing had to be some *thing, some place*, surely?

And then I hit the rocks.

DISORIENTED, I was slow to react to the chill creeping up my neck. The ground was black ice, and I lay facedown, my cheek pressed against it. As I pushed myself up, my skin ripped, like Velcro being peeled apart. I flinched, but it was at the thought of it, not the sensation. Pain was a feeling I hadn't felt in so long it was almost forgotten.

It belonged to a girl who hadn't known her real name.

A girl who both sought out and hid from change.

A girl I'd said good-bye to.

Now, with my Angel and Vampire lineage joined in the perfect balance of light and dark, my gray being made me superior to anyone and anything to walk any of the worlds. No amount of darkness would be able to blind me from the truth of what was here.

And with that thought, the dark veil that shrouded my surroundings began to lift.

I bent my knees and stood, brushing an object as I did.

Caught off guard, I jolted backward on my unsteady feet

at the sight of a Pureblood Vampire. He loomed above me, his arm stretched out, with his razor talons pointed dangerously above curled claws. I raised my hand defensively, but a second later I realized he wasn't moving.

The Vampire was a statue, but he was no monument— he was a real demon.

At least he had been, once.

Present in body but not in mind, the Pureblood was frozen from the inside out—he had perished in this place.

I stepped around him, quick to continue on. Beneath my feet, the black ice shimmered like a dusting of stars in a night's sky. All around, there was nothing more than the same, just a landscape of freezing, dead rock. But as I followed a line of cracks and splinters running into the distance, out of the ground a tower grew, giant and magnificent in its perfectly cylindrical design. The same speckles twinkled along the tower's exterior, twisting all the way up the building's curves. There were no windows or doors, no joins or seams, no evidence that it had been constructed piece by piece. Instead, it appeared to be formed from only one material, as though it had once been a lump of clay molded into this.

Whatever *this* was.

A massive cloud sat static, covering the peak of the tower, and elongated raindrops fell from it like stringy tar. Each drop was collected in a moat that circled the base of the astounding structure. In the river, the liquid churned clockwise at a sluggish speed. Two shoots branched out from the moat, allowing the river to flow farther, but from here, I couldn't see where they went. Everything beyond the tower remained shrouded in shadow.

I shivered at the bitter cold running the length of my fingers, but my attention quickly refocused. High above me, the sound of rifts opening rumbled through the atmosphere, and in this former vacuum where sound could not exist, now it demanded to be heard.

I tried to make sense of it all.

Malachi, an old and wise fallen Angel, once known in Styclar-Plena as the Ethiccart, had told me to "bring the Arch Angels and the *worlds* they exist in to an end," implying that the Purebloods had once been Arch Angels. That they were the ones who had fallen through to the third dimension and then emerged as Pureblood Vampires; that it was not the fallen Angel Descendants, as Gabriel had once believed, who became Purebloods.

And Malachi had been right.

When I ended the Pureblood Emery, I was able to catch a glimpse of the form he once took—that of an Arch Angel—thus confirming what Malachi had said. I believed Malachi was also correct about the third dimension. Cold, dark matter might well be the makeup of this world, but whenever and however it had happened, a being created organically from the light of the crystal in Styclar-Plena—an Arch Angel—had ended up here and become the first Pureblood: Zherneboh.

After the Arch Angel arrived, this place that had once been a void wasn't one anymore.

As the rifts continued to form, the ground beneath my feet vibrated and then cracked. From over my shoulder, a rattle grew into a roar. Overhead, a round object flew out of the nothingness, tumbling over three times until finally it stopped midflight high above me. The creature's bulging throat weighed down its head, causing it to use care as it uncurled each bony limb. It rocked backward as though it were gaining momentum to catapult forward, but then stopped. The creature could smell me. It angled its face and then turned in my direction.

I would have met its eyes, if it had any.

A scavenger.

I had seen one before, and I knew the contents of what it was carrying—the dark energy released in death from a human in the second dimension. But for what purpose Zherneboh wanted it brought here to the third, I didn't know. I tried to focus on the space from which I'd heard the rumble of a rift opening, from where the scavenger had emerged, but I couldn't discern one in the darkness.

My instinct was to remain deathly still, but I had evolved beyond simple instinct.

I was no longer afraid.

I had given my life in exchange for Jonah's, balancing the universe's scales and equalizing out the equation. I hadn't come here expecting to be able to escape.

And with that thought in mind, as the scavenger plummeted and scuttled across the barren land heading for the tower, I followed. I looked to the moat, willing myself beside it, and with ease I traveled there by thought. I was perched next to its banks when, like a ball shooting out of a cannon, another scavenger whipped past my shoulder. It was moving so fast I expected it to collide with the tower, but an invisible force caught it midflight above the moat. The scavenger stopped and, curled tightly, began to ascend. As far as I knew, scavengers could not fly, but something was causing the creature to levitate.

As I searched for an answer, I realized that with every passing second that I was here—that I was accepting that *here* was in fact a place—the clearer my surroundings were becoming. Much like a photograph being developed in a darkroom, the image at the center was being exposed, allowing me to process the picture.

There wasn't just one lone scavenger being dragged up toward the thick cloud at the top of the tower, there were many. So many that I lost sight of the one I had been observing. The creatures were like magnets, each one being pulled in and up, narrowly missing the others that were dropping out of the cloud.

Next to me, a scavenger smashed into the freezing rock, causing a huge crater in the ground. It clawed its way back up to the surface, finally stretching out on all fours. This creature's throat was not hanging heavy, and it darted with superspeed across the land, sniffing the air in search of another rift.

I didn't understand what I was seeing. Why were the scavengers levitating up toward the cloud? And why was rain falling into a contained river?

It struck me then. I was thinking about this all wrong.

This wasn't Earth—this was the third dimension.

That was no ordinary cloud, rain, or river.

The scavengers collected the dark energy released in death from a human, and that dark matter left the human form in a plume of smoke. The scavenger's throat was no longer bulging because it was now empty; it had just deposited that very smoke into the cloud.

And now that gas cloud was releasing tarlike raindrops into the moat. Why? My train of thought was interrupted as my skin rippled with a sharp, scratching sensation. My hands were beginning to freeze from the cold. The cold . . . the cold . . . *this world existed in a state of cold, dark matter. . . .*

Just like my hands, the smoke was cooling in the freezing climate. Only it was a gas, and so it was turning into liquid form—into the tarlike rain. And the rain was pooling into the moat, running into the river, but where did the tributaries go? What purpose did they serve?

Distracted once again by the bitter sting on my skin, I tried in vain to shift my weight. My hands were weighed down at my sides, and I had to concentrate to bring them to my face.

I flexed my fingers, and one by one, they broke. Wanting to devour me whole, the frost was not satisfied with just a bite and quickly spread through my veins. I had to think quicker. Gabriel had always been able to control his temperature, and now I knew that the Angels commanded their gifts simply by using the power of thought. And so I closed my eyes and imagined the ancient fireplace in the derelict house in Creigiau. I recalled the stifling heat as the logs burned next to me, scorching my skin. I willed the warmth to move out from my chest and down my body, until my hands grew hotter and my palms sticky.

My bones healed, and I was able to move my limbs once more.

Now I had to make good on a promise. I'd made a deal with the universe to turn back the clock, to exchange my existence for Jonah's, and it was time to pay up. But if I was doomed to die here, then I would take this world and the Purebloods that inhabited it with me.

Speak of the Devil, and he shall appear.

"Zherneboh," I called.

On the ground, the scavengers stopped in their tracks. Every last one of them cricked their necks toward the sound of my voice.

But Zherneboh did not come.

I spoke his name again.

Still, he did not emerge.

I considered the moat of dark matter. It fueled the

Purebloods and their Second Generation Vampires. It even fueled me. This might be the third dimension, but on Earth, fuel was flammable, so maybe, just maybe . . .

Rubbing my hands together, I created some friction, generating the smallest amount of heat. The scavengers remained still, and as I regarded the hundreds of them before me, through the crowd one moved forward. Uncurling its spine, it stood upright, and though its shape was deformed, oddly, it resembled a person.

The scavenger had no eyes, but I was sure that it could see me. Maybe it was going to try to stop me? And then a strange thing happened. The creature tilted its head and, as though it were willing me on, nodded. I'd assumed that the scavengers had somehow been created here in the third, that they belonged to the darkness and knew nothing else. If they had been born here, then this was their home. Their task of moving the souls of mortals here would be their purpose. So why was this scavenger asking for death? Unlike me, he had a choice, and he was choosing to die.

Over the lone scavenger's shoulder, in the distance, the frantic flap of a raven's wings came into view. The scavengers dispersed, but the one in front of me stood tall and absolute. It yawned, dropping its jaw low and allowing the skin that covered its orifices to tear. Fleshy, slimy tentacles spat from the hole, but this time the scavenger was not trying to suck up dark energy, it was trying to speak.

I stepped forward. Reaching up, I put my hand behind the

scavenger's head and brought its face down toward my ear just as the raven swooped in a vengeful descent. The moment my skin met the scavenger's, the raven stopped. I hadn't intended to, but my will to hear the scavenger's message had been strong enough to distort time. The scavenger's slimy hand slid over the top of mine, and now its voice was crystal clear as it simply said, *"Please."*

The scavenger's appearance may have been one born of children's nightmares, but its sweet plea was entirely Angelic. I remembered something else Malachi had said to me then: "Things are seldom ever what they seem."

My eyes shone, and I was able to see through the scavenger's translucent skin, beyond the darkness that had consumed him, to the face of a young and beautiful being.

I knew then *what* the scavenger was. Sadly for him—for all of them—*who* they had once been was surely gone, lost forever.

I considered his request.

The scavengers did not take human life as the Purebloods did, they merely mopped up the remains, and the fact that this one was asking for death told me that this existence had not been its choice.

I would honor his now.

So to the fallen Angel Descendant, I replied in a whisper, "Be free."

TWO

THE FALLEN ANGEL LINGERED in the gray area between the past of what he was and the present of what he had become, and it was in that suspended state that I saw his smile. Having heard his plea to free him from this world, I let my hand fall from his and began to summon a glow from within me to fulfill his request.

But the moment my skin left his, time resumed.

Not as it should. It did not simply "play" but began to fast-forward, moving at rapid speed, while I was held on pause. The raven returned, spreading its wings wide over the once-fallen Angel's shoulders and sinking its jagged claws into his back. The raven retracted its talons, and liquid from the Angel's perforated form spewed onto the ground, merging with the black ice. As the last drop of dark matter drained from the fallen Angel, he froze and turned into sparkling stone.

The raven rose high in the air and then darted forward, smashing through the statue, obliterating what remained of the fallen Angel, including his smile, which fell away only when he had turned to dust.

The raven beat its wings one last time before it shape-shifted into a form I was familiar with: that of a Pureblood.

The glow I had been summoning rose to my surface, and as it electrified through to my fingertips, I was brought back into sync with the speed of this world.

My gaze fixed on the Pureblood and the protruding lesion above his eye that marked him as one particular Pure-blood: the Devil, Zherneboh.

With everyone I cared about safe in the second dimension, I didn't hesitate in preparing to destroy all Zherneboh had created, myself included.

I wouldn't even pause to take a breath; I had already given my last for Jonah.

I was ready.

In the second dimension, embracing my gray being had made me untouchable, but here in the third, I would need to divide if I were to conquer.

The only way I knew how to rid a room of darkness was to turn on a light. And so I called on my Angel abilities and flipped my inner switch. Bolts of lightning left my fingertips, joining together and amassing into a single sheet. But Zher-neboh anticipated my action. As my light rushed forth, his almighty force met it. Like an elastic band, my light snapped back and propelled me away. I stopped speeding through the air only when my back hit the invisible shield above the moat of dark matter.

Then I knew what had levitated the scavengers. I knew because I felt it. A pulley system began to drag me up, and no matter how hard I struggled against it, still I rose to the gas cloud above. Scavengers plummeted past my face, dropping one by one to the ground far below me, on the "down" side of the pulley that I was now riding up. As they met the black ice, they scurried away from Zherneboh, who towered above them. He followed my assent with his steadfast stare, while I remained ensnared by silk strings I could feel but could not see—a fly caught in a spider's web.

Zherneboh lifted his arms, and his cloak billowed below as he began to levitate all of his own accord. I'd entered his house through the front door, but not as the girl in shadow. She was gone. I was in control of my own soul. He couldn't command me to do his bidding, which would leave him with one choice. The same one that Orifiel had been working toward since the day I was born—killing me.

He did not rush himself as he climbed higher to meet me, content perhaps that I was trapped. He reigned over this world; here, he held the home advantage.

But as I neared the cloud, a prickle of heat danced across my hands. Zherneboh may have caused my sheet of light to recede, but he hadn't snuffed it out completely. Like the yellow flame at the end of a sparkler, my glow, though reduced to a flicker, still crackled.

You only need a spark to start a fire. . . .

A smile twisted at the edge of my lips. Concentrating, I shot embers from the tips of my fingers. They hit the threads trapping me, sending an electric current through them.

In the blink of an eye, Zherneboh was level with me. But my thoughts were faster than his flight.

I added fuel to those embers and flames shot up, down, left, right. All around me, the web I was stuck within lit up, with me beaming in the middle.

Zherneboh fixed his eyes on my own, but I would not be distracted. My entire body warmed, the blood in my veins beginning to bubble, and I fanned the flames with the power of thought.

Rings of white light manifested one by one, starting at my ankles, encircling them like cuffs. More rings appeared in succession up my body—from my calves to my thighs to my waist and, finally, to my chest, where the halos spun with super-speed, multiplying and intensifying into blue blazes of heat. By the end, my torso and my every limb were surrounded by deadly rings that spun, waiting.

Once again, I was the witch and this world was my pyre, but I needed it to burn out before I faded away.

The pulley system continued to draw me up, but the

invisible threads began to lose their integrity. My white and blue flaming rings whipped across and melted the silks, which began to drip. As the searing heat intensified, the threads began to snap, and bit by bit, they fell into the moat below.

I willed my rings of fire to spread, and high above me, my electric flames soared, meeting with the peak of the tower hidden within the gas cloud. Pieces of the tower enshrouded in charged rings of light spiraled down, smashing into the frozen rock below.

The tower must have housed the mechanism responsible for churning the liquid in the moat, for as the structure began to break apart, so too did the dark matter in the moat stop moving.

Though the pulley began to disintegrate, I tried to hold on to the strings keeping me in place. I needed to stay here. It was only from this vantage point, high above all that existed in this plane, that I could destroy it. The energy to maintain my rings of light was exhausting me, but still I kept on.

Both the moat and its two tributaries caught fire. The explosion blasted through the riverbanks, revealing what had been previously hidden.

The river was actually flowing out in the shape of a star. A star now ablaze. At each of the five points stood smaller versions of the tower behind me. But as the dark matter boiled at each of their bases, halos of light rushed up the cylindrical structures, only disappearing from view when they met with the gas clouds that hung atop their peaks. One by one, they began to cascade like waterfalls of oil.

The world around me was falling to its knees.

The threads I was clinging to were about to give, but one final push was all it would take. I just had to find it in me to give it.

The only motivation I needed was straight in front of me: Zherneboh.

He must have known then that I had no intention of trying to escape. Despite the halos spiraling around my body, he came in close. Grabbing the back of my head, he squeezed his thumb against the corner of my eye, his skin meeting mine.

My body stalled, and the halos became stationary. His negative energy was attracting the positive charge of my electric light, pulling it up toward him. The rings reabsorbed back into my skin, and my insides began to sizzle as Zherneboh's touch drew them up through my veins.

Like a lightning rod, he was pulling my strike to one single spot, preventing me from ejecting any more of the charged particles through the web.

But just because he was drawing out my light, it didn't mean I had to let it be smothered by his darkness when it reached him.

It was my decision; I could still choose to burn.

And burn I would—bright and brilliant.

I would not falter.

But then Zherneboh cried out. Only it wasn't the same cry

I'd heard leave him on Earth. This cry did not belong to him. Never had I heard such a terrible sound. It surrounded and then engulfed us both, binding Zherneboh and me together with one single note. I spilled bloodied tears as I wheezed, but without knowing why. And as the note emanated from him, through me, I met Zherneboh's eyes, which for the first time told me a story.

The only story he had to tell.

One of rocks, rivers, and *revenge*.

The Devil was appealing to my duplicity.

I realized then that he was attracting my light to him, to buy him time to persuade me—not command me—to do what he had created me for: to end Styclar-Plena and to deliver Orifiel to him in the second dimension.

But then, from somewhere inside me, a tremendous thud hit my chest.

It silenced the cry and released my gaze from Zherneboh's.

The explanation of where the cry originated would remain a mystery. I was left ignorant of its importance and the rest of the message Zherneboh was trying to share, the reason he was at war. Without it, my resolve would not be weakened.

My rings of white light looped around one another like an atom, creating a bomb inside me.

Zherneboh knew what was coming.

The tangled threads frayed and disintegrated, but Zherneboh kept me suspended, struggling once again to im-prison my gaze. Charged light rose within me, dragged toward

Zherneboh's opposing force like a magnet. Zherneboh shook me violently as though he was trying to make me see sense, but as my head bobbed back, what I saw instead was a change in the previously dark sky. Swirling ribbons of luminous oranges and greens twisted like streamers on a curtain of red, creating the most beautiful aurora.

I was humbled that even here in the depths of Hell, I was gifted a glimpse of the heavens beneath which I would fall into my final sleep. . . .

But just then, the thud that had hit my chest and silenced the cry returned, stronger and louder than ever.

It came in bouts of three.

Trump pump.

Trump pump.

Trump pump.

The beat of a drum.

I remembered the bonfire erupting in the garden of the Henley house, how it seemed to melt the entire world around me. And a lone soldier was marching, calling out through the darkened wasteland. Calling out for me.

The scene below me unfolded in slow motion.

The star was smoking, the towers that had stood at its points had become molten, and a blazing ball of blue flame glided, forming a circle around the outside of the five points, connecting the rivers together.

Making his claim to this world, Zherneboh's signature

swirled below me, spelling out his name in the form of an inverted pentagram.

Tens of thousands of scavengers flung themselves at the riverbanks, dismembering one another's limbs in a frenzied fight to drink the fueling substance before it evaporated. Nearby, the frozen Pureblood with whom I had been faced was obliterated as yet more scavengers charged. But against the glow of the orange hue, I was enlightened. As I sought out the soldier I could hear but not yet see, I came to understand the meaning of the cloud, the rain, and the rivers.

On Earth, the Purebloods drank the blood of mortals with dark souls. From this blood, they would extract the dark matter that sustained their forms and grow their power when they were in the second dimension. But here in the third, they had created a never-ending supply. The science, the engineering, and the architecture all around me, manipulated and constructed, to create one thing . . .

A sea of souls.

And as I observed every last inch of Zherneboh's masterpiece, I convinced myself that far below me, there was nothing but death.

Just like the memory of the bonfire, I thought the beat of the drum was imaginary.

But then, there it was again.

My eyes searched the grounds below until . . . through the destruction and chaos, I found him.

To this being left behind, this lone soldier far below, I must have shone like a beacon—someone in the nothingness.

The figure, illuminated by a flare over his shoulder, strode across the barren landscape. The hood around his head slipped down, and he stared up, his eyes finding mine.

"Jonah," I whispered.

The rumble of the rifts continuing to open silenced all sound. The light within me rose, heating Zherneboh's hand, which was still pressed to the back of my head. If I was going to end the Purebloods and their world, I had to do it now, before they were able to escape through the rifts. But Jonah was down there, and he would be ended, too. I'd sacrificed myself to save him once, but to do it again, I would have to sacrifice the lives of the many I might save by not killing Zherneboh along with this world.

Jonah's was but one life. One life in exchange for the many—*the greater good* . . .

But sometimes it's for the good of the great.

And to me, there was no one greater than him.

Zherneboh and I were magnets, getting too close. In my neck, my veins swelled and splintered as my light—my internal bomb—rode up the side of my cheek. Drawn to Zherneboh's clawed thumb, luminous stripes forked before flashing out of my left eye. A flare struck him, sending an electric shock down his hand and arm.

I screamed.

Static crackled in my left eye as my sight was taken with

that single sheet. Zherneboh fought to pull away, and I had to work hard to stop my light from leaving me. I had to get Jonah out first, even if it meant letting Zherneboh escape.

Finally, Zherneboh was able to break the connection, and he retracted. His form shifted into that of the raven once more, and he swooped. Springing from my shoulders, he used me as leverage to gain traction. The force sent me into a spin, and I somersaulted as I fell. The flight of the raven blurred across my impaired vision as it headed toward the dispersing cloud that had surrounded the peak of the main tower.

Unable to see light against light, the Arch Angels were unaware of the rifts between the first and the second dimension. And here in the third dimension, despite being able to hear them, I hadn't been able to see the dark rifts opening against the black. But now with an arc of autumn color swirling in the backdrop and no structure concealing it, the fixed gateway to the second was revealed.

Without Zherneboh's force attracting my own, my electric energy stopped rising and fizzed, waiting for me to detonate or disarm.

At first, I drifted like a leaf riding the breeze, a part of the autumn, but all too soon the wind dropped. I plummeted toward the smoking moat below me with no threads left to grab onto.

But I didn't need them.

The same as always, Jonah was there to catch me when I fell.

He leaped through the air and met me, so when we landed on the bank of the moat, I was pressed into his chest. Jonah planted his feet firmly into the ground, placed his chin to my forehead, and, with a sigh, murmured my name.

Smoke swirled around us, but Jonah tightened his arms around me, keeping me safe at the center of the cyclone.

"Up there," Jonah said with a heavy breath.

Squinting, I peeked up from my refuge. High above us, and stretched out across the spectacle of luminous greens and burnt oranges, was the fixed gateway. A way home—but only for Jonah.

I had to finish what I'd started.

I locked Jonah's arms in mine, and together we levitated into the air. I couldn't risk meeting his eyes; I knew how easily they could change my mind. So when he rested his chin back on my forehead, I let him.

In line now with the fixed gateway, the world below us smoked in ruins, but it could be rebuilt. I had to destroy what was left and seal the rifts once and for all.

I delayed, indulging myself for a final time by breathing in Jonah's fragrance. Then, without warning, I thrust him away from me, aiming for the middle of the gateway. But as his arms slid down mine, he snatched my wrists and tugged me back to him.

My hesitation had been warning enough.

I opened my mouth to speak, but I didn't have to explain

myself. He knew me too well. Raising his finger to the middle of my lips and shaking his head, he quieted me.

"No, Lailah." His eyes were the windows into his soul, and he dared me to peer inside, where, stripped bare, was his truth. "You stay. I stay. We live or we die together. There is no in between."

Taking my hands up in his, he placed them on his chest and the *trump pump* of his heartbeat sounded in time with mine. "I always get the last word, do you understand? *Always*."

It was nonnegotiable. He wasn't leaving without me.

And so I willed my atom bomb to break apart and for the rings of light to disperse. I threaded my fingers through Jonah's; and without a word, I led him back home.

THREE

THE DARK GATEWAY SUCKED US IN, only to spit us back out into black.

I barely noticed.

In the shadows, I ripped my hand from Jonah's. I smacked it to my left cheek, trying to quash the simmering sensation that was vibrating under my skin. Dizzy and disoriented, I dropped to my knees.

"Lailah," Jonah said, bending before me and squeezing the tops of my shoulders.

I couldn't see him. My vision was blurred. He tried to pull me up, but I was too unsteady. I crumpled onto all fours. I tried to claw my way forward, but my feet slid underneath me, and I hit a rectangular stone that rose up from the ground. Exhausted, I crawled on top and turned onto my back. I fought to find balance inside and out.

I possessed the abilities of both Purebloods and Angels, which made me more powerful than either race. By embracing my gray being, the mix of the two that lived inside me, I had set myself apart from the Purebloods and the Angels. This had allowed me to end a Pureblood here on Earth, but in the third dimension, I had to divide myself—to separate out the lightness from my Angel side—to stand a chance of defeating Zherneboh. But that meant the current of electric white light that had shocked him had also shocked me—my own dark side—and the damage was still sitting on my skin here in the second.

I took a deep breath as I stared at the rock above my head. The rift through which we'd entered the second had churned us out into a cave that shimmered like stars, just the same as the rock in the third had.

"Zherneboh . . ." I warned in a raspy voice. The Pureblood had left through the gateway only minutes before Jonah and I, which meant he couldn't be far.

"No, there's no one here. I'll get you out and into the sun in just a second," Jonah promised.

My stomach rumbled in response to the word *sun*, as it had when I still had a hunger for sustenance in the form of food. I'd depleted most of my light energy, and Jonah knew I needed to refuel. I realized then how dangerous it was to split my soul in two. I needed to retain my balance of light and dark, not only to fuel my body but also to remain a greater force than my enemies. But then, when I'd made that choice, the state of my soul hadn't concerned me; I'd had no intention of returning to the second. I should have been dead by now.

The scrape of heavy stone fighting against flint was as cruel to my hearing as a knife dragging across a bottle. But for every second it sounded, with every inch Jonah shifted the stone above my head, more sunlight cascaded in, stretching ever nearer to where I lay, until finally I was bathing in sunlight.

I no longer wore around my neck the ring that housed my crystal. I had left it for Gabriel. It didn't matter. I didn't need it. My skin warmed as a golden hue surrounded me. The sunlight sank through my skin, absorbing at superspeed, feeding my soul. Twinkling crystals exuded from my body as I basked in the sun's rays. Then, with a whoosh and a burst of light, I stopped glowing.

The light merged with my darkness, and once again, my soul was painted gray.

My vision was still hazy, and it took me a moment to realize that Jonah had taken himself out of the way of my light and was waiting aboveground. Now that we were out of immediate danger, half of me expected him to reappear, shouting, blasting me for undertaking a suicide mission. The other half hoped he might take me in his arms and tell me that he had come for me because he loved me, not because he couldn't bear to be alone in the darkness.

Staring down at me from what was now a rectangular hole above my head, Jonah reappeared, his lower lip parted from his top, but no words came out.

"Jonah?"

In a flash, he was kneeling down at my side, and as he pulled me up into a sitting position, he said, "It'll be all right."

I shook my head, confused.

Jonah's Adam's apple bulged as he swallowed, and he helped me up from the stone slab. Visible only because of the glow of the sun spilling in, to my far right the fixed gateway to the third dribbled with black ink.

The stone Jonah had shifted to allow the sun inside acted as an exit. I bent my knees and sprang up high, landing outside in a catlike position. Shadowed stripes crisscrossed over my skin as daylight strobed through wilting tree branches. The ground around me was covered in a carpet of leaves. They lifted in the bitter breeze, twirling, before scattering through the air.

Gabriel had told me that the fixed gateways to the third and first dimensions were both positioned in Lucan, Ireland. And here on the Emerald Isle, it was fall, but it had been winter when I'd left through a rift in England. The shift in season didn't make sense.

I inspected the world around me, searching for clues.

The aged tree the leaves had fallen from stood centrally, raised up as though it were a monument. The land around it sloped dramatically from either side of its enormous trunk. A thin, light dusting of discolored topsoil spread as far as I could see. There was no grass nor any other plants; it was as though nothing else could grow here.

The structure we'd been catapulted into, housing the gateway to the third, was buried deep in the ground. It appeared to be constructed from the same material that made up the landscape of the third dimension. Cold, dark matter. Manipulated, presumably, by a pureblood.

The heavy hunk of rock concealing the gateway had been cut to resemble a tombstone, one only visible from this exact angle and positioned in a concerted effort to disguise what lay beneath it. Strange, I doubted a Pureblood would care.

In the distance, the land rounded off into a point. I strode toward that cliff's edge, gesturing for Jonah to stay. I needed time to collect my thoughts.

With my failure to destroy the third, nothing had changed since I went through the rift that morning. The Purebloods had survived me, same as I had survived the third, meaning no ground had been lost on either side. The only difference now, perhaps, was that I understood what Zherneboh wanted, and, to a degree, why he wanted it.

Anger twisted in the pit of my stomach. Everyone I loved would be safe now in a world without the Purebloods if Jonah had just listened to me when I'd told him not to follow. It was my choice to exchange my existence for his, a decision he hadn't respected. Worse still, I owed the universe a debt. And

I expected that when the universe came to collect, it would want interest.

A part of me wished to forget all this, but all this was a part of me. And there was no escaping any of it.

Because of him, I had failed.

Because of him, the Purebloods were free.

I glanced back at Jonah. As our eyes locked, a thought— no, a *feeling*—surfaced that didn't belong to me, at least it didn't belong to me yet. . . .

Because of him, I was afraid.

Unnerved, I rubbed my bare arms. Jonah had stolen my ending, and in doing so, he'd taken me straight back to the beginning. What was I supposed to do now?

At the cliff's edge, I stared up at the sky, silently searching for an answer. Below me, waves whistled as they lapped at the base of the cliff, the river working hard to wear down the rock.

And, like the river, the answer was clear. I had no choice; I had to start all over again.

I turned and faced Jonah. His huge hazel eyes drilled into mine, refusing to leave me as I circled back to him. As I watched him watch me, a cold tingle came over me as though someone were walking on my grave.

In an all-too-familiar fashion, the scenery around me began to warp, and I halted.

As though an artist were sketching an outline with charcoal, shapes were drawn against the autumn backdrop, morphing, one by one, into ghostlike silhouettes. Faceless bodies smudged together in small clusters, dotted around the oak tree's roots, ready to be colored into life.

The clouds above drifted and the river still whistled, but everything stretching down from the cliff's edge was still, simply *waiting*. The only thing untouched by the changing picture was Jonah, who remained with his foot perched atop the tombstone, regarding me with a puzzled expression.

Over my right shoulder, my name sounded, and I twisted around.

The scenery bounced.

I became unsteady as, outside my own skin, I watched myself begin to fall.

Just as in a dream, I woke before I hit the ground.

I knew immediately what I'd been given: a window in time. A vision, one not of the past but of the future. I swayed in place. It was oddly serene.

It was so quiet.

It was so still.

I heard her before I saw her. Screeching Jonah's name, she disturbed the tranquillity and yanked me back to reality.

The carpet of leaves sprang into the air as fast feet tore over them. She leaped onto Jonah's back, her arms meeting around his chest as she clung to him tightly.

Brooke.

Relief coursed through me. *She was okay.*

When Brooke had fled with Fergal, he was near death, despite my best efforts. I doubted he had survived. Despite his double-dealing and carefully crafted deceptions, I knew Brooke loved him, and I worried how she would cope if he died.

I had started toward Brooke when the smallest change in the flow of the river below caught my attention. I leaned back, and though the water undulated, whatever had caused it was now gone.

I made my way over to Jonah and Brooke.

"Lailah!" Brooke said, sliding off Jonah's back. Stopping just short of hugging me, she glanced at Jonah instead.

"What are you doing here?" I asked, not giving any consideration to her hesitancy.

"I sensed Jonah and came straightaway," she replied, tucking the wayward strands of her red bangs back into her purple beanie.

"Straightaway?" I said, confused. "The fixed gateway opens in Lucan."

"Yeah," she replied. "That's where we are."

"I know, what I don't understand is how you got here so fast." The rift Jonah and I had traveled into the third from originated in Henley. With the Irish Sea to cross, even with her Vampire abilities, she couldn't have arrived here in Lucan in a matter of minutes.

"After you disappeared, we moved here." She punched Jonah in the arm. "Thanks for leaving me, by the way."

"I didn't leave you for long," Jonah said, scraping his hand through his messy dark hair.

Before I had a chance to interject, Brooke replied, "Three

years might seem a drop in the ocean when you're immortal, but a gal gets hungry! Thank feck, I learned how to feed before you did one."

"*Three years?*" Jonah and I repeated in unison.

"Yes, three years. You won't believe what's been going on here, the world's gone mad," she enthused, as though she had the biggest piece of gossip that ever existed.

But before Brooke had a chance to tell us anything, heavy footsteps sounded, and all three of us turned in the direction of Ruadhan's voice, which met me before he did. "Little love."

I jumped as burly arms pulled me in from the side. It was then that I realized I hadn't seen Ruadhan in my peripheral vision. He patted and then rubbed my back in a circular motion before parting from me. The lines around his mouth smoothed out as his smile receded, and his bushy eyebrows dipped.

I stroked my eyelashes with my fingertips. I couldn't see anything out of my left eye, and long, lumpy lines ran the length of my cheek. Now I understood why Jonah had tried to reassure me and why Brooke had hung back.

I kneaded my fingers into my skin and began to tremble. Jonah was quick to tug off his hoodie and wrap it around my shoulders.

"It's cold," he said, using the weather as pretext. He gripped my wrists, guiding my hands through the sleeves in a bid to stop me from clawing at my face any further.

Just as Jonah was about to slide the zipper up, the leaves that had been blowing around us dropped to the ground simultaneously. The river stopped whistling as though it had run out of breath. It was as if here on this hillside, unexpectedly and without warning, everything just died. Even Brooke, who had been shifting her weight impatiently, desperate to bend our ears with her chatter, said nothing.

Ruadhan was the first to break the eerie silence. "We best be on our way."

Jonah turned toward the hole in the ground. "I should move the tombstone back—"

"Lad, there's not enough time," Ruadhan said, cutting him off. "Come." He then curled his hand over mine, looking from left to right as if we were father and daughter about to cross a busy road. He stepped out first, a protective action that calmed me, and I squeezed the hand of the person who never let me down, thankful that he remained a permanent fixture in my life.

Dust rose into the air as we sped away, leaving the tree's lost leaves, the river, and the rock to watch as we departed.

FOUR

WE DIDN'T HAVE TO RUN FAR. Ruadhan led us down the hill through lush gardens at the back of a church. We followed the roadside for three miles, stopping just short of a detached house.

I let go of his hand and quickly backed up, bumping into Brooke as I tried to avoid being seen from the house's windows.

"Sweetheart?" Ruadhan said. He straightened his trench coat, and then ambled after me.

"He's in there, isn't he?" I said, standing on tiptoes to peek over the hedge bordering the front lawn.

Ruadhan smiled gently. "Yes, love. He'd have come to see . . . Well, he'd have come to meet you himself, but he can't keep up like he used to."

It took me a moment too long to realize what that meant. "Brooke said we've been gone three years."

"Aye."

"*Three years,* Ruadhan, and Gabriel's still fallen?"

Ruadhan nodded. "He's been waiting for you. I told him to prepare . . . that it was conceivable that you might not be able to return." His small grin creased his cheeks.

"What?"

"I should have remembered that Gabriel's being wrong is the exception, not the rule. He told me *you*, Lailah, have always been inconceivable, that you make the impossible possible." He stroked his stubble thoughtfully. "Belief is a powerful thing, and his belief in you never wavered, not for one second."

Ruadhan delivered this news as though it was something I would be pleased to hear, when, in fact, he couldn't have been more wrong. I hadn't wanted Gabriel to wait for me. I'd let him go, hoping he would do the same. The conversation we'd shared before I went back in time, in which I'd spoken this intention to him, was one I remembered well, but for Gabriel, it had never happened. In the end, the only message he had received from me was short and without explanation. Worse still, Jonah was the one who had delivered it. But then, even if the words had left my lips, I'm not sure Gabriel would have listened. One thing I had come to know about him was that he'd never found a reason good enough to give up on me. Evidently, in the last three years, that hadn't changed.

"Love, he'll be waiting," Ruadhan said. "They will all be waiting."

"The Sealgaire?" I didn't need Ruadhan's confirmation. We were in Lucan—this was their home.

I breathed in as I studied the sizable brick house. A lawn with pretty flower beds bordering a wrought-iron fence spread out in front of the property. A paved path stretched up to a porch decorated with planters on either side of the royal-blue door. The lion's-head knocker could not have been less inviting—and it wasn't because it was made of silver.

"Before we do anything else, we should talk," Jonah said, coming up beside me.

The front door opened before I could answer Jonah's request. Gabriel set foot on the porch, and his eyes locked with mine.

My lips pulled in a tight line, and I battled to retain my composure at the sight of him. I had made my choice; letting Gabriel go was just the first of many. The decisions I would continue to make would no longer include him. They couldn't. Not as long as I wanted him to live and not as long as I wanted him to be free.

I bowed my head as Gabriel rushed toward me. Without a word, he wrapped his arms around the small of my back, bringing me in close. His cheek pressed against the top of my head as his fingers threaded through my short hair.

I didn't pull away immediately. It was strange. Somehow, he didn't feel as he used to. Maybe it was because that citrus aroma that I had loved so much hadn't just diluted, it had disappeared. Maybe it was because he didn't sound as he used to, either. My ear was against his chest, and his heartbeat was not as I remembered it.

Or maybe the thing that was truly different was me.

My arms were pinned to my sides. I knew I was cold and empty beneath him; he knew it, too, as, with reluctance, he parted from me.

"Come, let's get you inside. Let's get you both inside," he said, offering Jonah an almost respectful nod.

I lifted my chin, and Gabriel did a double take.

"Lailah! What happened to you?"

Once again, he reached out for me, and I withdrew, shaking my head.

Jonah stepped in front of me, protectively placing his arm across my chest. "What happened is that you sent her to death's door, and she was happily knocking on the damn thing when I found her."

Gabriel's faded blue eyes left mine, and he turned his attention back to Jonah.

"Don't," I said. This was one fight I had no interest in being at the center of.

Jonah relented. "It doesn't matter what happened; all that matters is that she's here. That she's still alive."

Ruadhan shuffled me forward. "Come, let's go inside, as Gabriel suggested."

I followed Ruadhan through the gate, and we walked

around the outside of the house, making our way from the front to the back garden. Jonah and Gabriel trailed us, and Brooke, unusually, hung back, quiet.

"We don't tend to go into the main house—that is, Brooke and myself," Ruadhan said.

"Not Vampire-friendly?" I replied. Although I was blind in my left eye, the sight in my right was still sharp enough to detect the glint of silver weapons hidden within the gardens. I especially liked the creative use of the unassuming, decorative garden gnomes. Though they appeared innocent, they had murder on their minds; each one was molded around deadly silver saber claws.

"Not in the least," Ruadhan said.

At the end of the backyard, behind the fence, was a field upon which sat the Sealgaire's home away from home, in the form of their large, well-equipped motor home. Positioned seventy feet or so behind that was Little Blue—the Winnebago. To the left was a dirt track, leading out to the road at the front of the house. Numerous trucks and bikes were parked next to one another, standing by and waiting for action.

"Sealgaire HQ," I stated, and Ruadhan nodded.

Ruadhan nudged me in the direction of the larger motor home, where, chivalrous as ever, he held the door open for me. The place hadn't changed. In the open-plan sitting room was the dining table where I had first broken bread with the members of the Sealgaire—the surviving members. So many of their group had perished the night they'd traveled to Wales at the request of an Angel—my mother—to rescue me. I could almost smell the chicken casserole Iona had prepared that evening. So inviting, it had warmed me through despite the cold shoulder Phelan had offered. In the corner of the van, the same sofa Iona had pulled a silver blade from when she'd felt threatened by me—not knowing then who I really was— still wrapped around the walls. Though the motor home seemed untouched, it had been repurposed. As ludicrous an idea as it would have been back then to the Irish band of slayers, this place was now residence to a demon and a fallen Angel.

We were barely through the door when a familiar voice sounded behind me. "Feck me, so you were right then, she made it out alive." Phelan's smooth words rose up along- side the twirl of smoke from his cigarette.

I spun around, startling Phelan, and the roll-up dangling between his fingers fell to the floor.

"Sorry," I said, "but I don't trust you when my back is turned." I might have placed my belief in the wrong O'Sileabhin brother, resulting in Fergal capturing me, but I hadn't forgot- ten the revelation about Phelan. He had been the one who had shot me in the back the night I had found Jonah in Creigiau.

He gathered himself quickly. "And I don't trust you *full stop*. You take being two-faced to a whole new level, like." He tipped his head as he stared at me. "And I told you before, I was aiming for the Vampire." He glanced at Jonah as he stamped down on the cigarette beneath his feet.

"Sorry, *what*?" Jonah growled.

"Now, lad, leave it be," Ruadhan interrupted. "All water under the bridge. With things as they stand, arguing among ourselves is wasted energy."

"And how do things stand?" I asked.

Before anyone could answer, a polite tap at the door sounded twice, followed by a low voice requesting permission to enter. "Phelan?"

"Just get in here, Cam."

The young lad made his way inside. He shifted nervously beside Phelan, a silver blade pressed down against his leg. Believing was seeing. We had indeed been gone far longer than it had felt. Little Cameron was not so little anymore. Now taller than his brethren, he was lanky and lean, his red hair styled neatly, short in back and on the sides, and his voice had finally broken.

"'Lo, Lailah. Good to see you again," he said. As he looked at me square, I expected him to recoil the way everyone else had, but he didn't. He only smiled.

"Is it really? You're holding a blade in your hand," I replied softly.

Phelan cut in, "You've been gone three years, and it ain't Heaven you were paying a visit . . . not to mention the Jekyll-and-Hyde situation you've got going on. So before we tell you anything, you tell me, what the feck are you exactly—Angel or demon? Coz from here I sure as hell can't tell."

"*Don't*," Gabriel snapped.

Pulling a chair out from underneath the table, I gestured

for Gabriel to quiet. My reply to Phelan was honest. "Neither. The same as you, I live in the gray. Your energy, *your soul*, flips between light and dark, based on the nature of your day-to-day decisions." Some time ago Ruadhan had explained how an individual's soul could easily be tinged from light to dark and vice versa depending on their choices.

"On the inside, I have the same color palette as you. So as far as I'm concerned, that makes me human."

Phelan considered this, scratching his temple underneath his woolly hat. "Yeah, well, might need to add a *super* in front of that *human*. We can't none of us maim demons quite as effectively as you can."

"Then you'll be happy to have me on your side," I replied. "So how do things stand?" I pressed again.

Phelan looked to Cameron and then back to me. "All right," he said, taking a seat on the opposite side of the round table. He freed a roll-up from behind his ear and placed it at the corner of his lips. "Cam," he said. "Drink." And Cameron followed Phelan's order without complaint.

Ruadhan escorted Cameron to the kitchen, and Gabriel took the seat beside me.

When we'd all sat here before, Fergal was with us. His absence suggested he hadn't survived the attack in Henley. Then again, if that were the case, I'd have expected more reaction from Brooke. Still, three years *had* passed. . . .

Automatically, Gabriel reached for my hand, and I pretended not to notice as I leaned away. Jonah was gesturing for

Phelan to pass him a smoke, but I could tell he was watching me from the corner of his eye.

"Roll your own," Phelan said flatly, throwing a packet of tobacco and some Rizla paper across the table.

Jonah snatched them as he took a seat next to me, while Brooke sat down on the sofa. She was scowling, displeased that she might not be the one to deliver the detail about *the world having gone mad*, as she'd put it.

"First, I want to know why you've been gone so long— what you've been up to in Hell," Phelan said.

I should have known he would want me to show my hand before he'd even consider revealing his.

I sighed. "As far as I was aware, I'd been gone a few hours, not a few years."

"Time travels slower in *Heaven*—" Gabriel began.

I cut him off. "Wait, wait, wait. I'm sorry, but are we *still* doing this?"

"Still doing what?" Phelan said.

"Calling it *Heaven*?" I directed my question to Gabriel, as next to me Ruadhan placed down two tumblers and a bottle of scotch.

Before I had fallen into the third, Gabriel and Ruadhan had insisted we keep the Sealgaire ignorant of the knowledge we possessed. Deeply Christian as they were, there seemed no point in enlightening them to the truth of what they believed to be Heaven and Hell.

It appeared, in three years, Gabriel still hadn't felt it

necessary to have a religion-versus-reality conversation. But then, even Ruadhan himself was not in full possession of all the information. In their time together, Gabriel had kept things from him. I remembered then the reason I hadn't attempted to fill in the blanks for Ruadhan, either; I'd had no desire to diminish his belief, for it brought him comfort. Perhaps Gabriel hadn't wanted to shatter Phelan and his men's beliefs in much the same way. It was, after all, a belief they had devoted their lives to, something their nearest and dearest had died for. It seemed we were still working on a need-to-know basis.

"I know you call it something different," Phelan said as he gripped the base of the bottle Cameron had brought him. "Plenty of people do. But it is the abode of the Angels, of our Lord, and the place of divine afterlife. Paradise, Nirvana, the Promised Land . . . here, we call it the Kingdom of Heaven, and we offer our holy reverence, and our lives to protect it and all who serve it." Calm and collected, Phelan poured himself a glass.

His words echoed a similar conversation I had shared with Jonah. He had told me that no matter what name I went by, and I'd had many, I was still the same person underneath.

Phelan had a point, but it was a weak one.

What he didn't know was that an Arch Angel by the name of Orifiel sent his Angel Descendants here to claim, in death, the light energy—or souls—of mortals to fuel his world, Styclar-Plena—Heaven—to sustain its existence. Rewarding the human race with some distorted form of divine afterlife was not the principal design for his Heaven. Phelan and the rest of the human race were not the center of the universe as he believed.

I expected that his Bible stories did not explain that Hell was, in fact, another dimension existing in a state of cold, dark matter. That the Devil—Zherneboh—only came to be because the leader of the Arch Angels took it upon himself to cast another of his kind through a dark gateway. In essence, his Heaven had created Hell, which in turn led to the loss of so many mortal lives by the hand of the dark forces that now penetrated Earth.

Jonah's faith in me, in who I really was, might have allowed him to see beneath my name, but for Phelan, his faith would keep him blind as to what lay beneath Heaven's.

"The first dimension travels at a slower speed than Earth. One day there is around twenty years here," Gabriel reminded me. "You were gone a few hours in the third, and those few hours to you equated to three years here. Heaven and Hell are on the same clock; it's Earth that runs out of time."

"You don't say," Jonah chimed in, rolling his cigarette with exaggerated slowness; the same could not be said for the way he was helping himself to the scotch.

"So what were you doing there?" Phelan pressed, blowing a stream of smoke past my face.

"Taking the place of someone I care for." I paused, and even though I knew it would sting, I ripped off the Band-Aid. "Someone I love."

Gabriel said nothing, but the whites of his knuckles showed through the speckled spots that blemished the back of his hands as his grip tightened around the cuff of his black sweater. Jonah looked around the table, his hazel eyes widening, noticing for the first time that Gabriel was not between the two of us.

"I went there to die. And I went there with the intention of taking the Devil and all of Hell with me." I spoke in a language Phelan understood, one of both religion and warrior. It was too much for Gabriel; he got up then, making his way in the direction of the door. But he didn't walk through it. Instead, his shoulders hunched as he spread his arms out, steadying himself using the door frame, where he stayed.

"Well, you're not dead, like, so I guess that means neither is the Devil." Phelan sipped his drink.

I shot Jonah an unforgiving look. "No. Now that you know where I've been and why, what have I—what have *we*—missed?"

"Oh, you know . . ." A sarcastic grin edged up Phelan's cheeks. "Just the dawn of the apocalypse."

FIVE

AT MY REQUEST, Ruadhan fetched another glass, and I filled it to the top as Phelan began. "After you disappeared, we returned home, but by the time we arrived, already things had changed."

"Changed? Changed how?" I asked.

"The demons were everywhere, Lailah. They flooded out through the mouth of Hell, spreading across the world."

I would have looked to Gabriel for a more accurate explanation, but still he had his back to me.

"The day *you* went in, *they* all came out," Phelan added.

Okay, surely the time had come for "need to know."

"They didn't all come out, Phelan," I said. "Second Generation Vampires were human once. They were changed by the Pureblood Vampires who emerged from the third dimension, or as you prefer to call it, Hell." When I left, the Sealgaire were totally uneducated to the fact that the demons they slayed had been human once, and clearly nothing had changed.

"You're wrong," Phelan insisted, taking a sip of his scotch.

Jonah snorted, reaching for the matches on the table and lighting the end of his roll-up. Uninterested in the conversation that was unfolding, he fidgeted, and I thought then that he was growing anxious to speak with me alone. If I had tuned in a little more closely, I'd have realized it was because he needed to feed.

"I'm not wrong. You saw a Pureblood in Henley. You saw me end it. Differs somewhat from the demons you're used to killing, no?"

Phelan shook his head. "The Devil has many servants, Lailah, and they take many forms. Don't get it twisted—just because the demons disguise themselves to resemble us, it doesn't mean that they were once us. The Devil's own will never reveal—"

"Their horns," I said, cutting him off. "Yeah, I remember someone else in your family saying that."

Phelan finished his drink. "Aye."

"Have you bothered to ask Ruadhan or Brooke? They're demons, you know." As soon as I said it, I realized it was a silly question; he would never take the word of a Vampire, "reformed" or otherwise.

"Hey, who you calling a *demon?*" Brooke piped up from the corner, her nostrils flaring.

Ruadhan jumped in. "You're quibbling over semantics. Little love, what Phelan is trying to say, in the way he understands it, is that since you've been gone, the sheer volume of Vampires roaming around has increased dramatically. As have the number of people being found dead, drained completely dry."

A sudden spike in Vampires? Why? Zherneboh had left the third, but only right at the last second before I did, and only when he thought I was about to blow it all to kingdom come. The other Purebloods, and I didn't know how many there were, could have escaped at any time.

I ran my fingertip around the rim of the tumbler, tracing the outline of a circle, which reminded me of the blazing blue ball that had ridden the river.

That's it.

When I had struck the third with light, the towers, the moats, and the river had all heated. The scavengers had ripped one another apart to consume the dark matter before it was no longer in liquid form. By taking away their supply of dark matter, I had left the Purebloods and their scavengers with nothing to drink—their river had run dry.

"Lailah?" Ruadhan said, and I realized that everyone, Gabriel included, was watching me, waiting for what my mind was churning on.

"There was a river of dark matter, a sea of souls. . . ." I

trailed off, and Jonah exhaled a plume of smoke as he met my gaze, sharing the memory of the horrors we had seen in what felt like mere minutes ago.

"*A sea of souls?*" Phelan repeated.

Cameron came out from behind the kitchen counter, positioning himself more squarely in the room. I almost didn't want to offer my theory with him within earshot. He might now be legally classified as an adult, but I still saw the shy, lonely kid that I remembered from this morning—what was this morning to me, at least.

"Heaven might have Angels, but Hell has some help, too. We call them scavengers. They travel to Earth with the sole purpose of pulling in the dark energy, *or the soul*, of a mortal in death. They were depositing that energy into a *system*, which gave life to, and sustained a river full of, churning, dark matter. Or put another way, a sea of souls."

"You saw this, too, lad?" Ruadhan's eyebrows lifted as he glanced toward Jonah.

Jonah tugged on his cigarette before necking his fourth shot, his pupils dilating as he returned Ruadhan's stare, giving my makeshift father the confirmation he was seeking.

"I spread light into the darkness. I caused the dark matter to heat, and it began to evaporate." I sucked in a breath. "I took away the Purebloods' supply of souls." For Phelan's benefit, I added, "They feed off them. Without the souls, they are relying completely on the dark matter they take from a human, here on Earth, through their blood."

The Purebloods were creating more Second Generation Vampires, but not just to add to their armies: They needed the Vampires to steal more humans for them to drink from. Which would account for the increasing number of dead, hollowed-out bodies being discovered.

Jonah nodded at me in quiet understanding before exhaling smoke through his nose.

"Would certainly explain why so many mortals are being killed," Ruadhan said, confirming my thoughts.

Phelan leaned across the table. "So, what, did you destroy this sea of souls for good?"

Again, my resentful gaze settled on Jonah, but he didn't falter when his eyes locked with mine. "Maybe, maybe not," I said. "Jonah pulled me out before I had a chance to—"

"Before you had a chance to what, Lailah?" Gabriel demanded, pushing the sleeves of his sweater to his elbows.

An expectant silence descended. "To destroy the darkness. To finish what I started. To end it."

"To give your life for it." The veins in Gabriel's neck jutted out. I might have lost half of my sight, but his pain was all too easy to see.

"I had already bartered my life away before I entered the third. I saw an opportunity to take the Purebloods and their world along with me, so I took it. At least, I tried to take it."

Gabriel's brow creased in confusion. He had no idea I had

rewritten the past and what I'd had to offer to strike that deal with the universe.

"So you didn't defeat the Devil, and you didn't close Hell's gates, but you did manage to bring about the apocalypse. Not an altogether successful trip, now was it?" Phelan said.

I tipped my glass back, letting the warm scotch burn the back of my throat before swallowing. "No."

Cameron piped up with childlike enthusiasm. "It doesn't matter. Lailah will save us all. She's said the Savior."

"I'm sorry, *the what?*" I said, unable to stop myself from shooting Ruadhan a glance. That was a word he, too, liked to pair with me.

"The Savior—"

Phelan cut Cameron off. "She's not the Savior, Cameron."

Now I looked to Ruadhan for an explanation.

"Christianity teaches of the Second Coming," he said. "Of a time when Jesus Christ would return to Earth, at the Last Judgment. The Sealgaire have awaited the return of the Savior for centuries, believing that she would once again die for our sins, sacrificing herself so that God and mankind could be reconciled." He pawed at the stubble on his chin. "We believe the Savior will destroy the Devil himself, and in doing so, she will expel the evil from this world, thus delivering freedom to humanity."

"And you think that your Savior, Jesus Christ, would

return as a woman?" I said with a hint of sarcasm. As far as I was concerned, religion was entirely man-made, a product that packaged women as second-class citizens. It was rather strange that the Sealgaire would suggest that their Savior would undergo a gender swap.

"Long ago," Ruadhan said, "a seer foretold of the apocalypse, and with it, the return of Christ. He was clear in his description that the Savior would walk among us, *female*."

"A seer?" This was not the first time I had heard of a prophet who foretold the story of the end of days.

"We saw what you did. . . . To that demon, I mean." My attention shifted back to Cameron as he cut in, hope and excitement spread across his face.

I couldn't help but feel like that rotten person who delivers the news that there is no Father Christmas. "Sorry, Cameron, it's just a story."

"You're wrong," he replied swiftly.

I yielded a little. "All right, if you believe there is a Savior due your way, then I'm not going to argue with you, but I will tell you that it's not me."

"Too right it's not you," Phelan grumbled. "I think I'd know the Savior when I saw her."

"Now, now," Ruadhan said. "Are you sure about that? You thought Lailah here was a demon when you first met her."

"Actually," I said, "I think for once, this is something Phelan and I can agree on."

Phelan sighed. "You're not the Savior, but my men are tired and the Devil resides here, on our doorstep. If you are on our side, then you want the same thing we do." Though it wasn't a question, it was a statement Phelan expected some form of agreement with.

I looked at Ruadhan, Gabriel, and Jonah. "I want those I hold dear to be safe. I want them to live in a world that is free. In Zherneboh's eyes, I saw his story firsthand. I know what he wants. As we thought, his desires are set on bringing Styclar-Plena to an end. But perhaps even stronger is his desire to force Orifiel out and into the second. He doesn't care about mankind; he'll do anything to succeed. We have to stop him." I glanced at Ruadhan and said, *"I have to try."*

Gabriel shook his head but said nothing, and Jonah's defensive body language said it all. Neither welcomed my decision to fight. Ruadhan, however, placed his hand on my shoulder and squeezed, reminding me that he was true to his word—he would stand beside me.

Phelan slid his chair back. "Well then, while here in this room we can agree that you are not the Savior, to my men, to the people of Lucan, they need to believe that's exactly who you are, because right now, they could do with some hope."

He swiped his tobacco products off the table and stuffed them into his cargo pants pocket as he stood.

I rose to meet him.

"Brooke," Phelan said, eyeing me, "do summat about her face."

Turning to leave, he pushed Cameron out ahead of him.

"Do what with it?" Brooke said with a tone.

She'd never been one for taking orders. Skip ahead three years and nothing had changed.

"I don't fecking know," Phelan said. "But do something. Paint it, dress it, whatever, just make her look how a Savior should. *Make her look beautiful*." For my benefit, he added, "No offense, like, but folks buy things more easily when they come in a pretty package."

My appearance was a trivial matter; the lack of sight in my left eye was my paramount concern. But as my gaze found Jonah's, I flinched. I cared what he thought, and despite myself, I didn't want him to think of me as ugly. When my time here was up, and death came to call, there was only one face I wanted him to remember me by, not two.

"You've got until this evening. We leave for the North Star at six o'clock." With that, Phelan ushered Cameron out of the motor home, slamming the door behind him as he left.

I didn't know whom to address first—Gabriel or Jonah. Both seemed as anxious to have a private conversation with me but I wanted to speak with Ruadhan too—jump straight into discussions about how to begin waging our war to protect this world.

Brooke hustled me across the living room and made my decision for me. "You heard him, let's get to work."

"Where do you think you're taking me?" I said.

"Brooke stays in the Winnebago," Ruadhan said. "Her things are there. Gabriel and I reside here."

I pushed my weight down, shrugging Brooke off easily. "Gabriel, you don't stay in the house with Iona?"

Gabriel scraped his hand through his blond hair as he shook his head. "Why would I?"

"I . . . I guess . . . Never mind."

Brooke tugged my wrist. "Come on."

"Go, little love, take some time, catch your breath," Ruadhan said. "We will be here waiting for you when you're ready."

I was hesitant to go. As angry as I was with Jonah for pulling me out of the third against my will, I couldn't deny the nervous flutter in the pit of my stomach, born from the knowledge that he had come for me, that he had risked himself to save me. When I had thought he was lost, he had felt so far away that now I just wanted to be near him.

Jonah winked at me, letting me know he'd be okay. He wasn't about to disappear into thin air; our conversation could wait a little while longer. Gabriel, on the other hand, didn't know where to put himself. The dark circles under his worried eyes showed how tired he was, as though he had aged more than the three years I'd been gone. Guilty as I felt to be the cause of his sadness, I knew deep down it was for the best. Short-term pain, long-term gain, I reminded myself.

Once outside, I made a point of walking slowly to Little Blue. I breathed in the fresh dew from the grass and welcomed the cold air against my bare arms.

For just a second, I savored being alive.

SIX

Unlike the larger motor home, the Winnebago had changed. The stained flooring had been replaced with a hard-wearing carpet striped in pastel tones. Heavy white wooden shutters had taken the place of the filthy orange suede curtains. The small table that sat in the corner had been upgraded, painted in a duck-egg blue and finished with a cracked varnish. A variety of fragranced candles sat clustered together in the center. Most noticeable, though, was the smell. It no longer reeked of stale cigarette smoke. Instead, a pleasant aroma of chamomile drifted through the air.

Brooke's makeover had given Little Blue a new lease on life. Now it was time to see if she could do the same for me.

I placed my hand on the sideboard next to the door as my mind continued to catalog every change to Little Blue—from what I assumed to be the purposely staged scattered deck of cards to the newly reupholstered sofa. Examining every detail wasn't a deliberate intention, but these days my brain processed things more keenly than it used to.

Brooke walked toward the linen curtain that separated the living area from the driver's quarters. "Want a mirror?"

"No."

Brooke stopped. "You sure about that? I think I'd want to see."

I took a seat at the table and shook my head. "I'm more bothered by the fact that I'm blind in my left eye."

Brooke removed her beanie as she sat down across from me. She scrunched her short red hair back into place. She'd taken out her dark hair extensions and now looked the same as the first time I'd met her. That in itself might not have been a big deal, but what it signified was that she was no longer trying to make herself into something she thought more attractive to Jonah.

"Really?" she said. "You've got no vision in it at all?"

"You can't tell?"

Brooke studied my left eye intently. "No. Your skin's all messed up, like, but your eye looks all right."

This wasn't the first time she'd sounded like one of the Irish. "Right, well, perhaps keep my vision problem to yourself then." If it couldn't be seen, then there was no need to highlight the chink in my armor to anyone.

Brooke nodded. "I'll keep your secret. I understand—better than most, you might remember."

On first glance, I had failed to give any real attention to the most important change in Brooke's appearance: She wasn't wearing shades. My crystal had been my security blanket, and likewise a pair of glasses had been Brooke's. When Brooke was human, she'd been blind, and back then she'd always worn a pair. When she became a Vampire, her vision was restored, but her glasses had been a comfort she'd relied upon, and one she'd found difficult to leave behind.

"You don't wear your shades anymore?" I said.

"It's not like I need them," she said flippantly. Though it was very subtle, I detected an undertone of pride, like a kid who had finally handed in her pacifier. "Anyway, I guess I owe you one, you know, for not telling you about your mom sooner. . . ."

When Fergal was still the leader of the Sealgaire, he had thought Brooke was me. He told her that not only did he know where the Angel Aingeal—my mother—was, but he'd also arranged a meeting at her request. Of course, that mother was my mother, not Brooke's. When I'd asked Brooke if Fergal had told her about my mother's whereabouts, she barefaced lied to me. Then again, neither Brooke nor I knew that Fergal's claims were actually a trap. He'd been preparing to hand me over in exchange for his brother, Padraig. A brother who, unbeknownst to him, had been turned into a Second Generation Vampire, a possibility that would never have occurred to him, because he, just like the rest of the Sealgaire, didn't believe Vampires had ever been human.

I shot Brooke a disgruntled glare. "Sooner? I think you mean *at all*." But remembering she had suffered, too, I softened. "I'm sorry that you lost Fergal."

She didn't respond, wrinkling her nose instead and bringing us back to business. "I've got a job to do."

She moved out from behind the table, and I swiveled in my chair to face her. She reached out, tucking my short strands behind my ears before tipping my chin up. Running her gaze over my face, she said, "So what does beauty look like to you?"

I thought on that for a moment before offering a reply. "I think the more important question is, what does beauty look like to them?"

"I really don't care. We're not doing this for Phelan, the Sealgaire, or anyone else, we're doing this for you." She brought her hands together. "Regardless of how low a priority you deem your appearance to be right now, trust me, you walk around looking all *frazzled*, and folks will stare. Then you might give a shite."

"Give a *shite*? You live in here, keeping well away from the people who *slay demons*?" I said, confused.

Brooke took a step back. "Yeah."

"So why do you suddenly sound like one of them?"

"Dunno." She pushed the curtain out of her way and disappeared behind it. "I guess you just pick these things up. Been here awhile, you know." She reappeared with a makeup bag and a hairbrush in hand. "You've gone *waaay* off topic." She gestured for me to stand. "So when it comes to what's beautiful, surely the only opinion that matters is yours." And then she added with a grin, "Yours *and mine*, that is. What do you care whether anyone believes you're this biblical Savior? It's all a load of tosh anyway. Ain't no way you're Jesus!"

"Phelan wants to give his people hope. I can appreciate that."

Brooke tapped her foot rhythmically. "And . . . ?"

Maybe she was smarter than I gave her credit for. "*And* it won't do any harm for the Sealgaire to believe I am their long-awaited Savior. Particularly if a need should arise for them to take direction from me."

Brooke reached past me, setting down the makeup bag. "Instead of Phelan, you mean?"

"Perhaps."

"Good. He shouldn't be in charge anyway," she grumbled as she began to brush out my hair.

I mustered the courage to again broach the subject inherent in her words. "Brooke . . . what happened to Fergal, I'm sorry."

She didn't reply but simply tugged the brush more slowly. The silence grew awkward as she slicked back my hair with product and focused on her work, moving on to my skin. "You know, I don't think makeup is gonna cut it. We might have to come up with something a bit more creative."

Something creative meant answering that question of what beautiful would look like to the Sealgaire and their community. Nothing was more beautiful to these people than their belief. But how would you symbolize that? What would belief look like?

For me, for so long, it had been the sapphire blue eyes belonging to my Morpho butterfly, to Gabriel.

For Jonah, it was *"el efecto mariposa,"* or "the butterfly effect"—words that acted as a sign, giving meaning to the chaos.

And when I had needed hope the most, Jonah's long-dead sister, Mariposa—the butterfly girl herself—had delivered it to me.

Beauty, belief, and hope all took on the same form.

"Brooke," I said quietly. "Can you make me look like a butterfly?"

Brooke pushed up the sleeves of her cashmere sweater and crossed her arms in thought. When she met my eyes, there was a spark in hers. "Right, let's package you pretty, shall we?"

I WAITED PATIENTLY ON THE SOFA while Brooke sat with her back to me, working at the table. Twice she left in a blur to gather items for her self-proclaimed "masterpiece."

Though Phelan had beaten Brooke to the punch of recounting the noteworthy events of the last three years before she had been able, it wasn't long before she was reveling in her version of events, a chunk of which Phelan had failed to mention.

Brooke told me that a war between mankind had broken out, one between the Western world and the Middle East, but that the conflict had been short-lived, brought to an end with the use of chemical warfare in a coordinated attack across ten major cities, and though it was unrelated, it had happened at the same time as the number of Vampires had increased. And assumptions and connections were made where there weren't any.

"You gotta remember, the Sealgaire believe that Second Generation Vamps are demons straight outta Hell, disguised to resemble human beings. But the rest of the world doesn't think that. And it's not like the Vampires could hide, there's just too many of them."

The world's intellects, not being in the "know" like the Sealgaire, offered a different explanation—the use of chemical warfare—for what these "creatures" actually were. "They call them Spinodes. What does that even mean anyway?" Brooke rambled. "They reckon that Second Generation Vampires were human beings that came into direct contact with the toxic gases released in the attacks." She paused for dramatic effect before finishing with, "The whole world is in a state of emergency. It's all that's ever on the telly now." She huffed.

Brooke went on to tell me that the majority of countries had a strict curfew in place, restricting the population to the confines of their homes, while military tanks and personnel patrolled the streets. The Vampires stayed out of sight during daylight hours, but at night would strike, abducting people. Of course, none of that could be seen here in Lucan; the Sealgaire ran this town.

Brooke had succeeded at having me dangle off her every word. I was caught up in the horror of it all when I sensed someone approaching the Winnebago; I got off the couch and headed for the door.

The familiar jingle of bracelets clinking together told me whom to expect, and I spread my hand over my left cheek before opening the door.

"Iona," I said.

"Hi," she replied, her plump lips stretching in a nervous smile. "Welcome back," she added quickly.

I nodded. Never one to wear jeans, today Iona had on a plain green dress, cable-knit tights, and flat ankle boots. She played with her thick blond hair, which cascaded in long, loose waves over the woolen infinity scarf drooped around her neck. She appeared no different from the way I remembered her, but then, unlike the others, Iona was Of Elfi—a child of a fallen Angel. The day I left, she had turned seventeen, and she hadn't aged a day since. Iona's big gray-blue eyes hadn't changed. They were a match for the new color of Gabriel's eyes, which *had* changed when he fell.

"Phelan asked me to bring this to you," she said, removing her backpack and passing it to me.

I took it from her. "What's in here?"

"Clothes, shoes, and some other bits and pieces. He said you should wear them tonight at the pub."

I should have guessed Phelan would prefer I wear one of Iona's outfits instead of borrowing something from Brooke's less traditional wardrobe. "Perception is reality. I guess jeans and sneakers don't quite say Savior, now do they?"

"Aye," she said.

"I'd invite you in, but—"

"That's all right, like, I'm sure you're very busy."

Iona hovered, and I got the feeling she wanted to ask me something. I wondered if the question sitting silently on her lips was one that concerned Gabriel. I wasn't sure how much he'd shared with her since I'd been gone. Did she know that he and I were Angel Pairs? Maybe he'd put it in a way he thought she'd understand. "Soul mates" perhaps? Or maybe he'd said nothing at all. I turned to leave, thinking better of being cornered into having to offer an explanation for something without knowing what picture had been painted in my absence.

"Lailah—" Iona said, gathering her thoughts. It was strange hearing her speak my real name. She'd only ever known me as Brooke, but I guess she'd had plenty of time to adjust to the truth of my white lie, whatever Gabriel had deemed that truth to be.

"Yes," I said with encouragement. Oddly, she seemed to be waiting for permission to speak.

"I wanted to say thank you."

Whatever I was expecting her to say, it wasn't that. "You have no reason to thank me, Iona."

"I do."

I leaned against the doorway, hesitant to hear her out.

"I don't know why Fergal turned his back on the Lord, but I do know that in doing so, he put you in grave danger. But

Brooke told me that despite what that meant for you, in the forest you forgave him. You showed him mercy, and you tried to save him. Brooke said that because of you, at the end he repented his sins."

Iona didn't know Fergal's motivations for deceiving me. I'd already surmised that none of the Sealgaire did, either, since Phelan still claimed that Second Generation Vampires came from Hell itself. Brooke hadn't shared the details of Fergal's death with me. I had no idea if he had "repented," as Iona put it, or even if that made any difference to anything anyhow.

I saw no benefit in telling Iona the truth about why she'd lost her twin brother, because if I did, she'd also know that neither Fergal's nor Padraig's souls had made it to her Kingdom of Heaven. I would spare myself from being the creator of the scars she would surely wear if she were enlightened to the truth.

I would spare us both—from each other.

"Your forgiveness, your mercy, and your love restored Fergal's faith. So I want you to know that I now place mine in you, Lailah."

I considered her statement, before challenging it. "You mean you place your faith in the Savior?"

"No," she replied swiftly. "I have faith in *you*, whoever *you* are." Her words were strong, and they took on a life of their own, becoming immortal just like her.

I hesitated, but then nodded gently before turning and clicking the door shut softly behind me.

Little Blue was compact. Since it had no bathroom, shower, or bedroom, I changed in the living area. Brooke ran out of steam on the whole "the world's gone mad" topic and was now purely concentrating on her creation. I had listened to it all, but I hadn't wanted to. Such horror, and such a massive loss of life, all of which could have been avoided if my intentions had been realized in the third. I was relieved when she had eventually changed the subject.

"Are you going to be much longer?" I asked Brooke, peeling off my T-shirt.

"You don't rush art, Lailah," she tutted, peering over her shoulder. "And are you seriously not going to use the main house to shower? *Technically*, you haven't had a wash in three years, you know."

"And risk being seen like this?" I said, pointing to the left side of my face. "I don't think Phelan would like that too much, now would he?"

"Fair cop," she said, her attention returning to her craft.

Stripped down to my underwear, I pulled out a rolled-up dress from the backpack. The cream chiffon unraveled until the pleated skirt skimmed the floor. "Oh, yikes."

Brooke twisted back around. "Halter neck, dropped waist, and a full-length skirt . . . *very boho chic*. Never goes out of fashion, you know."

"It's *very* . . ."

"Boho chic, I just said that," Brooke snapped.

"I was going to say *Angelic*." Fingering the delicate material, I wasn't sure why I was surprised. What else would Phelan expect a Savior to be seen in?

I placed the dress down carefully and pulled out a pair of ballet flats and a large box. I opened it carefully to find a stunningly ornate crystal hairpin.

Assessing the outfit, I sighed. "I can't wear this."

"Of course you can, and you will. Now stop distracting me, I'm just finishing the final touches." Waving her hands in the air, she went back to work. "We'll dress it down, just put the damn thing on before you catch your death." Before I could reply, Brooke added, *"You know what I mean."*

After Brooke's creation was complete, she turned her attention to my outfit.

With a chunky chestnut-colored leather belt around the waist and knee-high sheepskin boots, Brooke managed to style the traditional dress in a way that made it more current and more appropriate for a bitter fall. She only allowed me to add her long tan designer coat—her most treasured piece of clothing—after I promised to guard it with my life.

She slid the leaf-shaped hairpin through my slicked-back hair over my right ear, saying it would work well to balance out the mask she'd made.

"That should do it," she said eventually, as she finished dabbing a cotton bud covered in some sort of sticky adhesive to the left side of my face. She gingerly picked up the prosthetic mask she'd worked so hard on, positioning it carefully before pressing it to my skin and holding it long enough for the mask's inner latex to stick firmly to the resin. Then, with an oval mirror in one hand, she said, "Mirror, mirror on the wall . . ."

I didn't react to the reflection staring back at me.

Brooke had been successful in concealing the entire left side of my face. First, she had hand-painted the mask with an array of butterflies and then further added individual, three-dimensional versions made out of fabric and wire. She'd cut a long slit for my eye so as not to draw attention to the fact that my sight was suffering. Each carefully designed butterfly was fluttering outward, away from my nose, giving an impression of freedom. Brooke did symbolism quite well, it seemed.

"So?" Brooke asked, impatient for a response.

I clutched the sides of the mirror, taking one last glance, before dropping the looking glass onto the sofa. I'd been struggling to recognize the reflection in the mirror since my resurrection on New Year's Day, having died on the mountaintop. Today, I wasn't the person I was yesterday, and tomorrow I would be different still. Covering my face wouldn't change that, but I still wanted Jonah to recognize me, to see me the way he had before. So I would go to the lengths of wearing something beautiful on the outside, not only to satisfy Phelan's request but also to stop me feeling ugly on the inside when I was with Jonah.

My fingertip glided down the edge of one of the butterfly wings. "How did you know?"

Brooke batted my hand away from my face. "Know what?"

"To make them blue?" My belief in Gabriel, and my hope born from Mariposa, both took the form of a Morpho butterfly—they both took the color blue.

"It's a holy color, seemed suitable for a Savior," she answered with a shrug.

I remembered then that Iona had told me the same thing when answering my question as to how the Winnebago got its nickname. In fact, even the front door of the main house had been painted the same.

For a moment, Brooke and I stood facing each other, not saying a word. It was the first time a silence between us had felt comfortable.

I fastened the coat and made my way to the door. Squeezing the handle, I smiled and said, "Thank you."

As I stepped out, a small gust of wind blew past me, causing a pile of papers on the sideboard to scatter onto the floor.

I reached down to collect them. It was then that I noticed the book they'd been resting on was a leather-bound copy of the Bible. And the papers appeared to be handouts from church.

"Really, Brooke?" I said, turning to her.

"Yeah, well," she said, "Ruadhan, you know. Makes me go."

I had never known Brooke to take direction from Ruadhan— or anyone for that matter. She was a law unto herself most of the time. No, there had to be another reason for her attendance, and as my mind whirled looking for it, she said, "It's not all bad, some of the stuff they talk about is, well, I dunno, it kinda makes you think. Maybe we have a purpose, all of us."

"*Right*," I said, unable to keep the surprise or the sarcasm from my voice.

"They say God is all around us, that he communicates by sending hidden messages, but both your heart and your mind have to be open to see them."

Hidden messages.

I had heard those words, that theory, before. I sifted through my memory, and it threw up Darwin, a chap who dealt in just that, as he was a theoretical scientist. He was a gentleman I had served in the pub I was working in a few days before finding Jonah injured in the woods in Creigiau. Darwin's father just so happened to be Gabriel's business associate, who'd hosted a party in Chelsea where I'd again met Darwin. We'd shared a conversation on the landing of his home, and Darwin had said his father saw signs in things, that they were hidden messages.

I shook my head. "Okay. I need to go, but later you and I are going to *talk*."

What on earth had they done with the girl I knew?

As I reached for the door with one hand, I pressed my other on top of the papers to stop the wind from blowing them off again. Something caught my eye. The outline of a butterfly drawn with a black sharpie. I studied it and that's when I saw what was written below.

A proverb: *When the caterpillar thought its life was over, it became a butterfly.*

SEVEN

THE DAY HAD ALREADY DRAWN IN, and here in early evening, I was left with very little time to tackle the conversations that awaited me. Jonah, unwilling to take a spot at the back of the queue, appeared in front of me as I strode across the field.

"Wow, Brooke really went to town," he began. "All you need now is a cape."

I could always count on Jonah to return to his default setting, far more comfortable with banter and innuendo than anything deep and meaningful. But I could tell from the way he was tousling his untidy, dark hair that he was nervous, that he knew there wasn't a way to say the important things without having a real conversation.

My smile was small, and he straightened himself, following up with a predictable "Looks good on you, beautiful." He'd changed into dark jeans and a long wool coat, but as ever his collar was turned up. "Gabriel's closet," he said before I could ask.

"Right" was all I said—all I was ready to say. My feelings were more than a little confused. Where Jonah was concerned, I was always caught in conflict. He'd forced my hand and made me leave the third, which made me furious, but then he'd also risked his own life to save mine, which made it impossible to be furious.

I lingered, affording him the opportunity to say what he wanted. Unable or unwilling, he looked away, and I shook my head. *He had his chance.*

I sidestepped him, but he squeezed the top of my shoulder. "Wait, just . . . wait." He bent down and in an almost-whisper said, "I don't know how you managed to get to me so fast, how you were able to move me the way that you did. But I guess how you did it isn't as important as *why*. You said that you chose me. I don't understand. After what I said to you . . ."

I stepped back to see him face-to-face. "I know you didn't mean the things you said, but I understand why you thought saying them was the right thing to do." I paused. "But here's what I don't get. You didn't mean them, yet after I drank your blood you denied me. Why?"

His answer was quick and it was honest. "I know that pull, when you drink from another Vampire, and I didn't want you to give in to it, only to regret it." He reached for my wrists, bringing me toward him. "I never want you to regret anything about me."

I might be an ice queen on the outside, but Jonah's touch caused my insides to melt. He could wear down my resolve all too easily, which meant that no matter what terrible things awaited me, nothing could be worse than what I had right here—Jonah was the most dangerous thing of all.

I took my time, searching for the right way to tell him. "I'm going to stay, and I am going to fight, but you know that already. And whether you believe me or not, I need you to understand that I am doing it for you, for all of you, and that it's for the best." I looked away. "I can't give you what you want. I'm sorry."

With that, Jonah reverted back to his flippant self. "And you're an expert on what I want? Maybe you should share? Maybe say it all real slow . . ."

I didn't rise to it, and instead I thought carefully. "What you said to me in the third, and the way you've been looking at me since we got back to the second, there's only one thing you want, Jonah, and it's the one thing I just can't give you."

"Which is what, beautiful?"

"Me." My voice wobbled. "*Forever.*"

He opened his mouth, but nothing came out. He pressed down gently on my wrists as the weight of that word sank to depths even he couldn't reach. And with every second that he remained silent, I became more confident of one thing: What Jonah wanted—what he'd allow himself to want—was companionship. Perhaps for a being such as himself, the need for a companion was the closest he could come to an emotion such as love. Condemned to a dark and lonely existence, finally he thought he'd found someone who could share it with him.

Someone he wouldn't be able to drink to an end.

Someone who understood.

I turned away, but he snatched me back, pulling me in close. Locked in a belligerent war of wills, neither of us was prepared to concede. Regardless of how we felt for each other and why, I couldn't relinquish. My life did not belong to me anymore. I was on borrowed time. And as the hands of the clock ran down, taking away my forever, I would make it my sole purpose to ensure that my families were safe. I was clutching the lapels of his coat so tightly that my knuckles turned purple. I wished things could be different but knew in my bones that they could not.

There was no amusement in his tone this time as he said, "One night. That's it."

He surprised me, and I faltered. "Just one?" My second question escaped in a barely audible whimper. "That would be enough?"

"That's all I'm asking for."

I tuned in to his body's rhythm. Connected to him by blood, I was able to feel the rising anticipation pass through him to me. I didn't give much thought to it at the time, but I'd had to concentrate far more than I should have needed to.

I dared to meet his hazel eyes, and a wicked spark flashed, acting as both a warning and an invitation. He ran the back of his hand over my jaw and down my neck, kneading my collarbone seductively. When I didn't protest, he grasped the back of my head, bringing his cheek to mine. His breath escaped at my ear, causing me to struggle to catch my own, but as I did, a floral bouquet bloomed, the scent wrapping around him like bindings.

My chest sank, and I drew back. "Why can I smell a woman on you?"

He arched his eyebrow, brought out of the moment too fast, but his answer was easy. "I needed to feed."

There was no rhyme or reason as to why that caused me to feel winded, but it did.

"I didn't kill her," he added, as if that's why I was now retreating.

I wasn't about to tell him that honestly I didn't care about the girl's well-being, that truthfully, it was the thought of his sinking his teeth into someone else that caused my unease.

I snapped myself out of it. I was being foolish. What difference did it make anyway? The universe was coming to claim me. My time here was limited. Giving in to Jonah, giving in to myself, would only muddy the waters.

"Lailah—"

I cut him short. "We should go. I don't want to be late." Listening to my head, not my heart, within a blink I'd thought myself away to the safety of the motor home.

If the interaction with Jonah proved anything, it was that I needed my own space. After a quick conversation with Ruadhan, it was agreed that I would stay in Little Blue and Jonah would move into the much larger motor home, where Gabriel, too, was staying.

I had barely recovered from my conversation with Jonah when Phelan let himself into the motor home without even knocking.

"Let's see this then," he said, blowing cigarette smoke out his nose. With my dress covered by Brooke's coat, his eyes studied only my butterfly mask. "You'll do."

"I'm so very glad you approve," I said sarcastically.

Just then, Gabriel stepped into the living room. "She won't just simply *do*, she's the most exquisite being to ever grace this world. Savior or no Savior, you and your men should consider yourselves nothing short of privileged to be in the presence of her company."

Dressed in a black sweater and dark jeans, Gabriel was a shadow of his former self. He strode over, and this time he didn't give me the chance to pull away when he took my hand.

"Yeah, well, let's keep it more *Savior* than *no Savior,* shall we?" Phelan said, gesturing for us to follow him outside.

I pulled forward, but Gabriel tightened his grip. He whispered, "Stay close to me."

Several years had passed, yet Gabriel wasn't treating me any differently, and I knew our conversation was going to be a difficult one.

Outside, our group gathered, and after Brooke had been met with the news that Little Blue had been repurposed as my private abode, which meant she had to stay with the men in the motor home, she stropped off, deciding she had better things to do than to join us. So Ruadhan, Jonah, Cameron, Gabriel, and I followed Phelan back onto the main road that had taken us here. Like an army, we marched onward into the heart of a village that was anything but ordinary.

Terraced bric-a-brac shops and tearooms were squashed together, slanting as they stretched over the cobblestone street, each one appearing slightly more crooked than the last. Each building had rotting wooden beams crisscrossing over the front. They reminded me of a cell block. I could just imagine inmates trapped inside, watching as, one by one, prisoners walked the green mile when death came to call. Like wardens, streetlamps lined the route, armed only with bright bulbs that shone a white light onto the cobbles.

Taking prime position at the end of the road was a well-lit public house whose sign read THE NORTH STAR in big, curvy letters. Loud voices, the clatter of pint glasses, the scrape of forks against platters—not a drop of the noise spilling out could escape me.

Gabriel drew me to him and said in a hushed voice, "They might want you to say something."

"It's fine if they do," I replied easily.

Though Gabriel had been holding my hand for more than fifteen minutes, it was still ice cold against my own. I wondered if he missed being able to control his temperature now that he was fallen. I wondered what else he might miss.

I peered behind me to Jonah, but he looked away quickly when he realized I'd seen him staring at Gabriel's hand clutching mine.

Phelan came to a halt outside of the pub's double doors. "Lailah—"

I stepped forward, my fingers slipping from Gabriel's. "What are we waiting for?"

Phelan pointed to the bars running down the door. "They're made from silver, like. They ain't the only thing."

"I can tell when there's silver nearby, you don't have to warn me."

"Good. My men, the men who you met before, know what you are."

I played with the wing of a butterfly on my mask. "You mean they know that I have some sort of demonic heritage?" It hadn't been that long ago that Phelan had thrown a silver net over me when he and the rest of the Sealgaire had come to suspect that I was some form of demon.

"Aye. Jack, Riley, Claire, Iona, and Cam here, of course, know that you were the girl we were sent to save, and they also know that you're not altogether *celestial*. But that's it. The rest don't know the details, and that's the way it's gonna stay. There's no need for complicating things, like."

Phelan, as usual, was telling, not asking. Three years of being in charge of this ragtag band had clearly only added to his superiority complex. Though Phelan was heavy-handed, I thought he'd come to respect me, if only a little, when we'd spoken long ago—what was long ago for him, at least—next to the bonfire. I was about to point this out, when I realized something.

"Jack, Riley, Claire, Iona, Cam . . . You're missing someone."

"We are missing many, and Dylan is one of them." Phelan's lips thinned as they formed a tight line. "You ready?" he asked.

I looked to Ruadhan, who gave me an encouraging nod, and then to Gabriel, who held his arms out expectantly. "Your coat," he said.

I slipped my arms out of Brooke's treasured possession. Adjusting the lace at my chest and the pleats of my skirt, I nodded to Phelan, whose hard eyes softened at my appearance. But only for a moment. A nice, traditional dress would not change what he knew about me. And who I was prevented him from being able to even consider that I could actually be the Savior that he was trying to make everyone else believe me to be.

Phelan pulled open one of the doors and gestured for Cameron to open the other. I stepped from the crisp cold air into a hot room filled with twirling smoke.

The noise stopped immediately.

Phelan had failed to mention his recent recruitment drive. There must have been more than two hundred men, and every last one of them was gaping at me.

Phelan stood at my side and addressed the room. "We

asked the Lord, and the Lord delivered. Yesterday, the world belonged to the Devil. But today marks a new chapter. With the Savior's help, tomorrow we will win this war." Phelan paused. "For she has arrived."

It was so quiet that we could hear the squeak of the hinge that preceded the swing of the bathroom door. A twenty-something man stumbled out into the room.

"Who died? At least say it was Stephen. I had twenty euros on him!" he hollered, oblivious to what was going on around him. Snatching a pint glass off a table, he was in his own little drunken world. A taller, broader lad pinched the drunk's collar and pulled him to face us. The drunk's grip on the pint glass began to slip.

I thought myself across the room, and to the human eye, I dissolved into thin air, reappearing nose to nose with the drunk lad and catching his full pint as it fell.

I willed my light to appear, and a soft golden hue framed my form. "I think you've had enough, don't you?"

I let my light flicker and then die, and in the blink of an eye, I raced back to Phelan. With a nod, I handed him the pint of Guinness, showing respect for the officer in front of his troops. Phelan liked that. With a "Cheers," he raised the glass and glugged it down.

The room erupted in conversation, and Phelan, now happy, led us to the back of the pub, where a large rectangular table and benches waited for us.

I sat down on the worn leather, and before Gabriel could take the seat next to me, I said, "Ruadhan?"

My makeshift father, most happy to oblige, joined me.

"That's it?" I said to Phelan.

"Aye. For them, for now. Cam, get the drinks. Lailah, your tipple?"

"Wine might be most suitable." I smiled sarcastically.

"Aye, Cam, a glass of red."

Cameron plucked his checked shirt from his chest, staring at the bar, clearly distracted.

"You tryin' to catch a fly, like? Close your mouth, lad," Phelan snapped, shaking Cameron out of his daydream.

I followed Cameron's line of sight. He was eyeing a young, petite brunette who was trying to carry a round of drinks from the bar to a group of guys huddled around a table.

Cameron collected himself and then scurried away, passing some familiar faces as he did. From the packed crowd, Jack, Riley, and Iona appeared and took up stools at our table. I noticed Iona's hesitation as she looked to Gabriel for confirmation that she should sit herself next to him at the end of the table.

I didn't notice Gabriel answering her unspoken question, but she sat, crossing one leg over the other, and straightened her jacket. She offered me a sincere smile, and I had to twist my neck to return it since the side of my face closest to her was blocked by the mask. Her expression changed then from happy to solemn, and it was only later that I'd come to understand it was because she'd seen the crystal leaf hairpin, which I would learn had belonged to her mother.

Phelan cut through my thoughts. "So here's a sentence I never thought I'd fecking say. Let's discuss how the Sealgaire, a fallen Angel, three reformed demons, and the Savior are going to save the world then, shall we?"

EIGHT

WHILE I SIPPED MY GLASS OF WINE, Phelan filled in more of the blanks for Jonah and me. He explained how he and the others had returned to Lucan and grown the group. He'd spread word through the church, reaching every last congregation up and down the country, and welcomed men by the bucketload who came to join the fight against the Devil and his servants.

His recruitment had been aided by the war that had broken out while Jonah and I had been gone. The one between the Western world and the Middle East.

And with that war at the top of the agenda, Riley wasted no time sliding his smartphone across the table. His browser was opened to a news page that showed images of dismembered bodies piled on top of one another, discovered by the authorities just this morning.

"That's how they find them, like," Riley said. "Never just one or two, always tens of hundreds of bodies, just slung together, pulled apart so bad they can't even identify the people to put them to rest."

I swallowed hard as I scrolled through the images of men and women lying across the ground, mercilessly slaughtered. I'd taken away the Purebloods' sea of souls, and with no prepared supply of dark matter, I'd inadvertently forced their hands. They'd had no choice but to turn a vast amount of light-souled humans into Second Generation Vampires, who would then pillage for them. Whether human beings were being turned or drained dry, it was all the same.

It was all death.

And it was all my fault.

Riley brought up more news reports, this time from America, Europe, Russia . . . on and on he went, and eventually I tuned out. I leaned back, and as I did, I noticed Cameron collecting a second round back at the bar. He had a tray full of drinks, but his focus was elsewhere. He was watching the young girl again.

Phelan had no tolerance for Cameron's delay, and his piercing whistle cut through Riley's rambling about bodies on the train tracks in Munich and the buzz of conversations around us, causing anyone who wasn't already looking at us—which wasn't many—to focus on me. I was less a butterfly and more a goldfish in a very, very small bowl.

Cameron fumbled with the tray, nearly tripping over a

broadly built fella's foot as he rushed over. Riley coughed, thrusting yet more nauseating photographs under my nose.

"Excuse me," I said to him and to Phelan, who was discussing how best to utilize my abilities with Ruadhan and Gabriel. Jonah stood when I did, but I shook my head. "Ladies' room."

Phelan pointed beyond the bar into the far corner. "The jacks are over there."

Ruadhan and Riley slid from the bench, and I escaped before anyone could offer me an escort. Along the way, Cameron collided with my shoulder, almost dropping his tray. I caught it, and his cheeks flamed red.

"You know," I said, "there was a time when spilling drinks was my specialty." For years, I pulled pints in pub after pub as I searched for the apparition who appeared in my dreams, hoping he held the answer to what or who I was. I'd only found out recently that the one in my dreams had been Gabriel. I hadn't realized it at the time, but as complicated as my existence had felt back then, compared with now, it had been simple.

"You waited on people?" Cameron said, tentatively taking the tray back.

"Yes. Difficult to believe this Savior of yours worked as a waitress?"

Cameron wriggled his freckled nose. "Nay. Might have been yonks ago, but the Savior served food and drink at the

Last Supper. Don't see nothin' wrong with you serving it now." He smiled, and I laughed.

"If you say so, Cameron. But word to the wise, don't go handing me a glass of water hoping I'll be able to turn it into a nice merlot." And then I added quietly, "I'm afraid you'd be rather disappointed with what comes back."

He shrugged. "Fair play. Skill sets change, I guess."

I rolled my eyes, but Cameron's focus had already shifted from me—to the brunette. "If you like her, why don't you go and talk to her? I can take the drinks to the table."

At my suggestion, Cameron's body tensed, and the rhythm of his heartbeat quickened. "Nay, that's Molly. We went out for a while, but she got grabbed by one of Doc O'Daly's lads, so . . ." He trailed off, his shoulders slumping.

"You mean she kissed another guy?" I asked, trying to make sense of his Irish slang.

"Aye." He sighed and then, shifting his weight, whispered, "Everyone was talking about it."

I considered his crestfallen expression and then asked the only question I thought really mattered. "When did you fall in love with her?"

"The first time she smiled at me." Cameron's *when* didn't require a date stamp; moments like that were eternal.

I looked to his Molly, who, same as everyone else, was staring at me. Our eyes caught, and she turned, fidgeting uncomfortably in her seat.

I said to Cameron, "What happened, happened. What you choose to do now is up to you. It doesn't matter what anyone said or what they might think." Considering my own romantic situation, I added, "It's your decision, no one else's. Don't get in the way of yourself. For all you know, it might have been a silly mistake. Have you even asked her?"

"Nay."

"Then maybe you should."

"I dunno. Maybe she wanted to kiss him. Or maybe she didn't." He exhaled slowly. "You might be right, mighta been a mistake. I guess we're only human. Can't all of us be saints, like."

I smiled and said, "If you love her the way you say you do, then forgive her, find out where you stand, and if it's right, fight for her."

"I don't even know what I'd say."

Jonah had followed me into the third dimension, his silent action speaking volumes. "Words can be weak, so don't just tell her what she means to you, *show* her."

Cameron took a breath. "Sage words from the sage . . . Kinda hard to ignore, like." That lovely grin of his came back then. With a nervous but excited childlike enthusiasm, he seemed to forget himself as he pecked my cheek. He then swiftly turned beet red.

I laughed, as Phelan shouted from behind me, "For feck's sake, Cam, drinks!"

Cameron rolled his eyes but started toward the table. I

plucked the tray from his hands. "I've got this. You get Molly. No time like the present."

Cameron scratched the back of his head. "Phelan ain't gonna like that much. I'll have to ask her to meet me later."

"Wait—" Balancing the tray one-handed, I grabbed the back of his arm.

"Yes, Lailah?"

"What you said before . . . It's important that you know that there is absolutely nothing *only* about being human."

Cameron took heed and then left in Molly's direction. Just then, the pub doors swung open. The chatter of conversation hushed as a group of men walked in. Dressed smartly, these gentlemen were clearly not members of the Sealgaire. The tall, dark-haired man at the front removed his scarf from around his neck before pushing through the thick layer of smoke that filled the air. As he stepped forward, the chap behind him came into view.

I did a double take.

Here we were, yet again, in the same place at the same time. The theoretical physicist, self-confessed geek, and son of Sir Montmorency, Gabriel's business associate. Darwin. What were the chances?

Darwin waded through Phelan's soldiers, pushing his way to the bar. He scraped back his blond hair and pressed his finger down on the bridge of his glasses before gesturing to the bartender.

Concentrating so intently on Darwin, I jumped when

Gabriel's hand found my shoulder. "Lailah?" he said, his voice sounding an octave higher than usual, acting as the question mark to the end of my name. Never one to forget his manners, Gabriel took the tray from me. "Ah, Darwin," he said.

"Yes, Darwin. What's he doing here?"

"The same as the group he travels with—working."

My mind tumbled. From the conversation I had shared with Darwin at his home in Chelsea, I knew his work had crossed into the realms of the supernatural. With the fixed gateways to the first and third dimensions in Lucan, it seemed unlikely that his presence here was coincidence.

Gabriel changed the subject. "I need to speak with you."

Still thinking about Darwin, I replied absently, "I'm sorry, you've been waiting a long time."

"Three years is nothing. I would wait an eternity, and you know that."

Sadly, I did. And it was the primary reason I wasn't pushing our pending conversation to the top of the pile.

Darwin was shuffling on the stool at the bar, and as he paid for his drinks, he looked past the barman at me. He scratched his head, but as a smile spread across his face, I knew he had placed me. I would find out what Darwin was doing here myself.

Three years Gabriel had waited for me, and his wait wasn't over.

I excused myself in a hurry. "I'm sorry, would you mind taking the drinks? I'll just be a minute, please."

I couldn't be sure how much of my enthusiasm at seeing Darwin had to do with further procrastinating my heart-to-heart with Gabriel and how much was caused by getting a glimpse of a friendly face, one that I had known, albeit briefly, at a simpler time in my life.

Either way, I left Gabriel and eased my way through the crowd.

By the time I reached Darwin, the pub was eerily quiet, so I whispered Darwin's name when I greeted him.

"Cessie," he said, using the name he knew me by. He slid his fingers through mine, regarding me in that familiar way of his. As he squeezed my hands in his, the wooden bar top and the faded paintings hanging over his shoulder on the far back wall all warped. My vision became tunneled. The world around me wobbled.

Like a drawing, ink spread out before me, creating shapes. Two hands, reaching forward . . .

I was experiencing a vision.

Lines continued to form, creating two upside-down triangles that flashed bright green.

I was falling. . . .

As Darwin released me, I was brought back abruptly, and I steadied myself.

Experiencing visions was hardly new. Before I had realized what I was, memories of my past would come to me, activated by my senses—sight, sound, taste, smell, and touch, any of which could take me back to a previous life. But this vision wasn't of what had gone before; it was of what was to come.

It must have all happened so quickly that Darwin didn't notice that anything had transpired. He stepped back to get a better look at me. "I think I might start calling you Psylocke."

I gathered myself quickly. "I'm sorry?"

"She belongs to the Marvel Universe." He emphasized his next words. *"She's a superhero."*

"I'm not sure what would qualify me as a superhero."

"Well, firstly, you do rather look the part. I told you once before that your blue and black contacts were a little too X-Men even for my taste, but then, I hadn't seen them paired with this rather fantastic mask." He fiddled with the wing of one of the blue butterflies next to my ear. "Of course, that's just surface stuff. Scratch to reveal what's underneath, remember?" He was referring to the conversation we'd shared the night we met, when Darwin sought to uncover my true identity.

Under close surveillance from Phelan's private table, I fidgeted as I offered Darwin a small nod. "Forgive me for saying, but you seem a little out of place here. What brings you to Lucan?" I asked, changing the subject. Darwin gestured for me to take the stool beside him but I shook my head. "No, thank you. I won't keep you from your friends." I tipped my chin toward the four men he'd come with, who were unsuccessfully trying to find room at the bar.

Darwin snorted. "You'd think after five years coming back and forth, this place would be a home away from home. You might even expect the locals would be used to me by now, wouldn't you?"

"Five years, that long?"

"I was on my way here when I made your acquaintance, in fact."

The night we met, Darwin's car had broken down outside the pub I was working in. He'd been on his way to Holyhead to catch the ferry across the Irish Sea, saying he was on business. I knew from our second meeting at his father's home in Chelsea that his "business" involved assisting with the study of the singlet particle, a particle that was able to exist and travel through time and space. The crystal from Styclar-Plena contained that very matter. Darwin and the scientists at the European Organization for Nuclear Research, also known as CERN, had discovered it within a crystal taken from the neck of a fallen Angel, which had one way or another ended up in the hands of Darwin's father, Sir Montmorency. Thankfully, the crystals taken from the necks of Angels who requested to fall were virtually void of any light, but there had been residue traces, enough for the physicists to discover the singlet particle when they'd placed the crystals in the Hadron Collider contained within a tunnel deep underground in Switzerland. But how any of that had managed to connect Darwin to Lucan, I didn't know. If I wanted an answer, I was going to have to ask bluntly.

"What business could you possibly have here? It's hardly a place for science."

Darwin regarded me again, deliberating perhaps how much information to give away. "I've always believed that the answers to mankind's most profound questions aren't out there. I always thought they could be found right here. The universe is an ever-expanding entity as it moves forward and spreads out." He demonstrated with his hands. "Many fields of study explore that expansion, but I prefer to delve into the layers that make up our universe, or as we call it in the business, M-theory."

Gathering his change from the bartender, he placed a number of coins corner to corner, creating a small circle. "Other dimensions, Cessie." Picking up the euros one by one, he created a stack. "Lucan is, shall we say, a very interesting place, one that keeps calling me back." Cupping his palm behind his coin tower, he slid it off the bar and then discarded them into a tip jar.

The gateways to the first and the third dimensions . . . were they bringing Darwin here? Did he know they existed? If he knew and if he had been coming here for five years, clearly either he'd never managed to locate them or someone was preventing him from doing so.

"I'm surprised you've left Chelsea, what with everything that's going on in the world." I was fishing, throwing out my line to see if I might catch something unexpected. Still, the fresh knowledge of what was happening to humans made my stomach roil.

Darwin raised an eyebrow. "You know, when we met, you reminded me of the person I lost, the person I wished more than anything I had been able to save, and so I wanted to help you." He thought carefully. "So I'm going to tell you something very few people know, in the hope that you'll let me do for you what I couldn't do for her." He looked me straight in the eye. "The government is lying when they say that the Spinodes are people affected by the fallout from the chemical explosions. Of course, they are affected by something, but it has nothing to do with the poison gas. The world's leaders know the truth, and they've known it for a very long while now."

I waited with the appropriate amount of bated breath one might expect from someone not in the know.

Darwin nodded, continuing, "They don't come from the farthest corners of space. They exist in dimensions that are stacked above and below our own, places where time doesn't touch them. Interdimensional aliens, Cessie, and I am not talking 'little green men.'" He was right, of course—not that he knew that I knew it. "I couldn't save her, but maybe I can save you." Searching, he dug deep into his blazer pockets, revealing his T-shirt, which had the number 42 printed on the chest. To anyone else it might not mean a thing, but Darwin had informed me that this number was of paramount importance. That it was "the answer to the ultimate question of life, the universe, and everything." Well, at least according to *The Hitchhiker's Guide to the Galaxy.*

Finally, he produced a business card. Embossed in fancy lettering was "Dr. Darwin B. B. Montmorency, PhD, SM," followed by his job title, "Senior Theoretical Physicist," and his place of work, "CERN." In a plain font, Darwin's cell number and e-mail address were printed at the bottom.

"PhD . . . SM . . . That's a whole lot of letters," I mused.

"You can be impressed when I've added 'ScD'—my doctorate in science. Hopefully my contribution to CERN will soon take care of that."

He slid a Mont Blanc fountain pen out of his back trouser pocket and pulled the top off with his teeth. He scribbled something on the back of the card before handing it to me. "In case you don't remember, this is my address in Chelsea. I'm leaving in an hour, and I don't suppose I'll be able to convince you to come with me this evening." He didn't wait for a reply, assuming my answer would be the same as the night he had met me. "Please think on what I have told you and follow me to London."

He squeezed his hands over the top of mine, causing the business card to crumple within my palm. That same feeling I'd experienced during the visions on the hilltop ran beneath my skin, turning my blood cold as he offered his final words of warning.

"Please believe me when I tell you that I have seen and I have known a great deal of unfathomable things in my short years, and listen to me when I say that there are some threats even the greatest of superheroes cannot overcome." He eyed me carefully and tipped his chin as he once again focused on my butterflies. "Whatever this is all about, you should rethink it. Go back to being Betsy Braddock and leave this place, because if you stay here . . ." He released my hands and voiced the very words I knew in my soul to be true. "You will die here."

NINE

AFTER DARWIN'S HAUNTING ADMONITION, he left swiftly. A few hours later, my group was on its way back to the main house. With Phelan beside me, Jonah, Gabriel, and Ruadhan trailed behind. I could sense unrest within Jonah, but I didn't know why. More than once I glanced over my shoulder to see if he was okay, and it was only when he winked at me the third time that I was reassured.

More than twenty members of the Sealgaire accompanied us. Apparently the Savior required close guard day and night. I'd insisted the men concentrate their efforts on protecting one another and the townspeople, not waste their energy on me. I could more than take care of myself. But Phelan had over-ruled me, and though he'd said it was for my safety, I mostly thought it was so he could keep a close eye on my movements while plans were hatched to win this war. Despite several hours of discussion, ideas on how to do this were sparse. With hundreds of thousands of Second Generation Vampires now roaming the Earth, how a single individual would be able to effect any kind of meaningful change was a question no one had a definitive answer for.

Not far from the main house, or Sealgaire HQ, as Phelan preferred his home to be known, a teary-eyed Molly suddenly appeared on the pavement. Calling after her as she hurried toward us, Cameron wasn't far behind, but it was Phelan raising his hand in the air that made Molly halt. Before he had a chance to address her or Cameron, I shouted, "Wait!"

Ruadhan picked up on the slightest shiver within the tree's branches overhead only a second after I did. And as I twisted around, he'd already stretched his arms out protectively in front of Gabriel and Iona. Then, bending his knees, he jumped and curled into a forward somersault, propelling the Vampire away. To the human eye, a mere shape blurred as Ruadhan's feet thrust out into the air, but I had seen and cataloged every feature, from the Vampire's emerald-green eyes before they began to burn to the scar running down his cheek and over his lip.

The three soldiers marching ahead of us spun around and raised their shotguns, searching for something to shoot at. Electric light sizzled at my fingertips, but a sharp sting scraped in my throat, distracting me. I whirled around, and in the second it took me to check that Jonah was still with us, the three men were taken, pulled up by their shotguns and stolen into the night. Carried on the breeze, their cries lasted longer than they did.

The remaining men clicked their shotguns' safeties off in unison and took up a defensive stance, spreading out to provide us with coverage.

Jonah wasn't where I'd last seen him, and as I sought him out in the inner circle, I ran through my register: Gabriel, Ruadhan, Iona, Riley, Jack, and Phelan, all present, but no sign of *my* Vampire.

I growled.

Vampires, plural, now moved above us like shadows, disguised against the darkness. Branches bowed and snapped as the demons leaped from one tree to the next. Low, pained moans accompanied their dance. As I ran my eyes once more around the circle, looking for Jonah, stringy, sticky drool pooled on one of the soldier's shoulders. I shouted, "Get down!"

The fair-haired boy ducked immediately, narrowly avoiding the Vampire's bloodstained hungry hands, which swiped erratically into empty air. My streak of light reached the Vampire's chest midflight and he lit up like a firework, exploding in a ball of flame. The toasted embers of his remains scattered as they turned to ash, and it was as if he had never existed at all.

Though they hesitated, taken aback by my work, the Sealgaire took aim at the starving savages atop the trees. My light was just enough for them to aim and fire their weapons.

The Vampires overhead were not strong and stealthy. They

were sickly and sluggish, their skin rotting from their bones. Starving and malnourished, it seemed to me that the ones who were stopping to attack were acting out of desperation.

I listened for the *trump pump* of Jonah's heartbeat, trying to distinguish it from those of the demons, now fleeing in a frenzy, but he wasn't among them.

There was a shrill hiss as a Vampire darted from above us, careening in my direction. Phelan knocked me away, pulling a silver dagger from his back pocket, and he rammed it into the demon's chest. The impaled Vampire gurgled and a thick tar bubbled from the corner of her discolored lips. Phelan forced her chin back with the ball of his hand, retracting his blade in one clean and concise move. The Vampire's form burst, soaking the pavement and turning into nothing more than a gooey puddle.

Behind me, Gabriel broke away from Ruadhan, leaving Iona in his care as he rushed to my side. Iona's expression should have been filled with panic, but as she watched Gabriel leave, her plump lower lip hung open. She was upset that he would abandon her so easily for me.

"What are you doing?" I snapped.

"Protecting you." His reply was swift as he yanked me toward him, attempting to shield me with his body.

Drawing my face into his chest, he clipped my butterfly's wings, and as I pushed him back, the butterfly stretched and took flight. "No, Gabriel," I said.

Undeterred, he reached for my waist, fighting for me.

It was a fight he would lose.

"I don't need you, *she does*—" I was stopped short, interrupted by Molly's hysterical scream that cut through the cold as a wounded Vampire dragged her along the roadside by the hem of her skirt.

I didn't need the protection of this circle of soldiers, but Molly did.

Neither did I need the protection Gabriel was trying to afford me, but Iona did.

Molly, Iona, and the members of the Sealgaire, all considered collateral damage to Gabriel.

My hands grew warm as I willed my light, but being surrounded by the Sealgaire and their silver weapons made this a struggle. The quickest way out was up. I crouched and launched high into the air, meeting two Vampires and taking them both with me as I hurled back down to the roadside outside of the protective circle. I held each one by the scruff of its neck. Their skin fried under the fire burning in my palms. A blinding glow projected like the sun's rays out from in between the gaps of my fingers. The Vampires' limp bodies dropped, followed by their heads, which had been torn straight off from the force of my light.

Stepping up beside me, Cameron shakily pointed a crossbow at the Vampire dragging Molly. The silver arrow whipped through the air, narrowly missing its target, hitting the demon in the arm instead of the chest. Still, the Vampire dropped to the ground, wailing as the silver sparked against his skin.

Cameron drew a nervous breath. His big, soft eyes sought my approval, and then I understood why. "Show her, right?" His voice wobbled.

Running over to Molly, he pulled her up from the ground, but it wasn't Cameron's arms from which she sought solace. She fled to one of the soldiers behind me, calling "William!" as she grabbed and then clung to him.

I met Cameron's crestfallen expression with an apologetic one. He may have loved Molly, and maybe Molly had loved him once, but seemingly she had moved on.

A twitch on the ground drew my attention, and I anticipated the Vampire's action a second before he sprang to his feet. Cameron, however, was staring after his Molly, totally unaware that this demon's claws were only inches from his throat. My light pulsed, bouncing between my fingers, and I concentrated, joining the bolts together. I commanded the white light to stretch out in a single, deadly sheet, but then the flutter of Jonah's heartbeat resounded inside me, distracting me. I zoned in on the origin of the sound, finding him up ahead, slumped against a stone wall.

I should have been able to sense where he was long before now.

I choked like an old, useless car as I tried to pull back the throttle. Jonah was in the line of fire. He was too close. I couldn't guarantee my sheet of light wouldn't hit him, and if it did, he would be ended along with the Vampire at Cameron's back. It took all my concentration, but as the white flickered into a blue hue, I managed to break the sheet apart, creating small halos that ran up and down my fingers instead.

But as I expelled the rings, I was knocked clean off my feet, tackled to the ground by Gabriel. Another Vampire had swooped to attack me, but as he came from my left I hadn't seen the demon in my peripheral vision, but Gabriel had. My halos missed their intended target, striking the concrete instead. One second was all the Vampire behind Cameron needed to grab him, and I was two seconds too long willing a further bout of light to stop the demon from stealing him away.

A whoosh of wind lifted the leaves beside me as the Vampire Gabriel had just knocked away swung back toward us. I thrust Gabriel off me, and he landed on his back as I catapulted myself into the air. On course to meet the Vampire, I recognized the scar slicing down his cheek. This was the same Vampire Ruadhan had fended off. Lean and muscular, he was not like the others. He was able and clever. Meticulous in his execution, at the last moment the Vampire changed course, diving toward Gabriel's chest instead of meeting me in the air.

The Vampire didn't want me. He wanted Gabriel.

"No!" I shouted. Twisting midflight, I swiped my hand out, just able to grab the tail of the Vampire's jacket. Now that Gabriel was a fallen Angel, the best thing he could do was get the hell out of the way, but gifts or no gifts, Gabriel wouldn't let me fight his battles.

Clutching the Vampire's jacket, I flung him backward, and below me Gabriel called out to William.

The young lad must have thrown Gabriel a weapon, because just as the Vampire's ascent brought him to my eye level, my superior strength stalled. A silver arrowhead shot past me, missing the Vampire's chest but striking him through the cheek. The demon slapped his gloved hand to his jaw, a heinous cry escaping him, and in the moment it took me to regain my focus he had disappeared.

An acrid scent permeated the chilled air as the last of the gunfire sounded. The Vampires fled, heading in the direction Jonah and I had come from this morning.

On his back, Gabriel clutched a speargun in his right hand. I pulled him up by his left, shaking my head.

While the men behind me collected themselves, I zoomed using the power of thought to Jonah, who was struggling to stand.

"You're hurt," I said, forcing his hand away from his neck.

"I'm fine," he snapped, using the stone wall to steady himself.

"Silver?" As soon as I asked it, I knew it wasn't, but then I didn't understand. An injury caused by anything but silver shouldn't sit on a Vampire's skin for more than a moment. The skin on Jonah's neck had been split, and it hadn't healed yet. That wasn't right.

"I'm fine," he growled. Somehow, someone had gotten the better of him, and Jonah didn't like that one bit. Running his gaze over me hurriedly, he said, "Are you okay?"

I furrowed my brow. Jonah should know without having

to ask. We were connected by blood, which caused physical sensations as well as elevated emotion to pass between us.

Phelan's deep voice came from behind me. "You shouldn't have left the circle."

I turned to face him, but as I opened my mouth to reply, my gaze fell to Cameron's crossbow, which lay strewn on the ground, broken in two. I knelt down, collecting the wooden pieces and snapped string. Splatters of the little red-haired warrior's wet blood freckled over the tiller, the fragrance as sweet as he was.

"Cameron—" I uttered his name in a whisper. "Which way did the Vampire take him?" I demanded, facing Phelan.

Phelan pinched the bridge of his nose, but then shook his head slowly. "The demon killed him, Lailah. I saw it myself."

Rusty dark-brown liquid pooled under my feet. Mixed together, it was impossible to tell how much was Cameron's blood and how much had been the Vampire's.

I didn't have to search far to find Ruadhan, and his hand stretched behind my back comfortingly. "Cameron was a light soul," I said, knowing Ruadhan would understand. The Purebloods fed from humans with dark souls and turned people with light souls into Second Generation Vampires. The demon at Cameron's back wouldn't have wanted to feed from him, but as I looked to Molly cowering at William's back, there was no luminous glow framing her body. It had been her whom the Vampire had wanted to make a meal of.

"Aye, love. He didn't drink from the lad, but Cameron had shot him—" Ruadhan didn't finish his sentence and I knew what he was implying. The Vampire might not have wanted to drink from Cameron, but it had wanted him to pay for the silver arrow Cameron had struck him with.

"We can't be sure—"

Phelan cut me off. "Like I said, I saw it myself."

My mind whizzed, ready to argue, but then Jonah spitting up blood took my attention. His eyes met mine. He needed my help, and I didn't think he could wait.

"You did all you could do, love," Ruadhan said as I stepped away. Still clutching Cameron's broken bow, I walked toward Jonah.

Done all I could do, indeed. Cameron's death was my fault. I had judged the situation—no, I had judged Molly—wrongly, and my stupid advice had caused Cameron to fight for someone undeserving. I narrowed my eyes at Molly, but before she reacted, Gabriel grabbed my arm, blocking my view of her and my path to Jonah at the same time. My upset was replaced with anger.

It might have been my fault that Cameron had gone after Molly, it might even have been my fault that he had tried to show her that he loved her by defending her, but it sure as hell was Gabriel's fault that my halos of light had missed.

"His blood is on your hands, too, Gabriel." My tone was callous, and before I could go any further, Phelan interrupted.

"We should get inside." He began instructing his men to form a protective shield around me, but I didn't move; I was too angry and too upset to hold my tongue.

To Gabriel I said, "You shouldn't have jumped on me. I missed my shot because of you."

"I didn't have a lot of choice. You didn't see the Vampire," Gabriel started, his voice soft.

I shrugged off his comment, unprepared to confirm what he suspected—that I was blind in my left eye, that I hadn't seen the Vampire coming, that I was weak.

Phelan interjected a second time. "Lailah, we've just lost Cameron. I can't stand here and risk losing any more of my men."

Though he tried to disguise it, there was a quiver in Phelan's voice when he said Cameron's name, and I relented. "Fine."

Ruadhan and Phelan collected Iona and Molly, hurrying them ahead of us.

As we marched forward, to Gabriel I said, "Clearly you've been making friends while I've been gone. That Vampire wanted you, not me. He lured you out from the protection of the circle by coming at me, knowing you'd be stupid enough to take the bait because you got a case of the heroics trying to defend me before! He was cool and calculated and he wanted *your* blood—" I stopped myself as nausea swelled in the pit of my stomach. I looked over to Jonah, who was steadying himself against the wall. "I don't have time for this, I don't have time for you."

Gabriel's tone was as angry as it was sad. "There was a point when you had all the time in the world for me, Lailah.

When I was everything you needed. I don't understand. What happened to us?" His voice lowered. "What happened to you?"

I hesitated, rocking on the back of my heels. To be fair to Gabriel, only I could remember the conversation we'd shared, the one in which I had said that I no longer wanted to be with him, before I'd turned back the clock and saved Jonah. But it was not one that I desired to rehash. It had cut deep the first time, and I suspected with the way I felt now, the wound would prove fatal if I tried to have it again. "I changed. I had to change, to save you, to save him." I waved my hand in Jonah's direction. "To be able to save everyone."

"Everyone but yourself," Gabriel replied.

"In the end, yes." We neared the gate of the main house. "Go in," I said, calling the soldiers around us to break formation and filter inside. Ahead, Phelan was ushering Iona and Molly through the front door; this time he didn't argue with me.

As the last of the men marched by, I turned to leave, but Gabriel blocked me.

"You'd leave me here with nothing, wouldn't you? What did I do to make you hate me?" he said.

Gabriel had murdered Hanora, had tried to murder Jonah. He had always been prepared to sacrifice anyone and everyone in my name. And here we were, the first day reunited after three years apart, and he was still doing it, only this time the forfeit for my life was Cameron's. I was so angry, but the pained rasp in his voice caused me to remember what we had once meant to each other—how he had saved me, how he had led me to the answer I had sought for so long, the answer to what I was.

His ends did not justify his means. Yet I knew he only did what he did out of love. I couldn't agree with his choices, but then, I knew all too well what love could make one do. I'd just proved it, saving Jonah at the cost of another.

"I could never hate you, Gabriel. I love you. I will always love you. And it is because I love you that I let you go. And it's because you love me that you let me leave. You just don't remember it happening."

Gabriel's confused, faded blue eyes made me sad. "And Jonah?"

I didn't want to hurt Gabriel, and so I hesitated to answer.

"He loves you," Gabriel said.

I looked to Jonah, who, in the black of night, was waiting for me, and our eyes found each other's. I thought of the plea he made underneath the old oak tree as I took what I thought to be my last breaths. He had asked me not to leave him in the darkness all alone.

I hadn't realized what Gabriel had said was meant as a statement, not a question, and so I answered, "I don't know."

Gabriel's brow dipped and his bottom lip hung open ready to reply, but I shook my head. "Good night, Gabriel. Jonah needs me."

I left him standing in the street alone. We were no longer connected by light and so I didn't hear Gabriel trying to speak to my mind as he said, "So do I."

TEN

WITH HIS ARM DRAPED across my shoulders, I bore Jonah's weight and helped him through the door of Little Blue.

"Here," I said, easing him down on the sofa. Though I was sure that once Phelan had collected himself, he would instruct his best men to stand guard, I locked the door and fastened the shutters.

Jonah slipped his arms out of his dark coat and pressed his hands down on his neck. Rich, red blood seeped through his fingers, and cinnamon infused the air.

Automatically, my fangs cracked. I bit my lower lip, struggling to rise above my body's reaction. I continued on, helping him pull his T-shirt over his head, and grabbed a towel that I folded and used as a compress against the wound in his neck.

But my purest instincts betrayed me again. Even as Jonah

sat, bleeding when he shouldn't be, the sight of his toned torso made my blood warm. I swallowed hard and pressed the cloth harder against his skin.

It took me a minute to find my voice, and all the while I could feel Jonah silently staring at me. Finally, I met his eyes and said, "How did this happen?"

Jonah shrugged, but the movement caused him pain, and he hissed as he sucked in air.

I lifted the towel, expecting the wound to have at least decreased in size, but it was just as bad.

Jonah wasn't healing. The why plagued my thoughts and left fear in my gut, but at least I knew that I alone would be able to help.

I kicked off my boots and leaned into Jonah, who gently shook his head. "You don't have to."

"I want to. And there's no reason not to," I said.

I kneeled next to him on the sofa and assessed the damage. A lion might as well have mauled him. Four razor streaks tore through his throat, extending as far as the top of his shoulder.

"Are you in much pain?" I asked. For some reason, our connection was no longer enough to tell me what he was truly feeling.

"Stings, that's all," he said. But I knew Jonah, and it was causing him more discomfort than he was prepared to admit.

I cupped his cheeks in my hands. "Emery is gone, and with him your link to the Purebloods. Your taking my blood won't cause them to sense me, and it wouldn't matter even if it did. Zherneboh will know I am alive by now, because so, too, is his world."

Jonah held my wrists and squeezed. "I might find it hard to—"

"But you *will*."

His fears were understood—I knew them firsthand. When I had drunk from Jonah under the old oak tree, he'd become a stranger. My hunger took complete hold of me. But then I had heard his heartbeat, and it had led me home. My love for him outweighed my dark desires. It was an impossible struggle, and at the time, it had caused me to wonder how he had managed to withdraw on the occasions he had taken my blood. But then I later learned that both times a spark had ignited, shocking Jonah when he came too close to draining away my dark energy, preventing him from drinking me to an end. My built-in security system had served me well, but my safety came at a cost. Because of it, I would never know if the thief at my door would have been kind enough to leave his heart in place of my own.

Peeling back Jonah's heavy fingers, I brought my wrist to my lips. Gently, I kneaded my skin and then hooked my fangs into a thick blue vein.

I held out my offering, and Jonah took me by my waist into his lap. Squeezing my arm tightly, he hesitated, but then his mouth met my skin. He inhaled sharply and the tip of his tongue glided over the laceration, gently mopping up the taste of me. His dark, luscious eyelashes batted frantically, framing the bloodied explosion that was racing around his pupils. I dared him to take me with a low, encouraging growl.

Sharing blood was more than an exercise in necessity; it was the only way to truly fill the emptiness inside, to briefly breathe life down death's dark hallways.

That night under the old oak tree, Jonah hadn't thought twice about offering himself to me, and so today, I returned the favor in kind. I was happy to share a part of myself with him. At least then, when all this was over and I was gone, he would be left with something. It wouldn't give him the forever he wanted, but it was the best I could do.

Jonah's fangs scratched my skin, and though this was for him, I couldn't help taking my own enjoyment.

Jonah may have had a taste, but before he began to drink he stopped.

He lifted me off his lap and placed me beside him. My senses told me why. The last of his cinnamon scent evaporated as his skin stitched until it was smooth once more. Thankful as I was that his body had healed, my chest fell with disappointment at our connection being broken.

I stalled before standing. "Well, looks like you don't need me after all."

Jonah winked at me. "I wouldn't say that." He rose to his feet, and my eyes lingered on the rippled muscles of his stomach and cut lines around his hips, revealed by his low-slung jeans. My insides stirred.

"If this is about our conversation earlier—" I started, but Jonah raised his finger to my lips and shushed me.

"No more talking."

His hand found the dip at the bottom of my spine and he pulled me into his bare chest. He was soft at first, his bottom lip catching the top of mine. But as he pressed down, he stifled a low, animalistic groan that made me shiver. I leaned back, but his skilled fingers had already threaded through the back of my short hair and he held me firmly in place. The more he tasted, the more he wanted, and he invaded me more urgently now. His kiss was pure sin; and as our tongues tangled, I wondered what penalty I'd have to pay for it—surely nothing this good could ever be free.

Rising on tiptoes, I stretched to meet his six-foot height; and already dizzy from his carnal assault, I became unsteady on my feet. Jonah yanked me up and onto his boots, drawing me close enough to burrow into that sweet spot in the crevice of my neck. He skimmed his hand down my torso until it collided with the leather belt tied around my waist.

His breath hot and heavy at my collarbone, he parted the lace at my back. So close now, Jonah didn't smell like Jonah. He wasn't wearing his usual woody, summertime aftershave, and the way things were going, pretty soon that wouldn't be the only thing he wasn't wearing.

He clasped my hands together behind his neck, where beads of his sweat trickled over my fingers. His natural pheromone was musky and alluring, and I quivered deep down low.

He reached for the belt at my midriff and began to unfurl the hard leather. Watching me, he snapped the belt as he whipped it away. Breathless, I watched him back.

His eyes were dark and brooding, and as the leather hit the floor, my knees bowed.

My insides twisted with a wicked want. When Jonah's lips once again found my neck, I encouraged him by tipping my head back. His tongue rolled over my throat, and his fangs grazed my chin. But as he hooked his fingers underneath my cap sleeves, tugging at the fabric, I became nervous. Unlike Gabriel, Jonah was rough around the edges, but he wore it well, as though he had been deliberately chiseled that way. His expertise was written in his every move. Of course it was. He was intoxicating from the inside out, and I was surely not the first woman in the world to know this. And I began to fear that I would not live up—not so much to those others but to him, to the image that Jonah had created of me.

I pulled away, unable to find the words to express my fears, my pupils growing wide and worried.

Jonah stopped, and his Adam's apple bulged as he swallowed. "Are you scared of me?"

"No," I whispered.

Tentatively, Jonah tucked a wayward strand of hair behind my ear, waiting, now with the utmost patience, for me to tell him how I felt.

"I've . . ." I flushed. "I've never done this before."

A small, almost relieved snort escaped Jonah's lungs. "That makes two of us, beautiful."

I furrowed my brow. "You're seriously trying to tell me you've never had sex before? *You?*"

Jonah didn't reply immediately. Instead, he pulled a throw off the couch and spread it across my shoulders. "Sorry," he said. "That's not what I meant." He brushed the edge of a butterfly beside my eye, and then contemplatively with his fingertip he traced my facial features, only stopping when he reached the middle of my bottom lip. Then, and only then, did he finally finish: "But never like this."

Reassured, and wanting nothing in the world more, I exhaled the breath I hadn't realized I had been holding, and I nodded.

His huge hazel eyes never left mine as, more slowly, he peeled away my dress, which cascaded to the floor, leaving me bare but shrouded by the blanket. Pressing his steely body against mine, Jonah brought the blanket around us both, and we collapsed to the floor wrapped in each other's arms.

And what little I had left for him to take, I gladly gave him. . . .

A PIPE ORGAN RESOUNDED, causing me to stir in my sleep.

Uri—my fantastic white mare from a bygone life—manifested in the void of my unconscious mind. Her big, beautiful eyes glowed, her nostrils flared, and she reared. As her hooves lifted, her thick mane stopped flowing, and the shine on her glossy fur faded to matte. The life sucked out of her, Uri became inanimate before me, as if she were somehow carved out of wood.

Thick, colorful strokes painted tack onto her white coat, followed by pastel flowers that bloomed across the bridle at her forehead. A garland of pink roses grew over her body like vines, dressing her for show. A twisted golden pole appeared, sinking through the saddle, and the wooden replica of my once best friend started to bob up and down.

In time with the unmistakable sound of the fairground music, three more horses, painted in blue, green, and orange, joined her on the carousel, and now, with renewed life, round and round she went.

As bells began to ring, chiming in time with the organ, the image faded away. In the dark recesses of my mind, paint spilled, turning the backdrop from black to white.

Charcoal drew upon the newly white page, sketching a hillside, tree branches, and the basic outline of people scattered at the base of the tree.

What was this?

Suddenly, the scene began to animate like a stop-motion film.

The characters darted, disappearing and reappearing on the stage. From the bottom lip of the scene, the outline of a man's body appeared, his limbs moving bit by bit with each new frame until he jumped high, disappearing out of sight in the top left corner. Three frames later he reappeared, rejoining the story, towering over another person down on the ground.

Up until now the film had been black-and-white, but as the figure leaning over the body turned his head, bright red paint ran down the scene before the whole thing turned to black.

The fairground music faded, and a single sweet voice began to sing, manipulating me into thinking it was now safe. The blackness lightened and the chilling character was gone, replaced by a faceless man and woman sitting on the ground. Though the lyrics were different, the melody was familiar. It was the notes of the song that had once belonged to Gabriel and me.

Once again the image flickered to black and a three-dimensional figure began to draw itself, starting with a large circle colored white inside, followed by a smaller one that sat atop the first like a head on a round figure. Two upside-down triangles appeared inside the head, and though the image was white on black, the triangles—the eyes—lit up bright green.

It was so quiet now.

It was so still.

The figure blurred, the chalk was brushed away, and whatever story had been trying to be told finished. I woke up, my conscious freed, but "The End" never came.

ELEVEN

I woke up convulsing, Jonah's arms draped around my shoulders. I gasped, and Jonah's palm pressed down on my chest.

"Lailah?" he said. "What's wrong?"

He pulled me against his torso in an effort to help stop my trembling. I couldn't respond, as the last few moments of the vision had knocked the wind out of me. Dizzy and disoriented, I was able to ignore the fact that I had awoken wrapped up in Jonah, completely naked.

"Take three deep breaths," he said.

I listened to him and concentrated.

One.

Two.

"That's it. In through your nose, out through your mouth," he said calmly.

Three.

I closed my eyes, but in the darkness the green triangles flashed. My body tensed, and my toes curled against Jonah's calf as I tried to escape the image.

"You're freezing." Jonah pulled the edges of the red knitted throw together, helping to cover us both more tightly. When I said nothing, he pressed again. "Nightmare?"

My feet were like two blocks of ice and I tried to rub them together to warm myself, but my blood ran cold.

"I need to get dressed." Still shivering, I stood. He didn't protest and rose with me, taking the throw from around his back and tucking me inside, covering me completely.

I made my way to the table, feeling his eyes boring through my back as I sorted through the clothes Brooke had left for me. I pieced together an outfit, using the time to steady my nerves.

Once I'd calmed, I peered over my shoulder to Jonah, who still stood stark naked. My eyes on his, I released my grasp on the blanket, and the throw fell to the floor. Though he otherwise appeared unaffected, his breath hitched unmistakably.

A sudden dread crept under my skin. I turned my face before a single tear splashed down my cheek, and though I didn't know why, I knew that my sadness belonged to him.

I began to dress, and as I reached behind my back to fasten the clasp on my bra, my fingers met Jonah's.

/

He straightened the straps at my shoulders before he skillfully skimmed my curves. He turned me around, holding on to my waist. He murmured, "Stop trying to distract me. Tell me what's wrong."

I traced his defined muscles, wondering if there was really any point in rehashing the visions with him. Finally, I rested my hands at his chest, sighed, and then whispered, "I love you." My words were not meant to be an answer to his question, but little did I know that it was the most honest answer I could have given.

I didn't wait for a reply, assuming those were three words that didn't exist in Jonah's vocabulary, though last night the way he had held me, the way he had touched me, couldn't have felt like anything but.

No response came and we both turned our attention to dressing. I pulled on a pair of black jeans and a plain T-shirt.

After wriggling my feet into leather ankle boots, I reached for the square mirror set on the table and found the crystal hairpin on the sofa, tossed aside by Jonah at some point last night. He'd been more focused on me, covering my scars with his kisses as though he were trying to use his lips to take away the afflictions riddling my skin, and I'd let him. I'd been utterly immersed in him as he'd stripped me bare, and the only thing that had managed to pull me out of the surreal embrace was when the back of his hands had once again grazed the edge of the butterfly mask. He'd wanted to peel it away, but I'd stopped him.

Though the jagged scar Frederic had left running down my back had bothered me once, it didn't anymore. The same could be said for every last mark that brandished my body. If they had once caused me concern, they didn't any longer.

Jonah had seized up when he'd reached my midriff and the sight of the scars created at his hand. Though he'd once called them ugly, I couldn't have disagreed with him more. He was alive because of them, and I wore the lashes like a badge of honor.

While the mask was still in one piece, as I looked in the handheld mirror, I could see that none of the fabric butterflies had managed to survive. Brooke would be mad, but I knew she'd insist on making more even though the truth was that the painted mask was easier to wear without them.

I folded the red throw and rested it on the couch beside Jonah. "You said all I was missing was a cape. Looks like you found me one."

Jonah ruffled his disheveled hair. "Lailah—"

"Nothing about me is normal, Jonah, and that includes my dreams."

"Jeez, you went white as a ghost, you started fading in and out like you did—"

"Under the old oak tree," I said, finishing his sentence. I then reached across the sofa to open the shutters, letting the morning sun shine through. "I used to dream about my past." I laughed sarcastically. "I guess you could say that I used to dream about the beginning. Today I was dreaming about the end."

"The end?" he echoed.

"Yes." Since that first sketch appeared in my vision on the hilltop, I'd known that what was being drawn before me was my final scene; each vision I'd had since had only depicted the same.

Jonah stared at me, expressionless. "Explain."

I didn't want to tell him. I didn't want to take away from the night we had just spent together. So wonderful, but so wicked—one night with Jonah would never be enough. The light bounced and reflected off the crystal hairpin as I fiddled with it. "When we came out of the third, at the cliff edge, I experienced a vision, but it wasn't of the past, it was of the future. There were ghostlike shadows of people, and you were there, but then there was someone else. . . . I'm not sure who, but he called my name."

"He?" Jonah cut in.

"It was a deep voice, too deep to belong to a woman, and then I was falling." I shook my head, trying to recall the detail. "It happened again in the pub, but different. There were these *hands* . . . dressed in black gloves, and then above them there were two bright-green triangles." I scowled as my mind backtracked and then came full circle, recalling the haunting sounds and images from this morning's dream. "I don't understand how it all fits together, and I don't need to, because I feel it, Jonah. I feel it in my bones. What I'm seeing, what I'm dreaming . . . it is the end. . . . It's the day I *die*."

Jonah's eyes fell to the carpet, and when they returned to me, their hazel had turned blood-red. "What about just now? What did you dream, Lailah?"

I played with the hairpin, but then Jonah's hand was over the top of mine, forcing me to be still. "I don't know. It doesn't make any sense. What does it even matter?"

"Just tell me."

Taking my hand from under his, I slid the hairpin into place in the strands above my right ear. "There was music, really old fairground music. And Uri appeared." I paused. "My horse. I once had a horse in my first life, did I ever tell you that?"

Jonah shook his head.

"I guess there's a lot we don't know about each other."

"I know everything I need to. It's not a prerequisite to have shared a past in order to share a future, you know."

Why was he talking like this? I thought I'd made myself clear. "I told you before, I don't have a future. Which makes this conversation pointless. The details don't matter."

Before I could walk away, Jonah had me by the elbow, tugging me back toward him. "I need to know."

"Why? So you can save me?" I snorted. "There is no saving me, Jonah. Not this time."

Jonah growled in such a way that the hairs on my arm stood on end.

I said, "I should have died in the third, but you had to come wading in and drag me back here—"

"Yeah, and you seem real grateful."

"'Thank you' is the last thing you'll be hearing from me." My eyes narrowed. "You really want to know how I did it? How I was able to save you? I offered myself. I exchanged my existence for yours. I took your place."

"Bullshit," he said flatly. When I didn't argue back, he only became more agitated. "Exactly who the hell do you think you made a deal with?"

"The universe." I shrugged. "*God*."

"We both know damn well you're not religious. Try again, beautiful."

"What's religion got to do with God?"

Jonah shook his head. "So now what? You suddenly believe in some illusive, invisible force, so much so, in fact, that you're prepared to let it play puppet master with your life because you think you owe it something?" When I didn't reply immediately, Jonah cursed under his breath. "There's nothing wrong with having faith, beautiful, but there are better places to put it."

"Such as?"

His hand found my cheek then, and looking me square in the eye, he said, "Me."

"I do have faith in you, but I've learned to manage my expectations. There are three words you just can't give me, Jonah. They're beyond you."

My Vampire released me. "You need me to say them that badly?" he said.

He'd misunderstood.

I clarified for him. "I'm talking about 'happily ever after.' There will be only two words printed on the last page of my story. Two words, six letters, that simply spell out 'The End.'" I quietly added in a whisper, "Maybe, when all this is over, it's all I will deserve."

Jonah turned away from me as he swallowed my bitter pill, and a defiant growl rose in his throat. "Managing your expectations, huh? Nice, beautiful."

I didn't need to be connected by blood to sense I had pissed him off. The veins in his neck jutted out, and his fangs cracked, making it impossible to disguise his anger.

"There is nothing that is beyond me," he started, and the arrogant look on his face took me back to the Jonah I'd first known. But then he stopped, catching himself.

"Go on," I said, "don't hold back on my account. You always get the last word, remember? It's the reason we're all in this mess, and I'm starting to think it has nothing to do with me and everything to do with your distaste for losing."

Vampires move fast, but this was blinding. He hoisted me up and his hot mouth was against mine before the last syllable left my lips. His kiss was hard, and it was endless, and it branded me as his.

His hands tangled in my hair, and he released me only when the taste of my blood spread across his tongue. Bringing his finger to my bottom lip, he blotted where he'd nipped me. As he exhaled, he said, "If you're right, if there is a God, then even if he's the one holding all the cards, I won't fold. At the end, I'll be the one to deliver the only three words that matter."

Jonah surprised me, and I struggled to keep it together as I broke away. One more minute in his company and I might start to believe him.

I stumbled out the door of Little Blue. As I stepped into the path of the rising sun, countless crystals rose up and out of my body. The hairpin reflected and refracted the rays at every angle. Encapsulated by the light, to Jonah behind me, and to Phelan's men in front of me, I became invisible.

Though what Jonah and the Sealgaire believed in was different, each one did believe in something; they all had faith. So even though I could not be seen, they knew that I was still there.

TWELVE

I KNOCKED ON THE DOOR of the motor home and Ruadhan answered. "Good morning," he said, inviting me inside.

I greeted him and made my way into the living room, where Gabriel sat holding a mug of fresh coffee. He rose from his chair, an unsure smile welcoming me, and I stalled to return it, noticing how tired he looked. Angels, fallen or otherwise, were able to sleep, but the bags under his eyes suggested that he seldom did.

Just then, Brooke hit the side of the front door frame, using it to stop her momentum as she hurtled inside. Not expecting all three of us to be loitering in the living room, she gave a sheepish grin, but there was an underlying smugness to the way she puckered her lips when she said, *"What?"* I knew Brooke well enough to know that there was only one possible reason for it—a guy. She was like the cat that got the cream, and I was just about to ask her which particular brand of dairy she'd just treated herself to when Ruadhan said, "And exactly where have you been all night?"

Brooke was too busy giving me the once-over to reply immediately to Ruadhan, and I wondered if she could tell just by looking at me that I'd spent the night with Jonah. Would Gabriel know? Nothing on the outside of my skin was any different, but the same could not be said for what hid just below the surface.

"You promised me," Ruadhan scowled, refocusing Brooke's attention.

"I was with Lailah all night," she said, meeting my eye, almost daring me to call her bluff.

Gabriel's chest heaved with a sigh of relief. He didn't want to think I'd spent the evening alone with Jonah. It was for Gabriel, then, not Brooke, that I went along with her lie. My mind turned to the events of last night—to Cameron. "Have you seen Phelan this morning?"

"Ah, I thought my ears were burning," Phelan said, letting himself in. Dressed head to toe in camouflage print, he looked even more militant than usual. Tattoos, some of them recent, worked their way up and round his neck, covering the extra scars he had received while I was away.

"What's going on?" Gabriel asked, rolling up the sleeves of his dark cardigan.

Instructing his people to remain outside with a nonchalant wave of his hand, Phelan removed a roll-up from behind his ear, taking his time to light it.

"Do you have to do that in here?" Brooke whined. "It stinks!"

Phelan blew out a stream of smoke, deliberately aiming it in her direction.

"Lad?" Ruadhan said.

"Them demons last night were not the only ones to make an appearance." Phelan reached into his back pocket and pulled out a smartphone. "Got CCTV hooked up round Main Street, the house, and the church. It streams to my phone and tablet," Phelan said for my benefit.

"How many more?" I asked.

"Enough. The demons disappear out of sight from the cameras once they get past the graveyard. As the sun's up, we're going hunting."

If they'd waited out the night and were choosing to go and investigate now, Ruadhan must have told them that Vampires were at their weakest at sunrise.

Ruadhan looked at me. "Beyond the graveyard there's a vast and lush garden, with acres of land adjacent."

"I remember," I said.

"Then you'll also remember that at the very edge of it sit Hell's gates." Ruadhan put his hand on his trench coat and asked Phelan, "I assume that's where you're going?"

"Aye. Seems that's the direction they were heading."

"I'll go," I said. "You don't need to risk your men, not after last night . . . not after Cameron—"

"Nay, we're going, but you should come." Taking a long tug on his cigarette, Phelan gestured for me to follow.

Ruadhan had his arms through his trench before Phelan managed to step back outside.

Looping a wool scarf around his neck, Gabriel said, "Lailah, I don't think you should go. Zherneboh will know by now that you're still alive. It's not safe." He was quick to slip back into old habits, reaching out and touching me. I wasn't totally devoid of compassion and so I didn't shrug him off right away.

As I followed Ruadhan out of the motor home, I withdrew from Gabriel's grasp. "I'm not afraid of Zherneboh," I said smoothly. "He should be afraid of me."

Gabriel moved ahead and blocked my path. "I still think—"

"You saw firsthand what I did to Emery. I am more capable than any Pureblood and that includes Zherneboh. Besides, he still has unfinished business. I don't have anything left to lose. I'd say that alone makes me more dangerous." I paused and then repeated what my inner voice had assured me of in the third. "I'm ready to die." It took me by surprise when an uneasy flutter rose in my chest. I may have sounded confident, but all of a sudden I didn't feel it anymore, and I didn't know why.

Unexpectedly, the blast of shotguns roared all around, but

the only missile to reach its intended target was Jonah, as in a flash he appeared beside me and said, "We're not ready to let you."

The hurried slide of stocks snapping one by one as the next shells advanced into their chambers became my focal point. Instinctively I raised my hand and, as I willed them to, the guns on the shoulders of the six men accompanying Phelan levitated in the air. I swiped my hand as though I were clearing a misty screen. The guns flew through the air before bumping down to the mud.

Phelan reeled, and then, seeing Jonah, spat to the ground. "Feck sake, I know you're a demon, but round here you might wanna walk so you don't get shot at."

Jonah was a new addition to the reformed demons now living on-site, and the Sealgaire hadn't quite gotten used to seeing him yet. Phelan gestured to the lads around him, shaking his head in response to the blades they were pulling from their belts. "Get your gear and come round to the road," he instructed, marching in the direction of the dirt track.

"Ruadhan, you'll come with me?" I said, turning my back on Jonah.

He locked his arm in mine. "Aye, sweetheart."

Gabriel came up along my other side and I said to him, "You're not coming."

"Yes, I am," he said.

Which caused Jonah to draw closer and say, "And you know the score by now, beautiful. You go, I go."

While my divine and devoted Angel and my rough-and-ready Vampire were very different, they did have one shared interest: me. Though they'd each taken turns saving me, now our roles were reversed.

"No," I said, "both of you can stay put for a change."

I wasn't used to seeing lines in Gabriel's forehead when he scowled, but one thing that hadn't changed were his dimples. They were still perfect.

"And keep an eye on Brooke. Don't let her leave while we're gone, okay?" Whatever it was that she was up to—or whoever—experience told me that her judgment couldn't always be trusted.

"I'll look after Lailah," Ruadhan reassured them, and it was only then, though neither of them liked it, that they agreed to stay behind. It irked me that they would listen to him and not me.

Outside the house, near the main road, Phelan was talking with Riley. The six men who'd aimed at Jonah divided into two groups of three—one set ahead of Ruadhan and me and one behind. Ruadhan and I hung back, not keen on being sandwiched between the two crews laden with silver weapons.

"Lailah, Ruadhan," Phelan barked, calling us forward.

I shook my head. "If you want to speak with us, you need to get used to changing your formations."

Phelan didn't like being told what to do and grunted.

"Fine," I said, impatient to get started. "We'll meet you there then." I took off in a sprint. To the naked eye, I vanished into thin air, as did Ruadhan, who quickly followed. I came to a halt only when I reached the gates that restricted access to a long path leading up to the coffered doors of the church. A second later and Ruadhan was next to me.

"A little warning wouldn't hurt, sweetheart," he said, straightening his trench.

"Sorry, but his attitude stinks," I replied, scanning the area. It might be morning but the streets were empty, the townspeople not yet having left their homes.

"Someone's overslept. The gates are locked." I jiggled the bars.

"Careful, love." Ruadhan gestured to the speared finials at the top of the tall wrought-iron gate. They were cast in silver and clearly could double as weapons.

He explained, "The church only opens for Sunday mass. It takes too much coordination, too much time, and too many resources to make the area secure for the locals every single day."

"Ruadhan, the fixed gateway to the third is on the church's land. Why would anyone come here at all? And if the situation's worsened, why haven't the locals left?"

"It's their home, love. They won't let anyone, or anything, take it from them." Ruadhan's smooth tone suggested he agreed with the townspeople, but then perhaps he understood better than me. As far as I could remember, I'd never put down any roots.

"I've never had a home, at least not before now."

My home was not made of bricks and mortar; home was wherever my family was. Ruadhan understood what I meant without having to ask. "Well, the fact that we're mobile at the dawn of the apocalypse is an added advantage."

A gruff laugh left him, and I grinned. "Too right. Shall we?" I nodded to the gate.

"We should wait for Phelan. It's not altogether respectful to proceed without him."

"Yeah, well, he may rule the roost around here, but I don't answer to him, and neither do you, Ruadhan." Though he, Gabriel, and Brooke may have spent the last few years conforming to Phelan's way of doing things, we had been a team first. Still, Ruadhan hesitated, glancing over his shoulder, hoping perhaps that the members of the Sealgaire would have caught up by now. Ruadhan was scratching the bristle on his chin but stopped when I said, "You made me a promise once."

"And I will die before I break it," he said in a deep, assertive tone.

"Well then, to stand beside me, you'll have to keep up, old man." I elbowed him playfully, lightening the mood before springing up and catapulting myself over the gates.

RUADHAN AND I LANDED on the other side of the cemetery's fence. While the graveyard was no different from any other, providing a final resting place to the bodies of the damned and the saved alike, what lay behind it was what made this church, this location, unlike any other.

The church's land resembled circles, positioned side by side, separated by shrubbery. The central circle contained a lush garden, the circle to its right housed a dense forest, and finally, the circle to the left was only bare dirt, save for the ancient oak tree.

The outer perimeter of each circle combined to form a wave—a long, undulating cliff edge that led to the River Liffey below.

An ordinary human wouldn't be able to see what I could. This truly was hallowed ground. The one place on Earth where all three dimensions interlocked side by side—where Heaven met Hell, separated only by one garden, where the red and white roses bloomed brightly, untouched by the season.

I shifted my focus to the land on the left—the spot where Jonah and I had returned through the fixed gateway. The aged tree dominated, situated in the middle of the barren field. Its thick roots grew up and cut through the dead stone beneath it. And though from this angle it could not be seen, I knew what the drooping branches were helping to conceal: the cave.

"Sweetheart," Ruadhan said.

He was shaking me by my shoulder, which snapped me out of my deep concentration. I was so focused that I couldn't hear the now clear shrieks resounding around us. "Where's that coming from?" I asked.

Ruadhan pointed toward the land on the left, to where I had just been focusing.

I covered my ears, trying to drown out the harrowing howls. "I can't see anything, at least not around that tree."

"Let's try from the garden," Ruadhan said.

I nodded, and we ran at superspeed through the foliage into the central garden. And that's all it took—a change in perspective and we could see what we hadn't been able to before.

The tombstone Jonah had pushed remained where we'd left it; the hole in the ground was still uncovered; and, one by one, a group of Second Generation Vampires were plummeting down it, into the cave. Cloaked Purebloods roved around the demons, sniffing at their throats and hissing at their ears as the line moved along.

But these were Second Generation Vampires, not Purebloods. They could not pass through the fixed gateway, because if they touched the dark matter, they would immediately lose their forms and simply fail to exist at all. That couldn't be the plan. No, the Purebloods were sending them somewhere else, and I had an inkling as to where.

"Ruadhan, are you seeing what I'm seeing?"

"Aye, love."

Crows perched on the oak tree, and though I was conscious of the deathly flap of the birds' wings, it did not hold my attention for long.

Red, orange, and green smoke poured out of the oak tree's branches. Twisting into streamers, the breeze caught and carried the color upward, splashing it against the sky.

I had wounded Hell, and now Hell was bleeding.

I was certain the aurora I had left behind had somehow followed me here. The universe was indeed plotting a truly dramatic backdrop on which for me to die.

I smiled. "You've got artistic vision, I'll give you that." But as swiftly as I'd conjured the words, my inner voice was silenced by a troubling sensation—fear.

I glanced to Ruadhan. He stared straight ahead, his expression blank.

But I remembered what he'd said to me once, that if he were ever presented with an opportunity to rid the world of a Pureblood, he would surely take it. I swung my arm out in front of his chest. "No."

This was the closest I would ever let Ruadhan get to Hell.

Still staring straight ahead, he fumbled to find my hand. When he did, he pressed down, squeezing tighter than he had ever squeezed it before.

And I squeezed back.

A cloaked figure was watching over the proceedings; with his back to me he stood entirely still. I didn't need to see his face to know it was Zherneboh. I was connected to him. It was his venom that had changed the makeup of my soul, and though his intention had been to forge his own image upon me, when the girl in the shadow had perished, he had failed. I had asserted myself as my own person, one he could not control, but that didn't change the fact that the darkness that made up half of my gray being had come from him.

"Come then, before they see us." Ruadhan tugged at my hand, and I let him lead the way.

I'd seen enough.

Just then, leaves crunching under hurried feet met my hearing, and I glanced back the way we'd come. "Phelan and his men are passing through the graveyard."

"Aye, I hear them."

"Then it won't be long before they do, too. I'll get Phelan and his men, and we'll meet you at the church gates." I disappeared in a blur as I thought myself away. Phelan was the only one not pointing a gun at my head when I appeared next to him a moment later. "It's me," I said calmly, and the men lowered their weapons.

"How nice of you to rejoin us," Phelan snapped.

Leaning into his ear, I whispered, "I don't think that's how your men would expect you to speak to the Savior." Pointing to the church, I gestured for them to follow. "Come on."

"No," Phelan grunted. "We need to see what's going on." The three lads out front ambled ahead, but the bodyguards behind me had the sense to hang back.

"Every second you stay here, you're cheating death. Trust me, it's time to go." I changed my tactic when he still didn't budge. "I'll give you the lay of the land, but not here, please, Phelan." My plea was not for my benefit; it was for his, for Riley's, and for these men.

Phelan scratched underneath his camouflage beanie before nodding. "Right, back to HQ."

THIRTEEN

I PACED THE LIVING ROOM of the motor home as I explained to the group what Ruadhan and I had seen.

"I counted six Purebloods, including Zherneboh. That's six of the type of demons you saw me end in Henley. Plus one hundred and twenty-two Vampires aboveground."

From inside the kitchen where she stood with Iona, Brooke wagged a bottle of vodka at me, and I nodded, accepting her offer.

"I'll take one of those," Claire said, swinging her two-year-old from her lap to her hip as she rose from the sofa. Though the world was dangerous, still Claire and Riley had chosen to bring life into it—perhaps that was the definition of hope.

"You counted out one hundred and twenty-two exactly?" Riley asked.

"Yes," I said. "I don't think the Vampires from last night intended to attack us. I think we just got caught in the traffic."

Ruadhan grunted in agreement, but his attention never left the door. He was on guard.

Iona placed a chilled glass in my hand, and I took it gratefully.

"It'll help settle your nerves, like," she said, as if I needed justification to drink hard liquor first thing in the morning after what I'd seen.

I glanced at Jonah. The concern on his face and my reassurance back to him threatened to expose what we'd been up to last night, but right now I wasn't sure I cared.

"So what were they doing on the hill?" Phelan asked, throwing down his beanie and picking up the vodka bottle.

I took a breath, gathering my thoughts as my gaze rounded the room. It was just like old times. Gabriel and Jonah were both listening intently, though from different ends of the living room. The girls were coming in and out of the kitchen, Ruadhan was on lookout, and Riley and Jack were quietly taking stock while trying their best not to look too terrified. But things were not exactly as they were before; things had gotten worse, as evidenced by the forty other men surrounding the motor home for protection.

And things were different for me, too. Gabriel, Jonah . . . things with them were not as they were. I'd been to Hell. I'd seen things. I'd learned things. And all those things began to coalesce in my mind as I pieced together what I'd just witnessed. "The gateway to the third dimension, or Hell's gates as you'd prefer, is hidden underneath the tree on the hill. Within the ground there's a structure made from cold, dark matter. Basically frozen dead rock, and it's the same material that made up the third. There's a tombstone, which Jonah shifted for us to escape, but there was also another stone, exactly the same, directly below it."

"What are you getting at, beautiful?" Jonah said, stepping out of the shadows.

"The tombstones act as doors. We could see the Second Generation Vampires dropping down through the first one, and I think when they went belowground, they just kept on going through the second." I fiddled with the edge of my mask as I pondered. "Two tiers: tier one houses the fixed gateway to the third, and below it, out of the way, tier two . . ." I trailed off.

"Go on, love," Ruadhan said, encouraging me to finish my theory.

I pondered. "Do you know Pandora's box wasn't really a box at all? It was actually a jar?" A few heads shook and I continued. "Tier one is the lid, and tier two is the belly of the jar. I think the Purebloods are depositing their Vampires, collecting them inside."

"But why?" Phelan asked sharply.

"The last time we saw multiple Purebloods gather, they were joining their resources, their armies, to hunt me down. Only this time it's not me they're after." The memory of

Zherneboh's story, of his desire for Orifiel's death, came to the forefront of my mind, and the answer was apparent. "He wants Orifiel. Zherneboh's readying his forces for battle, the final battle."

"You've mentioned this Orifiel before. What part does he play in all this?" Phelan asked, taking a swig from the bottle of vodka.

Gabriel came forward then, perhaps feeling better placed to offer an explanation suited to their beliefs. "Hell's gates may be on your doorstep, but so are Heaven's." Though Phelan was Gabriel's target audience, he seemed more interested in Iona's reaction as his gaze fell to her. "The entrance is within your orchard, which means your garden is the only thing separating the two gateways."

"Really?" Iona said. Unable to contain herself, she hurried to Gabriel's side.

"Yes, really," he said.

Iona excitedly lunged forward to take Gabriel's arm, but he met her hands and brought them back down to her side instead. Before she had a chance to deflate, Gabriel squeezed the tops of her shoulders, and though he'd turned his back to me, I was certain he was smiling at her, as her plump pout stretched into a shining smile of her own.

"And this Orifiel fits into things how exactly?" Phelan pressed.

"He resides in Heaven; he is the highest-ranking Angel," Gabriel answered, giving as little detail as possible.

Phelan's chin jutted forward. "The Bible speaks of this Orifiel. He is named as one of the seven Arch Angels of the Throne of God. You think the Devil wants to kill him?"

"I know he does." I stepped in. "Zherneboh—that is, the Devil—wants Orifiel dead, but he can't pass through the gates to Heaven himself, so he must make Orifiel walk through to the only place he can challenge him—here on Earth." I gave Phelan the part he needed to know. "One way or another, he will draw Orifiel out, and when he does, he'll open Pandora's box."

"He can't keep Vampires contained for that long," Jonah blurted out. "They'd starve."

"Who says they won't be fed?" I replied. A chill raced up my spine as I considered that Zherneboh might not let what he'd trapped inside out, but it didn't mean that dinner couldn't be brought to them.

Phelan's brain was already in fifth gear, and though normally he was calculated in his approach, he was also hotheaded.

I got in first. "Trying to kill them all while they are buried inside isn't an option. The Purebloods would never allow you to get even remotely close enough."

"We might not be able to get in, but we can be prepared for when they come out," Riley said, his voice hoarse. He took his daughter from his wife and stroked her auburn hair, holding her tightly as she nuzzled her face under his chin.

Riley was a light soul, and as he held his little girl, his aura jetted out and pulsed, transitioning from white to seven vibrant colors: red, orange, yellow, green, blue, indigo, and violet. I had never seen light exude from a mortal's form like that. His love for his daughter was unconditional, untainted, unequivocal. And it deserved all the colors of the rainbow.

I sighed. Zherneboh was gathering the Purebloods and their armies, bringing them all to one place at one time. This might be the only opportunity we would have to destroy them for good. But Riley and his daughter changed everything I was about to say. "No. Take your family and leave," I said to him. "You won't survive it. None of you will survive it."

Riley looked from Claire to his daughter and then coughed, clearing his throat. "This is our home, Lailah."

"Your home is that little girl, and she can be anywhere in the world you choose to take her," I replied.

"Where would you have us go?" Though Claire's tone was almost accusing, she wasn't challenging me, she was asking, and I knew then that she didn't want to stay here, not now that she had a child to protect.

My initial response was to tell them to get out a map and find the place farthest from here, but then something else came to me. Something Gabriel and Ruadhan had once told me. "Get a boat, and get on the water." I locked eyes with her. "Rifts open from Heaven and Hell, here on Earth, and anyone and anything from either of those worlds can step straight through. But rifts cannot form and open over water, right, Ruadhan?"

Ruadhan didn't hesitate to answer. "Aye, love."

"The safest place is the sea," I said.

"You don't tell my men what to do. Riley is needed here—"

I cut Phelan off. "Yeah, you needed Cameron, too. He stayed and look where that got him. He was killed only yesterday, and yet you've made no mention of him today." Angry, I started to shake. Though last night I'd seen some emotion from Phelan, standing here now he seemed unaffected.

"Don't bring Cameron into this," Phelan said.

Brooke laughed. "She's right. For all you go on about family, you never talk about Fergal."

Phelan's fist clenched, and his right hand drifted toward the weapons at his belt. Ruadhan, though supposedly guarding the doorway, sensed the escalating tension. "That's quite enough," he said. "Let's take a breather, shall we?"

In a show of solidarity, Riley ushered Claire through the living room, nodding at Phelan as a sign of respect. Jack followed suit, but Phelan hung back as they made their way outside.

Fergal's name was the trigger for Iona's tear-filled eyes. To Gabriel, she said, "I should go."

Gabriel turned to me. "Would you mind if—"

"Please," I said, encouraging him.

Gabriel escorted Iona outside, leaving only Phelan here representing the Sealgaire. He scratched behind his ear and then stepped around Ruadhan.

Jonah growled in warning from the corner, but Phelan was softer this time, a lot less telling and a lot more asking as he said, "You might not really be *the* Savior, Lailah, but it doesn't mean you can't be *a* Savior."

I shook my head. "I can only do what I can do. If I knew how . . ." My gaze fell to the floor.

Phelan thought nothing of invading my personal space, tipping up my chin with his index finger, ensuring he captured my stare. "To be a Savior is to sacrifice, and sacrifice goes hand in hand with suffering. Be prepared to suffer, Lailah, and save us all."

"Get out," Jonah hissed, appearing at my side and knocking Phelan backward. But Phelan kept his eyes on mine. When I didn't reply, finally he cocked an eyebrow and swiped his beanie from the kitchen counter.

Before exiting, he took a roll-up from behind his ear. "I may do it in silence, but every time I put a member of my family into the ground, I suffer, and I will continue to suffer so that I may save." He knew he'd hooked me by the way I sucked in air, but it was his final sentence that reeled me in. "So babies like Riley's don't have to die."

Between the blindness in my left eye and the tears spilling from my right, Jonah became a watery blur beside me. I was weak, with a desperate quiver in my voice, when I repeated myself: "I don't know how." And I truly didn't.

For all my power, I was powerless.

There were so many now, and I was but one.

I may have ended a Pureblood, but it had taken everything

I had to do it. How could I take on so many of them at once and ensure they all became dust before I did?

"Suffer, and you will save," Phelan said once again, as though I were holding out on him. Finally, he left, slamming the door so hard the hinges rattled.

My skin itched with frustration, and I lashed out at Jonah. "You shouldn't have followed me," I said coldly. "It was okay for me to die, it was okay because I'd saved you, because taking Zherneboh with me would have saved so many more. You took that away from me."

Jonah shifted his weight. "Really? You gonna listen to the head of the pitchfork committee?" Coming in close, he took my cheek in his palm, but I turned my face away. So with nothing else to do, he adjusted my crystal hairpin and said spitefully, "Maybe he's right, but if Saviors must suffer, then you were sleeping on the job, beautiful, 'cause to suffer death, you gotta want to live in the first place. Maybe, instead, you wanted to be a martyr. Maybe all I took from you was the easy way out."

Jonah's words, as always, cut. I wasn't out of fight, or willingness to suffer, as Phelan was suggesting. I'd laid down my life for Jonah's, proving that I was more than willing to sacrifice myself. I was about to argue this point when I realized that he actually might be right. I was no Savior, because I wasn't prepared to sacrifice the thing that would cause me to suffer most; I wouldn't sacrifice Jonah or any one of my family.

They came first.

Though my legs had gone to jelly, I broke away first, staggering over to the table. Unable to get a rise out of me, Jonah swore and stormed out.

Behind me, Ruadhan said to Brooke, "Love, would you mind, perhaps you could wait in Little Blue?"

Brooke huffed. "Whatever. I got someone to see anyway."

She was gone before I could find my voice to warn her from straying away from the Winnebago, but then, I doubted she'd listen to me anyway.

I sat at the table and twisted the bottle of vodka by the base, lost inside my own head. Jonah had a way of being able to ruin me with just one sentence. It was a skill he was perfecting on what seemed like an hourly basis.

Ruadhan sat down next to me. "Are you okay, sweetheart?"

"Yes. No. I'm not sure anymore," I replied honestly.

Ruadhan waited patiently, giving me time.

"Did what you saw on the hilltop scare you?" I asked tentatively.

Ruadhan smoothed his salt-and-pepper hair, before placing his hands into a prayer shape on the tabletop. "No, love. But it scared you, didn't it?"

I didn't offer a direct answer. "I don't understand." I pinched my thumb and forefinger together. "I was this close to death, but I wasn't afraid. I was ready to die. When I came back, *still* I was ready. . . . But this morning . . . I don't get it."

"If you no longer feel the same, something must have changed?"

"Yes, I suppose so." A lump formed in my throat. "I'm frightened, Ruadhan."

He pulled me into him, and careful of my mask, he rubbed my back up and down. "Do you know, in my experience, sweetheart, death is something people fear only if they have something—*someone*—to live for." Ruadhan released me. "So, little love, who are you living for today that you weren't yesterday?"

I squeezed my puffy eyes together, and the face that manifested in my mind provided me with the answer.

I didn't offer it to Ruadhan.

"Why don't I make you a cup of tea?" he said, getting up.

I wrinkled my nose. "Doesn't really do anything for me anymore."

"Aye. But it can be comforting to hold something warm in your hands, and truth be told, I quite enjoyed making it for you. I've missed it while you've been gone." It was impossible to refuse him; I smiled and he left me to go in search of the teapot.

I drummed my fingertips on the table while I waited, considering Ruadhan's words.

The kettle whistled, and a spoon clinked into a waiting mug. I pushed Brooke's stack of fashion magazines aside, revealing a leather-bound book underneath.

I recognized it straightaway.

Jonah's sketchbook. I picked it up and a pencil rolled out from inside one of the pages. I caught it before it hit the floor. "You found Jonah's drawings?"

"Aye," Ruadhan said, fetching milk from the fridge. "Over the years, you get to know one another's habits. No matter where we go, or how long we stay, the lad always keeps his valuables in his pillowcase. Didn't know he'd started sketching again. Mind, was a bit of a surprise finding that when we left Henley."

Putting the top of the pencil between my lips, I ran my fingers over the suede leather cover, wondering what Jonah had drawn. I shouldn't look. It was his personal property, but then, given that I tended to be the focus of so many of his sketches, it was too tempting not to.

"I don't think he'd appreciate your looking through it," Ruadhan warned at my shoulder. He placed a mug down next to me as I opened the book with care. Off the first page, I read Jonah's full name aloud, and I recalled what it had felt like to let the syllables roll off my tongue when I had thought the person they belonged to was gone forever. "Jonah Cyrene."

"Huh," Ruadhan said.

"What?" I flipped through the pages, making my way to the one bookmarked by the charcoal pencil.

"In all these years, the lad never told me his surname. Funny . . ."

"What is?" Procrastinating, I stroked the edge of the page,

mustering the courage to turn it, unsure of what I might find. If he'd sketched me, how might he have seen me after he'd pulled me out of the third? After he'd seen me wearing the butterfly mask? *After we'd spent the night together?*

I flipped the page, and the pencil fell from my lips.

It wasn't me Jonah had drawn.

Two triangular eyes were set within a round head, with a round body to match, complete with two arms, hands, legs, and feet.

Jonah had taken the triangular eyes and the gloved hands I'd told him about, but somehow he'd seen what I hadn't. He'd sketched a complete figure. Jonah had sketched a robot.

One I'd seen before.

Refusing to feed, I had been suffering at the time. To numb the pain, I'd turned to the bottle, drinking more than I should have, but still, I remembered the image. The robot was on a painting in Darwin's house that depicted the apocalypse. Darwin had said it had been in his family for generations.

The portrait was a sign all right; it was the image of the day I would die.

And just then, another sign slapped me in the face.

"Jonah's surname," Ruadhan said. "*Cyrene.*"

I tore the page from the sketchbook and folded it into my jeans pocket. "What?"

"It won't mean anything to you, sweetheart, as you're not of the Christian faith. But the Gospel talks of a man named

Simon of Cyrene, you see." Ruadhan paused, scooping up the pencil and taking the sketchbook from my hands. "He was the man who helped Jesus carry the cross to his crucifixion."

I sat, mouth agape.

Okay, universe, I'm listening.

FOURTEEN

THE WINNEBAGO WAS EMPTY. With no sign of Brooke, I couldn't ask her permission to borrow her coat. She'd have to forgive me. I bundled myself beneath its warmth and pushed my hands deep into the pockets. There, I found the business card Darwin had given me the night before. I smoothed out the creases as I contemplated my next move.

Jonah had disappeared, so the downside was that I couldn't ask him how he'd come up with a robot from my brief description. But the upside was that I wouldn't have to argue with him about my decision to leave for London, alone. Even Ruadhan, who usually trusted my judgment, hadn't especially liked the idea.

Unable to travel across water by the power of thought, I'd have to take a ferry over the Irish Sea to Holyhead, but first I could at least use my legs to get as far as Dublin. I searched for the rucksack Iona's borrowed clothes had arrived in, but found an overnight bag stashed in the driver's cabin first. With little consideration, I emptied the contents onto the passenger's seat and stuffed the clothes Brooke had lent me inside. Halfway to the living quarters, I stopped. A metallic scent permeated the air. I went back and scanned the items dumped from the bag: a pack of old cards, some matches, aftershave, underwear, shirt, jeans, and a beanie.

The beanie—though a summertime aroma from a recent wash tried to mask it, the heady, coppery scent of dry blood remained, woven into the fabric.

The cards caught my attention next. They were plain, the kind you could buy for a pound at the local corner shop, with a linen finish and a simple red-and-blue diamond pattern on the back. I pressed my thumb against the top of the pack and fanned them inside my palms. I counted fifty-four cards in the deck. The ability to absorb specifics was, up until now, one I hadn't considered to be of great use, but then without it, I wouldn't have just recognized a tiny tear in the top right corner of the six of hearts. Though this was the same deck I'd seen when I first returned to Little Blue, this tear was new.

Brooke, it seemed, had a regular visitor, one who apparently enjoyed card games. No wonder she'd been upset at being ousted from Little Blue; clearly there was a reason she wanted some privacy. I scratched my head. Either she was hooking up with a human, or somehow, somewhere, she'd met another Vampire and was secretly sneaking him in and out of the Winnebago when no one was looking.

Both possibilities presented almost insurmountable difficulties.

I'd have to launch my investigation when I returned; there was somewhere else I needed to be.

I DON'T KNOW WHY I DECIDED to walk through the town. Maybe I was hoping Jonah would appear after all, or maybe it was because I was starting to get hungry and this time the fuel I needed was not solar-powered. The streets remained empty and I wondered if, given the influx of Vampires descending, Phelan had warned the locals to stay off the streets and remain in their homes. It was the best I could hope for. I highly doubted Phelan would evacuate—"Stand and fight" was his motto, not "Fright and flight."

As I walked parallel to the gates of the church, I noticed they were unlocked. Up ahead, one of the church's coffered doors was ajar. From inside, I recognized a low, mournful sob—Iona. Why was she inside the church when the Devil himself was filling up Pandora's box only a mile behind her? The word *reckless* came to mind, but then I couldn't hold it against her; there were plenty who'd have said the same of me on more than one occasion.

I kept a respectful distance from the silver and vaulted myself over the finials of the gateposts. With caution, I headed toward the heavy wooden doors. Even with my impaired vision, the precious metal popped out against the scenery like a 3-D movie. On the doors, every handle and hinge had been cast from solid silver. And though the centuries-old stained-glass windows remained intact, the Sealgaire had gone to some effort to encase the ledges, and, for added security, sheets of the stuff covered some of the stained panels themselves.

Though I wasn't religious, there was something awe-inspiring about the way the autumn sun streamed into the nave, spreading over the pews and casting a warm glow into even the smallest pockets of darkness. Iona sat at the very front, hands in her lap, her head bowed.

"Iona," I said.

"Oh!" She jumped. Then, realizing it was me, she wiped her eyes and said, "Sorry, you startled me."

"I was passing, and I heard you from outside."

She sniffed. "All the way out there?"

"Yeah, part and parcel of being all, well, you know . . ." I sat beside her as she foraged around in her bag for a tissue.

Finding one, she patted her cheeks and laughed. "Silly really. I was just thinking about Fergal, but when I think about him, I think about my daddy, and Padraig, and my ma of course." Iona's list was long, too long, longer than anyone like her deserved it to be. "It's wrong of me to be sad. I shouldn't be. They're in a better place. They're with the Lord now." She tucked her long, wayward strands back into her side ponytail.

"I guess it's just—now, now that I'm like this, it may be a very long time before I see their faces again."

Iona was Of Elfi. Both she and her twin, Fergal, were children of a fallen Angel. Unlike her brother, her soul had been clean and light when she'd turned seventeen, causing her form to become frozen, meaning that just like a fallen Angel's, the length of her life was now vastly extended. But with no abilities to protect her, if she wasn't careful, "a very long time" might be sooner than she thought.

"I try to picture their faces, when I close my eyes at night, but I struggle," she confessed.

I nudged her with my elbow. "Maybe that's the problem. It's hard to see when you're searching in the dark." My mind turned to the scavenger in the third. "Maybe, instead, think of the memory of them, and then open your eyes. Where the darkness ends, and the light begins, right there, in the gray, you'll see them." Gabriel came to mind next, all the years the memory of him had haunted me. How he had been so close, but so far away. "Remembering keeps the lost with us, until we can one day find them again."

Iona smiled. "Sometimes, just in case they can hear, when I'm alone, I sing. Then they'd know I was thinking of them, see, 'cause we had a song. My ma would sing it to us when we were small. It's the only thing I have left that connects me to them, to the people I love the very most." With kind eyes, Iona asked, "Will you pray with me?" She placed her hands together again and bowed her head. "Pray that they hear me, that my song reaches them?" I coughed awkwardly but nodded, and she whispered, "You do believe in God, don't you?"

Just then, the sun's rays struck the stained-glass window in such a way that the image of Jesus nailed to the cross glowed from within. My pending meeting with Darwin on my mind, I answered plainly, "I believe in the man wearing the jacket."

Iona regarded me quizzically, and as she did, the strobes of light hit her white blouse. The unmistakable sparkle of my oldest, and at times only, comfort glowed from under the silk.

"Iona, your necklace?"

Iona placed her palm to her chest and then pulled the chain out from below her top, revealing my crystal gem, still set within the engagement ring Gabriel had Ruadhan make for me. Gabriel had lost his light when his own crystal, which had been buried in the nape of his neck, had failed. Unlike him, I didn't need my crystal to retain my abilities, and so before falling into the third, I had left it for him. Gabriel had told me that light was love, and so I thought that when he let me go and allowed himself to love Iona, his light would be restored with my crystal. Then he would regain his immortality and could live happily, forever with Iona. But in the three years I'd been gone, evidently that hadn't happened.

"Gabriel gave that to you?" I asked, confused. Why, when Gabriel refused to give up on me, had he passed my crystal, set in an engagement ring, to Iona?

Rolling the platinum band over her knuckles, she said, "No, Ruadhan gave it to me yesterday for safekeeping. He said that it's very special and has great purpose—that I would know what to do with it when the time came." She paused. "Do you know what he meant, Lailah?"

Ruadhan must have been guarding the crystal since I'd left. It was only good sense that he did. Gabriel was fallen, but Ruadhan was still a Vampire; his hands were safer until, hopefully, the time came when Gabriel's gifts returned. But the fact that Ruadhan had now charged Iona with its safe-keeping meant he wasn't sure he'd still be around to continue to do so himself. He was preparing to fight, to be by my side as he'd promised, but clearly he was making provisions should he not be one of the last left standing when all was said and done.

"One thing about Ruadhan is that he says what he means, and means what he says. I'd take stock of his words if I were you. They are always wise ones. Even if you don't understand now, you will, I am sure of it. Just . . ."

"Yes?"

"Don't take it off, okay? And stay close to Gabriel."

Iona regarded my ring once more before slipping it underneath her blouse. Placing her hand firmly down on top, she said, "I promise. So will you pray with me?"

"If I do, then will you go home? You know you shouldn't be here alone. How'd you even get in? I was told the church was closed except for Sundays. Weren't the gates locked earlier this morning?"

"I had the caretaker open them for me. He works for my

family, so he kinda has to do what I ask, like." She blushed, almost embarrassed.

I nodded and shuffled my bottom side to side on the uncomfortably hard pew; I clasped my hands together and bowed my head.

Iona spoke aloud, and I recognized parts of the prayer from the one given by Fergal over the dinner table the first evening I had broken bread with the Sealgaire. But then at the end, she added her own words. "Lord, please bless and keep Lailah, bestow unto her the same grace she bestows to others. Forgive her sins and show mercy."

Not a selfish bone in her body, Iona wasn't praying for me to save them, she was simply praying for my soul.

"Thank you," I said, raising my chin, and I sincerely meant it.

THE DAY WAS DRAWING IN. It was close to nightfall now. I escorted Iona back to the main house. She promised not to leave again without protection. With still no sign of Jonah, I said good-bye to Ruadhan for a second time. Gabriel wasn't there, either; after Iona had given Gabriel the slip, he had gone in search of her. And so I left.

Though it took me no time at all to reach the port in Dublin, I'd had to use my ability to influence to get a seat on one of the few boats carrying passengers across to Holyhead. Due to the "Spinodes," the UK was on high alert, and gaining entry into the country without imperative reason was not easy—well, unless you happened to be me.

It had taken mere minutes to travel by thought from Holyhead to the exclusive road of Egerton Crescent in Chelsea, and though Darwin had handed me his business card with his address, I hadn't needed it to find the property. Using the power of thought, I'd only had to visualize the whitewashed villa and my legs had brought me here. It was a gray and drab evening in London, and from the muddy puddles, it was clear that it had been raining for some time.

Approaching Darwin's house, I thought myself invisible to shield myself from the private guards that patrolled the outside of the expensive four-story villa.

Using my abilities to travel here had once again reminded me that I needed to refuel, and so I slunk away, following Exhibition Road. It was nearly five o'clock, and most of the local residents had already locked themselves away for the evening curfew. I had never known London's streets to be so empty. The groan of heavy tanks and the march of military personnel broke the silence and set the scene for war.

I sniffed the air, searching for a scent that appealed to me, and I found one leaving through the gates of Imperial College. I continued to cloak myself, following the teenage girl as she headed toward Hyde Park. Once she turned off the street and passed through the arched gates, she was careful not to veer away from the path, passing by troops who were selecting their guard posts along the trails that ran through the huge park. Though something about her scent alone told me she was a dark soul, I squinted out of my good eye, ensuring there was no glow framing her body. There wasn't. Her energy was dark. She would do.

As the sun began to set, the brunette hurried, struggling with her heavy book bag and shifting the weight from hip to hip. At the path's curve, there was a small cluster of bushes and trees. That was where I waited.

I had only ever drunk from Jonah, never a mortal, and though I would take the dark energy along with her blood, it wouldn't be as powerful as taking it from a Vampire.

The girl was on the phone now, reassuring the caller on the other end that she was only a few minutes away from home. I took my opportunity. Her cell clattered to the ground as I stole her away from the path and into the cluster of trees.

My arm pressed against her chest, restraining her, and my left hand slapped over her mouth before she could scream. Only when I was ready did I stop concealing myself, concentrating now instead on the task at hand.

Tipping her jaw, I exposed her neck, and the girl's eyes widened as I breathed in the sweat trickling down her neck.

My fangs cracked, and I dug them into her flesh, propping the girl up when her knees bowed. Every mouthful of her blood revitalized me, her dark energy merging with mine, topping up my tank.

Though taking from this girl served its purpose, it was nothing like drinking from Jonah. She was nowhere near as satisfying. When I consumed Jonah's blood, he intoxicated me. I was left barely able to remember my own name. This girl's blood was hardly giving me a buzz. It was simply doing what it needed to. There was nothing enjoyable about it.

Jonah had been confused as to why the idea of his drinking from someone else had bothered me. Now I understood. There was absolutely no comparison.

Bright red blood dribbled down my chin as I unhooked my fangs and withdrew. I swilled the last of it around my mouth and swallowed before licking my lips, cleaning away the evidence of my crime.

As I loosened my arm across my victim's chest, she didn't struggle, and quickly I checked her pulse to make sure she'd just passed out. Carefully, I let her collapse in my arms and dragged her over to a tree near the pathway, propping her up against it. I couldn't risk leaving her hidden in the foliage. It was too dangerous to abandon her—exposed and vulnerable—out in the dark and cold, but no amount of shaking was waking her up. She remained alive but unconscious.

The girl might have a dark soul, but that didn't mean she deserved to die. Whistling loudly, I gained the attention of a nearby soldier, and masking myself, I waited until he'd found her before leaving.

I returned to Egerton Crescent, and I stood in the communal gardens, which looked onto the front of the villas. The face of my father, Azrael, flashed into my thoughts. The memory of following him through this very garden and of using my bare hands to execute him were as fresh as the blood I'd just consumed. The words that had left me, sentencing him to that death, still wet my lips.

I took a tissue from my coat pocket and dabbed away any remaining evidence of my crime from the corner of my mouth. Putting on my very best smile, I approached Darwin's front door.

FIFTEEN

I HANDED THE MAN IN BLACK Darwin's business card, and he eyed me suspiciously. Out in the cold, I waited patiently at the bottom of the steps. The clip-clop of Darwin's brogues against the granite floor sped up as he neared, and at the front door, the broadly built security guard turned away from me, blocking Darwin from view.

"Cessie!" Darwin exclaimed, patting the man on the shoulder as he stepped around him.

"Hi," I said smoothly.

"I'm so pleased to see you." Rushing down the steps, he stretched out his arms, preparing to take my hands by way of his usual greeting. But with a quick glance from left to right, he curled his fingers and withdrew, hurrying me inside instead. "Come, come."

After whisking me into the warmth of the house, Darwin

wasted no time in taking my bag and coat. The last time I'd been here, I was dressed head to toe in couture, while this second time around I was a little more mishmashed in my plain jeans and shirt but ornate crystal hairpin and butterfly face mask.

From behind me, Darwin rubbed the length of my arms up and down. "You're not wearing a jumper. You must be freezing."

"Thank you." I smiled. "I'm fine." Darwin didn't know that I could control my own temperature.

"May I offer you a drink?" Leading me through the hall to a reception room, he offered me a seat on a leather chesterfield in front of a Victorian fireplace. Darwin slicked back his blond hair and pushed his glasses over the small bump just below the arch of his nose. "Perhaps a glass of cabernet?"

"Sure," I replied, swallowed up by the worn leather.

The fire beside me crackled, the yellow and orange flames rising high, and for a brief second, the burning inverted pentagram from the third flashed in my mind.

Darwin returned with two wineglasses in one hand and what was surely a very expensive bottle in the other.

He was careful as he poured, and I found myself reading the text on Darwin's white T-shirt beneath his tweed blazer. "'Don't panic and carry a towel'?" I mused aloud.

Darwin handed me my glass, and then glanced down at his shirt. "*Hitchhiker's Guide to the Galaxy*." He grinned.

Of course. "A firm favorite of yours. I'd read it, but I'm short on time."

"Then make some. I guarantee it will change your life."

Darwin took a seat, leaving a small gap between us on the sofa, and swished his wine around his glass contemplatively. "You're not planning on staying, are you?" He surprised me by reading the situation correctly.

"And you know that how?" I sipped my drink.

"You're still wearing your mask. If you'd decided to take me up on my offer, you wouldn't be."

"I'm just passing through. I was hoping to take another look at one of your paintings, the one hanging on your landing that depicts the apocalypse?" There was no reason to make up an excuse for my visit.

Darwin regarded me quizzically, tipped back his glass, and then said, "Of course you may. Is there any particular reason it's of interest to you?"

"Lately, with what's going on in the world, and with what you said to me, I've been thinking about the end," I answered honestly.

"And so you thought about that god-awful painting? You think there's something behind it? Well, besides a madman?" When I didn't answer immediately, he said, "I had you down as a lot of things, Cessie, but not a fool. Seers, signs, sortilege . . . it's all hokum." He necked his remaining wine and I took another sip of mine.

"You said your own father, a respected man of great stature, would see signs in things, hidden messages. . . ." I paused, waiting to see if he would interject. When he didn't, I continued to press my point. "You'd brand me a fool for considering one man's prophecy, but you'd expect me to accept yours without question?"

"There is an incredible difference between my message and the one the creator of that monstrosity was trying to send. My warning is founded on truth, a truth formed from cold, hard facts. All we know about that painting is that it's terribly old and that the artist was a seer, which of course is not a real thing. No one can see into the future."

My eyebrows arched automatically.

Darwin continued with a dark undertone. "They say he experienced a vision so very dreadful that he actually blinded himself before painting it." He stopped, his tone lightening. "Makes absolutely no sense, and, though ugly as it is, I highly doubt a visually impaired person, and newly so no less, could paint something as delineated as that."

Darwin's thought process was in many ways similar to Jonah's. Jonah had discussed with me once before the expectation versus the reality of being dubbed a "Vampire," explaining to me that factual accounts over time had been reduced to stories, stories that through a game of telephone became distorted. The story attached to the portrait might not be accurate anymore, but if the painting was acting as a sign, there was a message waiting to be delivered within it.

"I'd still like another look, if you wouldn't mind." Placing my glass down, I rose to my feet.

Ever the gentleman, Darwin stood from the sofa and said, "Of course." As he escorted me back into the hallway, his hand drifted to the small of my back and he nudged me toward the left side of the wraparound staircase. Reaching out for the cast-iron rail, I glanced up to the chandelier hanging majestically from the ceiling, glinting and glimmering in place of its predecessor. I hesitated as I recalled the shrieks from the Vampires, drowning out the screams from the guests, as they'd flooded through the house in search of the crystals from Styclar-Plena, which Gabriel had come here to trade with his business partner—Darwin's father, Sir Montmorency. For me it had only been days ago, but for Darwin several years had gone by.

"Are you quite all right?" Darwin asked.

"Yes," I assured him. The light from the grand chandelier reflected off his retro glasses and caused me to squint. Rushing across the landing, I wasted no time picking out the artwork.

Darwin hung behind me, and the varnished hardwood floorboards squeaked beneath his shoes as he rocked back and forth on his heels. Pushing my hair behind my right ear with one hand, I swayed the other one in front of the portrait, imprinting the detail inch by inch into my memory.

The first time I had seen the painting I'd been hours from fading into nothing. It wasn't so much the images that had left an impression on me but the feeling instead. Pins and needles had traveled down my neck and rippled over my spine, and were doing so again. And as before, the vibration they created wasn't warm beneath my skin; instead it made my soul freeze.

Slightly off center, the robot Jonah had sketched stood on what appeared to be a blood-coated grassy verge, its upside-down triangular eyes a luminous green. The emphasis was placed upon the ball of white light shooting high into the air.

As I strained, searching for something, anything, to confirm what I suspected I knew, my right eye wandered. The portrait shifted out of focus until I was seeing double. Now there was the actual painting and a hazy version appearing next to it.

I took a step back, allowing the painting to fall even further out of focus. The distorted images were mere color blocks. I could see now what I hadn't been able to before.

The red and green were not blood on grass and the orange splashed across the sky was not some depiction of hellfire, it was the aurora bleeding out. Everything on the cliff edge was caught in its color.

The message that had been hidden in plain sight became clear.

As I blinked, the blazing ball became a blue hue. It unraveled like an orange peel and then stretched.

I blinked again, and this time the iridescent blue broke apart. I fluttered my eyelashes, and a billion butterflies were born, flapping their wings in time with me as they twirled, rushing up the strobe of light and disappearing off the canvas.

Startled, I tripped backward.

When I looked again, everything within the painting was a blur—everything except the luminous green triangles.

The painting was indeed a sign.

The message spelled out my end.

The warning was the robot.

Darwin steadied me. "Cessie, are you all right?"

It took me a moment to collect myself. "Yes. Sorry. You're right, it is god-awful, isn't it?" I said matter-of-factly. I turned and smiled at him. "Thank you for showing it to me. I better be on my way."

As I walked by, Darwin placed his hand on my arm. "You can't leave now. There's a nonnegotiable curfew in place. You won't get farther than the end of the street before a soldier spots you."

With the ability to mask myself, I could get as far away from here as I wanted, but I couldn't travel across water without a boat and someone to steer it, and finding an able person late at night with a curfew in effect would be damn near impossible. I frowned.

"My father is away on business. He won't be back until the morning. Aside from the staff, the house is empty, and truth be told, I would appreciate the company." He tipped his glasses to the top of his head. His jade-green eyes widened in hopeful anticipation. "I have good wine, good food, and . . . Jenga."

"You have Jenga?"

He grinned. "I have lots of games; Jenga is just one of them."

Though I had packed a bag, my intention, or perhaps my hope, had been to return to Lucan before the day was officially out. I didn't have to stay. I could still try to get across the Irish Sea.

"Okay. Look." Darwin reached into his pocket and pulled out a coin. "Heads you stay, tails you *try* to leave."

I sighed. I couldn't deny that Darwin's offer wasn't appealing. Finally, I nodded in agreement. "Okay, heads I stay."

Darwin flipped the coin high into the air, then stalled for dramatic effect before revealing the outcome of the coin toss.

"Heads."

As he said it, I realized that I'd been hoping that was exactly the way it would land. I liked Darwin, and I could do with one last evening of normality—some sort of human contact—before I found myself at the edge of the end. "Very well, uncork the wine and bring on the Jenga."

ONE IN THE MORNING and far too many empty wine bottles later, Darwin and I sat opposite each other on a woolly rug in front of the open fire, deeply embroiled in a game of chess.

Closest to the fire, Darwin had removed his blazer. As he pondered his next move, his brow crinkled. Long gone were the giggles and silliness the likes of Jenga and Operation had brought. Darwin's face was now entirely serious, and every so often, when he thought he was onto a winner, his triceps tensed under the short sleeves of his silly T-shirt. I'd laughed when he'd added a pair of Darth Vader slippers to his outfit, but then I hadn't refused the R2-D2's he'd offered me.

After necking the remainder of his wine and chewing on the last olive, he wiped his mouth, but the napkin wasn't big enough to disguise his third yawn in as many minutes.

"As much fun as I'm having, you look tired. We should call it a night," I said, getting to my feet.

"Very well, but I'm not letting you off that easily. We finish this game in the morning over breakfast." He used the small table to leverage himself up.

I eyed the pieces on the chessboard. If I wasn't careful, in five moves or less, Darwin would have me in check. When he'd brought the beautiful wooden chess set into the room, the idea of playing with anyone but Gabriel had felt strange. But Darwin wasn't just anyone. Despite my apprehension and the caution I'd exercised knowing his father did business with Angels, somehow he had become a friend.

I stood and moved to collect the empty bottles, but Darwin intercepted me. "Leave them, honestly. I'll sort out everything down here." Darwin strode past me and returned with my bag in hand. "I'll show you to a guest room."

"A," not "the." The house was as grand as I remembered it, so I wasn't surprised there were plenty of spare beds to offer.

Upstairs, toward the far end of the landing, Darwin presented a gorgeously decorated, lavender-scented room, complete with en suite. I walked through and placed my bag on top of the throw, covering what I was sure were expensive sheets on the four-poster bed.

"It's lovely," I said. The double-vaulted ceilings gave a sense of space, and the drawn suede drapes were easily twice my height. Darwin slid them back, opened the doors hidden behind them, and led me onto a small balcony that overlooked the gardens.

"Not a bad view," I said. The grounds were gently illuminated by the dull glow of solar lamps, and when I looked up into the night's sky, the moon was full, shining like Darwin's coin.

"I'll leave you to get settled. Would you like a hot beverage to take to bed?" he asked politely, stepping back inside.

I closed the doors behind us both and pulled the drapes together. "No. Thank you, though."

Darwin gave me a quick peck on both cheeks before leaving.

I headed for the bathroom. As I flicked on the light, my gaze settled on a roll-top bath—too inviting to ignore. I undressed and helped myself to the linen robe hanging on the back of the door, sliding my feet back into the silly slippers. Just as I was about to run the water, the thought of a nice, warm, familiar cup of tea came to mind, and though I didn't need one, somehow the thought of soaking in bubbles made me want one.

As I left the guest room, the clatter of glasses echoed through the hallway. Darwin was still in the kitchen. I had only taken a couple of steps when a creak from three doors down caused me to stop dead in my tracks.

I could put the movement of the door drifting open down to the wind blowing in from an open window perhaps, but that wouldn't explain the *plink-plonk* of fairground music that filtered out.

SIXTEEN

Sliding my feet out of the slippers, I tiptoed across the landing. I willed my glow from within to create a defensive barrier and, without hesitation, pushed the door ajar and peeked inside.

Ding der ding. The tinny vibration traveled in short, sharp spells as my light illuminated what appeared to be a girl's bedroom.

I pinpointed the origin of the music to a bookcase built into the alcove next to a chimney breast. I raised the dimmer switch beside me, ridding the room of the darkness. The room was empty. Confident there was nothing or no one untoward lurking inside, I allowed my glow to dissipate.

Sash windows were positioned on either side of a small double bed covered with a floral duvet. To my immediate right was a vanity desk whose top was covered with a large oval mirror, a makeup bag, and neatly placed pots containing lotions and potions. Though my heightened sense of smell picked up on the lavender scent that had also filled the guest room, it was almost overwhelmed by the aroma from the vase of freshly cut oriental lilies.

As I made my way around the bed, the wind seeped through the partially open window, causing the door to squeak behind me. I searched the bookshelves at speed, and starting from the bottom, I ran my gaze over the trinkets positioned in front of the romance novels, seeking out the source of the sound.

A cold chill brushed my arm as the unmistakable steam organ from my dream piped up once more.

I did a double take.

On a shelf just above my eyeline, a carousel music box sputtered. Four horses with twisted golden poles cutting through their saddles drifted up and down as they slowly turned. The horses were painted in different colors—blue, green, and orange—but the fourth was pure white, decorated with a garland of pink roses.

I knew her when I saw her: Uri.

I picked up the heavy wooden box and ran my fingers over Uri's smooth, hand-painted porcelain mane. Searching the bottom for a key, I found it next to a gold label that read "Four Signs Music Box Company."

I wound the music box, freeing the tune once more. I set Uri and her friends on the shelf, and the horses bobbed up and down as the carousel turned. A tear streaked down my cheek as I took a bewildered breath.

How could this be?

Why had I dreamt of this music box?

What did it represent?

This exact object had surfaced from my subconscious before the sequence on the cliff edge had played out. Trying to solve the conundrum, I didn't hear Darwin's footsteps until he appeared in the doorway.

"Cessie?" he said.

I wiped my eyes and patted down the mask at my temple, ensuring it was still intact before facing him. "I'm sorry. The breeze must have caused the music box to start. I followed the sound to see where it was coming from," I explained, shuffling backward.

Darwin came to my side, and his lips pulled in a sad smile. "I haven't heard that play in years. My mother couldn't bring herself to clear Rose's things—my sister, that is." And then he added, "The girl I couldn't save."

I hadn't realized that the night Darwin and I had met, when he'd told me that he, too, had lost a loved one, he'd been referring to a sister. A sister whom he said I had reminded him of.

"The music box was a gift from me for her thirteenth birthday," he said.

"I'm sorry, Darwin."

As the bells chimed in, the music grew louder and

Darwin's heartbeat thudded in his chest, adding a baseline only I could hear.

He scanned the shelves and then reached out, collecting a photo frame, his attention fixed on the young girl trapped behind the glass. After a moment, he passed it to me. In the picture, there was a discarded white gift box beside Darwin's sister as she clutched the carousel in her hands, a wide smile spread across her face. Though she was young, there was something very familiar about her appearance—about her big, eager eyes. Even though they were not as bright as Darwin's jade-green ones, I could be forgiven for assuming that it was he to whom she bore a resemblance—it was an assumption that would cost me later.

"She's very beautiful," I said.

"Yes, she was." He cleared his throat and placed the frame back down.

"How did she . . ."

"She battled with psychosis. In her late teens, she lost all grip on reality. The boarding school she was attending in Switzerland sent her home, advising my parents to seek professional help for her 'madness,' as they called it." He shook his head and then snorted with derision. "As you can imagine, my father was mortified. He was quick to pack her off to a private clinic. When she returned, he applied an enormous amount of pressure on her, concerned with what people might think. He couldn't have the Montmorency name attached to such a thing, after all. And for a time, she seemed well again. She stopped voicing her delusions as if she no longer had them, and so we carried on, business as usual." Darwin's voice was becoming hoarse; I took his arm.

As he stared out into space, remembering, the nostalgic music became the sound track to his and Rose's childhood. There was a sudden warmth radiating from him, and as I focused, a soft white hue framed his body. Darwin had a light soul, but the memory of his sister made his aura shine brighter than ever.

Gabriel had been absolutely right when he'd told me that light and love were one and the same.

Winding down, the carousel slowed, and Darwin came back to me. The glow exuding gently around his form flickered. "She took her own life." His jaw clenched, and he pushed his eyeglasses back to the bridge of his nose. "Selfish really."

My brow creased.

"She left no one to blame, no one to punish. . . . well, except for myself. Unlike my brother . . ."

What did he mean by that? I frowned; I didn't want to pry. The only talk of Darwin's brother that I could recall was Gabriel's discussion with Sir Montmorency. He'd said something about his youngest son having gone missing, but he hadn't appeared too worried, saying that it was not the first time he had fallen off the grid. But that was three years ago now.

"I don't understand," I said, shaking my head.

Darwin's lips pulled in a tight line. "Elliot was murdered."

"Oh, Darwin..." I fidgeted, but then asked, "What happened?"

Darwin nudged the base of the music box back an inch, setting it so that it was perfectly in its place. "My father has many business interests, but primarily he deals in *commodities*." Though I couldn't tell him that I knew, because then he would ask *how* I knew, I was well aware of what his father dealt in.

But while Sir Montmorency was concerned with the monetary value held in the crystals' flawless aesthetics, unbeknown to him, his son Darwin was concentrating on the scientific value they held, slipping CERN a number of them, which he'd stolen from his father.

"Elliot worked in the family business. He was in the south of France tying up a deal when he disappeared."

My mind whirled. That's exactly where I had been around the same time.

"My father thought Elliot had gone on a bender, expected he would return eventually. After the party here, my father let an entire week go by before he finally started to take Elliot's disappearance seriously." Darwin shook his head. "My father tracked his last movements to one of his business premises and obtained CCTV footage from outside the building. The camera was in the wrong place. It picked up only so much, but what it did..." He swallowed. "What I said to you, in the pub—"

"The interdimensional aliens?" I said quietly, in acknowledgment that what he'd told me was a secret.

"Yes. There was ten seconds of footage, maybe less." His voice trembled. "Elliot came into the camera's view. He stumbled backward before falling to the ground. But then . . . the creature descended upon him. It tore off his arms, before hauling his body away by his ankles."

"What did this 'creature' look like?"

"It moved at such speed it was almost impossible to see clearly. The only distinguishable characteristic was inked markings that ran up its arms. I've studied them so many times, but it's not enough." He paused, and then said, "The shriek that left it, Cessie . . ." He didn't need to finish his sentence. I could guess how it ended: *I'd know the sound anywhere.* I'd felt the same the first time I'd heard it, too. It was clear that Darwin was referring to a Pureblood. Zherneboh had hunted me down in the southern region of France. If Darwin's brother, Elliot, had been there at the same time as me, it was very possible their paths had crossed. And if I was right, then without even realizing it, I was inadvertently the cause of his brother's brutal death.

"I don't know what to say."

The dizzy sounds of the fairground began to quiet, and the white shimmer that had skimmed Darwin's body disappeared. "Elliot's life was taken from him, and all things being equal, an opportunity will one day present itself to balance out the scales. I told you once before—I'm just a man, capable of the very best and the very worst of my humanity." His entire body tensed. "When that moment arises, I suspect the latter would be most prevalent in me." He peered over his glasses. "Do you think that makes me a terrible person?"

Though the tremor in his voice was frightening, Darwin wasn't evil. He didn't have a bad bone in his body. I had killed Azrael, *my own father*, and I'd shown no mercy when I had ended Jonah's Pureblood Master, Emery, because Jonah and the thousands more like him deserved retribution.

I, of all people, understood. "The need to wage war against others in order to feel peace is a powerful thing."

He tugged at the hem of his T-shirt uncomfortably, perhaps because he thought I was judging him. "Quite."

With a difficult smile, Darwin gestured for me to follow him out of his sister's bedroom. As he reached for the doorknob, I lingered on the landing, knowing that it was wrong of me not to have expressed myself fully for fear I would expose the worst of my own *super*-humanity. I rose to tiptoes, and taking him by the shoulder, I looked into his eyes. He'd once quoted Shakespeare to me, and so I returned in kind. " 'If you wrong us, shall we not revenge?' " The haunting music from the carousel ended in one brilliant burst before fading. In a whisper I said, "Darwin, it's your right to take it."

I LOCKED THE GUEST ROOM DOOR behind me and slumped against it on the cold wooden floor. My head between my knees, I took several deep breaths in an attempt to steady my nerves and calm my overactive imagination. I nearly jumped out of my skin when I tipped my head back.

"Jonah?" I hissed.

My Vampire leaned against the bathroom door, twirling my knickers around his finger before casting them in the direction of the bed. "Yes, *Jonah*," he said, knocking down the hood of his dark jacket.

Springing from the floor, I shushed him. "You shouldn't be here," I practically growled. And then I realized something. "How did I not know that you were here?"

Nonchalantly, Jonah shrugged me off, striding forward in his biker boots. "What exactly are you doing with the toff? More to the point, what are you doing with the toff with no panties on?" His eyebrows dipped with a lighthearted scowl, but I was sure that underneath his sarcasm he was irked, anxious, maybe even jeal—

"I don't get jealous, beautiful."

I tilted my head. "Maybe we aren't out of sync after all."

I scooped my knickers from the foot of the bed and shoved them into the pocket of my borrowed robe.

"So?" he demanded.

I blinked heavily, becoming increasingly tired from the strain I was placing on my right eye due to the lack of sight in my left. Jonah never missed anything, and his tone changed. "Lailah, are you okay?"

"I'm fine. Why'd you follow me here?"

"Oh, I dunno, maybe because given the chance, you'd have told me not to, and you know how I like to ignore you."

He smirked.

Bad humor and ambiguous sarcasm were the closest Jonah ever really came to an apology. He had hurt me this morning when he accused me of trying to take the easy way out by going to the third to die.

I sat on the edge of the mattress, scratching my cheek. The resin securing my mask needed reapplying. It was starting to irritate my skin. "My jeans pocket," I said flatly.

Jonah hesitated, but then was in and out of the bathroom in a blink, producing the piece of paper I'd stolen from his sketchbook. Unfolding the sheet, he took one look and said, "You took this?"

"Yes. It's the reason I'm here."

Jonah tugged the back of his thick hair, shifting his weight.

"When you apologize for keeping things from me, I'll apologize for snooping," I added.

His hazel eyes narrowed, and he took a moment, but finally he said, "Fine. For the sake of not wanting to spend the night on the floor, I'm gonna let this go."

"You're very sure of yourself." I pulled a camisole-and-shorts set from my overnight bag.

He was quick-witted as always. "That's because I am always a sure thing, beautiful." He winked at me, and I rolled my eyes, but the action stung. Grimacing, I let the satin pajamas drop to my lap, raising my hand to my right eye.

Jonah lunged forward, his chest falling as he breathed my name. "Lailah—"

I cut off his growing concern with a wave of my hand.

"Can you please tell me how, from the little description I gave, you managed to piece together a robot?"

He hesitated. "Because I saw the same thing you did, only I saw all of it." He wandered over to the drapes and tugged them closer together.

"What? How?"

His answer was not forthcoming.

"Jonah?" I said in a sharp whisper.

He turned around. "Because I dreamed it, too."

"You're a Vampire, you don't sleep."

"Yeah, tell me something I don't know." Marching across the room, Jonah pulled off his jacket and launched it too hard at the chair in the corner, making it wobble and nearly tip over.

"Shhh," I warned, pressing my finger to the middle of my pursed lips. I racked my brain for any possible explanation, finding only one that made any sort of sense.

"I—" Jonah started, at the same moment I said, "Maybe—"

We both stopped, and Jonah gestured for me to go first.

"*Maybe* it has something to do with the time distortion. We were both in the third, after all." I paused, collecting my thoughts. "I don't have to be asleep to experience a vision. Maybe you weren't, maybe it just felt like you were."

Jonah's lips parted, but he stopped short of saying whatever he was about to. He swallowed and then stretched his lips into a small smile. "You're probably right."

"Was that all you saw?" I pressed. It was chilly, so I slipped under the duvet and untied my dressing gown.

"Yeah," he said, now more than a little distracted as I attempted to change underneath the covers. "So what's the tin man got to do with the toff?"

I shimmied the shorts up my legs, letting the waistband rest below my hips. I'd begun to pull the camisole on over my head when suddenly Jonah was pressed against me, the duvet the only thing separating us. I froze as his smooth hands wrapped over my wrists, the feel of his skin against mine heating me. Slowly, he tossed my camisole aside and leaned in, touching the tip of his nose to mine. He wet his lips as he slid his hand through my hair. My breathing hitched as he unclasped the crystal hairpin. All the while, his hooded eyes never left mine.

"On second thought, tell me in the morning," he murmured.

SEVENTEEN

I LAY ON MY SIDE, facing the drapes, with one arm under my pillow. My back was to Jonah as he traced his fingertips over the scar running down my spine. Then, bringing his arm over my chest, he nuzzled into the crevice of my neck. His fragrance was ever changing. Lately the summertime woods aroma I'd favored had been replaced by that vanilla cologne. But now as I breathed him in, he had a sweet, musky, manly sort of smell.

Jonah sat up and tucked my hair behind my ear, his hazel eyes growing wider. It was as though he were seeing me for the very first time. "You have never looked so beautiful, beautiful."

Squeezing my hand over his, I said, "Jo—" I didn't get a chance to utter the second syllable that made up his name because his finger pressed the middle of my parted lips, and he shook his head from left to right. *"Just one more minute."*

One minute became five as he silently stared at me. Finally, he leaned in and, taking advantage of my parted lips, molded his mouth to mine. His kiss sealed a promise, and though it was well intentioned, it couldn't be anything but cruel, because it wasn't one he would be able to keep.

"Before," I began, "when you said just one night—"

"I meant what I said."

"But you knew, didn't you?"

Jonah didn't reply.

"You knew that's all it would take," I said. "Just one night to break me."

It was slow to form, but a soft smile edged the corners of his delicious lips. *"Knew* is a strong word."

"What word would you use?"

He considered me before offering an answer. *"Hope.* I hoped one night would be enough. That one would lead to many. That it would give you reason to add another soul to your list of those worth fighting for."

"What are you talking about? I've been fighting for you ever since the day we met."

"No. Not me. You, Lailah." He took a breath. *"You."*

A shiver ran up my spine, and I knew for sure then what he had done to me. I brought my knees to my chest and swung my legs off the bed. Grabbing my jeans and shirt, I dressed quickly.

I stuffed my pajamas into the overnight bag. "I'm going to die, Jonah. *I have to die.* All you've done is made it that much harder, that much more painful to let go."

"I won't let you let go." Jonah's hands clamped over my hips, and he drew me into him, staking his claim. "You don't have to die."

Exhaling, I closed my heavy eyes, and the luminous green triangles were waiting. I fluttered my eyelashes to escape them. "There's a painting out on the landing that says different." I pulled away, making for the door. "Get dressed. I'll meet you out front."

"Where are you going?"

"To say good-bye to my friend."

I closed the door and headed for the stairs but was interrupted by a loud clatter coming from Darwin's bedroom. Though my Angel lineage meant I was capable of sleeping, Jonah's sudden appearance had put a stop to any rest I might have had. I didn't know what the time was, but perhaps it was a little early for breakfast. I drifted to Darwin's door and knocked twice.

"Darwin?"

"Come in," he replied quickly.

He was down on one knee, picking up a spoon and tray that must have fallen to the floor. Fortunately, the pot of tea that had likely found its way here on that tray was safe on his desk.

"You're working already?" I asked.

He straightened, setting the tray on his desk chair. "You know what they say, early bird catches the worm."

He was far too chipper for someone who had spent the night before knocking back as much plonk as he had.

He began to pour himself a cup of tea. "Sorry, let me get a second cup for you."

"No, thank you." Though the clock above his laboratory table read just after 6 a.m., I wasn't intending to stay. But then my eyes scanned the pile of books littering the table, and one in particular demanded that I remain a little longer.

"*Dark Matter?*" I said, noting the title. Given the state of the third dimension, I needed to see what he knew on the subject. "Has something to do with your field of study—with M-theory, was it?"

"You could say that. . . . Though it's part and parcel, really." He stirred his tea. "There've always been plenty of theories on the stuff, but it's only in recent years that we've gotten closer to finding evidence of its existence in the universe."

"How?" I asked.

Blowing on his brew, he answered plainly, "Light."

"*Light?*"

"Clusters of it, radiating from the Milky Way."

I wriggled my nose. "I would have thought there'd be plenty of light coming from the Milky Way, but I don't understand what that has to do with dark matter."

"You're quite right, but light comes in many forms, and a specific set of characteristics were present within some gamma rays emitted from the center of the Milky Way, which wholly supports the theory of dark matter."

My face must have given away my incomprehension.

When he took a deep breath, I knew I was in for a Darwin-esque explanation. "Dark matter is essentially made up of weakly interacting massive particles—otherwise known as WIMPs—and when they collide, they completely destroy one another. When that happens, naturally it creates an explosion." He took a sip of his tea. "What we're talking about here is highly dense pure energy, which, post-explosion, decays in the form of gamma rays. The characteristics discovered in the ones more recently detected can't be attributed to anything else. It's a real leap forward in proving that dark matter actually exists."

"Right." This may have been Darwin's version of simple science, but it was still pretty mind-boggling.

"You were saying before, at the bar, about different dimensions," I said. "Do you think an entire world could be made out of this dark matter?"

Darwin placed his cup in its saucer as he considered my question. "Yes, but I wouldn't say 'made out of.' Dark matter is just that; it's dark matter. We're only partway to proving it even exists because of the gamma rays. If you had a dimension that existed entirely in a state of dark matter and nothing more, the aforementioned WIMPs would eventually collide and explode."

That didn't make sense. The third was like a world of

freezing black ice. It certainly hadn't been exploding when I arrived. The fact that it was breaking apart when I left had less to do with dark matter and everything to do with me.

Leaning against the front of his desk, he said, "There is a difference, of course, between cold and hot dark matter."

"What do you mean?"

"The specifics would only bore you." He collected his glasses from the desk and began to clean them with the bottom of his T-shirt.

"Please, I'm interested, but perhaps give it to me in layman's terms."

Darwin fixed his retro glasses over his ears. "Well, the particles that make up cold dark matter travel at a speed far slower than the particles present in hot dark matter. Meaning cold dark matter has a lower energy that, along with its high mass content, would make it far more likely to form objects—if, of course, it were in the right environment to support it."

"Objects like structures?" I said, jumping in.

"Yes and no. In theory, though it could form something tangible, it would only be a random collection of mass. To create a structure, you'd need an entity that could control and manipulate the particles, and that's where we start getting into science-fiction territory."

I smiled, trying not to come across too eager as I asked, "And the hot dark matter?"

"It possesses a far higher energy, making it more fluid in its nature."

It all made sense. In the third, the structures rose up out of the ground, cold dark matter manipulated by Zherneboh. And the hot dark matter, brought to the third by the scavengers, was kept in a liquid state by being cooled; it was used to fill the sea of souls to keep Zherneboh and his Purebloods in constant supply. And it was being churned clockwise to prevent the particles from colliding and smashing into one another, to stop them from obliterating themselves.

Darwin's eyes narrowed from behind his glasses, his analytical mind assessing my interest, and so I quickly tried to make it seem as though I were merely being polite. "Well, it sounds like a really fascinating subject matter."

"Quite." He nodded. "Right, then. As we're both up, we might as well finish our game of chess while we wait for breakfast."

"Thank you, but—" A gentle warmth prickled up my neck, and I tripped over myself to escape the ray from the rising sun shining in through the open terrace. One little sparkle, and I might as well be wearing a glowing sign that read "Alien."

Darwin caught my elbow just as I bumped into his laboratory table. I stooped down to collect the equipment I'd knocked onto the floor, and he joined me.

"Sorry," I said.

Clonking down a pair of pliers, he asked, "Are you all right?"

A handful of what appeared to be flat-ended syringes lay

scattered behind my feet. As I gathered them, I was surprised at how heavy they were.

"Careful!" Darwin said, clasping his hands around mine, trying to help me carry the weight.

"What are they?" I asked. The tiny, button-size syringes should have been light as a feather, but instead they were like paperweights—with a shimmer I recognized. "Crystal," I said without thinking.

Darwin's eyebrow arched. "And what do you know of crystals, Cessie?"

I snapped back to attention. "Very little," I lied.

He stared at me, studying my face before finally saying, "I couldn't help but notice you're no longer wearing the one around your neck."

I stepped away from Darwin. "I'm sorry, I should probably go."

"You know, don't you?" he said, reaching for me.

Meeting his expectant expression, I murmured, "Know what?"

"They are the key." He dropped his hand to his side. "I saw you with my father's business associate. Gabriel, I believe was his name. Did he give you the necklace you were wearing? Where is that crystal now, Cessie?" In the pub, when Darwin had shared his secret about the dimensions, he had said he was warning me because I reminded him of the person he lost, and I now knew that person to have been his sister, Rose. And while I believed he was trying to "save" me where he could not "save" her, as he claimed, the mention of Gabriel and my association with him now made me think that Darwin suspected I knew more than I was letting on. Perhaps he had thought if he confided his secret in me, I might respond in the same manner.

I ignored his questions. "The key for what, Darwin?" How much did he really know and how much was he surmising?

He didn't hesitate to answer. "The doorways between dimensions."

Three years was clearly enough time for someone as smart as Darwin to have joined together a few more dots.

"You're still trying to find a crystal that possesses active elements?" I said. "So, what, you can open one of these *doorways* and walk into another world? You dislike this one so much you feel the need to put your life at risk to see if the grass is greener?"

What was Darwin's agenda?

"Not at all. I'm a man of science. I'm not trying to put myself in so much as I'm trying to take something out." Looking to the syringes, he continued on as though I might understand, as though I would give up the information he was starting to suspect I had in order to help him. "The crystals may not have contained enough active particles for study, but it didn't mean they weren't useful in another way. The material they're made from is unlike anything on Earth. We don't have an element on the periodic table to even begin to try to define it." He opened a large rectangular box and placed the button syringes inside it, next to a handful of needles. "If I could get a sample . . ."

My eyes fell back to the cover of the book that had been the catalyst for this entire conversation. "Dark matter?" I cut him off. "You think you can collect it from a doorway?" Worryingly, he was right. The rift to the third dimension dribbled with the stuff.

"They're there somewhere, Cessie. Extreme temperature readings have been coming out of Lucan for years—the kind of numbers that could only suggest dark matter. I'm still searching for the source."

"Say you're right. Say you could extract and contain it using those." I nodded my head to the box. "Why would you want to?"

"Dark matter makes up a possible five-sixths of the universe. It was created at the time of the big bang. If ever there was anything that might reveal the mysteries of our universe, it's dark matter. Scratch the surface, remember, to see what's underneath. If we could study it, maybe then we'd understand."

"We'd know the meaning?" I breathed.

Darwin nodded just once. "Mankind's most profound question, answered once and for all by science."

I squeezed my lips. Maybe in the beginning, Darwin had been content purely dissecting data in a bid to answer the "how" regarding the origin of life. Maybe after the death of his siblings, he could no longer settle for the how; perhaps now he needed the why. I didn't know what to say, and so I said the first thing that popped into my head. "And here I was think-ing it was the number forty-two."

"Help me, Cessie," Darwin implored. Though he was ig-norant as to who I was and what I could do, his gut instinct that I held information that could forward his pursuit was spot-on.

"I am sorry about your sister and your brother, Darwin. But the answer will mean nothing to you if you're dead. Stay away from Lucan."

Darwin's mounting protest was cut short by a shrill scream coming from the landing. He launched himself through his bedroom door and I followed. Jonah was picking himself up off the floor, and a plump woman dressed in an apron was desperately scrambling to get away.

I scowled at my Vampire for being so careless. Why had he allowed himself to be seen? More to the point, why was he still inside the house?

Protectively, Darwin's arm stretched across my chest, and he shielded me with his body. Jonah rolled his eyes. Darwin was not built to fight. He was a debonair gentleman, an intel-lect . . . and yet . . . he was pulling a Stanley knife from his waistband.

From behind Darwin, I gestured for Jonah to leave, and for once he listened to me. Yet, somehow, as he was heading for the guest room, Jonah lost his footing and slipped. Darwin sped to the top of the staircase.

"Yohan!" he shouted, calling for one of his guards. "Yohan, up here!"

Behind him, I thought myself into the guest room, so when Darwin spun around, I was gone. The balcony doors were wide open, and I rushed through them to the sound of Jonah cursing, but he wasn't in my direct line of sight.

"What are you doing?" I demanded, peering over the railing. "Are you hurt or something?" It was the only possible explanation I could think of as to why he had slipped on the landing and as to why he was now precariously dangling one-handed from the railing, trying to grab hold of the drainpipe on the brickwork with his available hand. A two-story drop shouldn't pose a problem for a Vampire; why hadn't he simply jumped? Heavy footsteps sprang along the landing, leaving me no time to press him for an answer. Vaulting up and over the cast-iron railing, I snatched Jonah, taking him with me as I landed, perfectly balanced on tiptoes, on the patio below. Redistributing his weight over my shoulder, I sped through the gardens before we could be seen.

I took us two roads away before stopping and taking refuge underneath a tree in the communal grounds across from the terraced townhouses. As I dropped Jonah, I punched him in the arm. "What are you playing at?"

Jonah scowled as he scratched the back of his head. "Don't ever do that again." He rooted around in his jacket pocket and pulled out a packet of smokes and a lighter. He cupped his hand around the end of a cigarette as he lit up, somehow inhaling and exhaling smoke all in one go as he tipped his head toward the sky. "I was taking a look at the painting that's got you so heated up."

Annoyed as I was at him exposing himself, it was more important to know what he thought of the painting. A scolding could wait. "And?" I said.

"Obviously, you're crazy."

Why I expected him to be anything but acrimonious I don't know. "You and I both saw a robot, the very same robot that a seer painted on that canvas centuries ago."

"*And?*" he said, mocking me.

I was about to fill him in on what was hidden within the image, sure he wouldn't have seen what I had, when he said, "I saw the butterflies, beautiful. I felt the flap of their wings as they took flight. And yeah, it's freaky, I'll give you that, but it doesn't mean anything. It doesn't mean you have to die."

Choking on the fumes, I said, "I think we'll have to agree to disagree."

He took a deep pull on his cigarette, and the ash fell away with the breeze as the paper burned. "For argument's sake, let's say you're right, let's say somehow that painting represents your death. Killer robots haven't been invented yet, *so*—" Stooping to my ear, he blew a steady stream of smoke out of the corner of his lips. "Perhaps you should find something better to do with your time than worrying you're about to run out of it." Jonah flicked his cigarette and then stubbed out the glowing orange bulb with his biker boot. He walked back to the road, turned his head from left to right, and finally flipped up his hood and whistled at me over his shoulder.

I wasn't about to come running when he called me like that, and so I made a point of strolling instead. "Don't ever do that again," I said with disdain, mirroring his earlier words and tone.

He smirked sarcastically. "Works for the Paddy kingpin, and you seem to listen to him."

"Don't start."

Taking my hand, he lead me across the road, stopping when he reached the passenger side of a shiny black Porsche. "Grand theft auto isn't as much fun when there's no one around to try to stop you." He sighed. Then, nearly pulling the door off its hinges, he said, "Nevertheless, your chariot, beautiful."

Jonah was right: There wasn't a single person in sight. I guess the curfew hadn't lifted yet.

He said, "I assume you're wanting to go back to the kid farmers?"

"You assume right, and the sooner the better. We'll be faster on foot." I turned away, but Jonah caught my elbow.

"What's the rush? They aren't going anywhere. Let me have my way for a change."

"*For a change?* Are you forgetting about the last two nights?" I'd meant to use a sharper tone, and I absolutely hadn't meant to grin at all.

Jonah gave me a devious wink before taking me by my waist and bundling me into the passenger's seat.

EIGHTEEN

By the time we reached Dublin, Jonah had had enough fun driving the Porsche that he was willing to dump the stolen car. It had taken us the better part of the day to drive from the southeast of England to Holyhead, where we had then driven onto a ferry and made our way by boat to Dublin's port.

Though I'd initially wanted to get back sooner, I couldn't deny that I'd found the journey refreshing. As Jonah cruised along the motorway, I'd wound down the window, letting the cold air skim my skin. No talk of Heaven or Hell, of war or religion, of life and death—no, we'd simply talked. Maybe for real for the first time.

Jonah had never spoken much of his life before he'd become a Second Generation Vampire. What I knew had mostly come from Ruadhan. I'd been led to believe that once a mortal had been infected with the venom of a Pureblood, the darkness took over, leaving little of the person that he or she had been. But Jonah was different. Through Brooke, he had remembered Mariposa, and that spark had been enough to grow a flame. With each day that he was parted from his Pureblood Master, it continued to burn. On and on, every day, it burned as he tried to find his way back to some form of humanity, to an existence that had been stolen from him. I admired him for that. Jonah had never let what he was define him; he'd made a choice, even though he hadn't been given one.

He told me about his childhood, how he'd enjoyed sketching from an early age; a God-given gift, his mum had called it. His father had had high hopes for him in the way of a soccer career, but as much as Jonah enjoyed playing sports, he'd dreamed of becoming an artist. He'd gone on to tell me about college life, for the short while he'd attended Florida State University, and of the time he'd wasted away playing drinking games with his friends. He didn't speak about his sister or of the night he had been changed into a Vampire. And I didn't ask. Instead, I sat, providing him with an audience while he reminisced about the good times, becoming more and more animated as the stories poured out. Somehow, as he regaled me with them, it felt as if it was the first time he was remembering them himself.

Eventually, he was doing all the talking, and I sat,

welcoming the sounds of the laughter that was increasingly leaving his lips, the same laughter that had caused me to fall in love with him, each new bout resounding in my soul.

WE DUMPED THE PORSCHE next to the rail track, and though we both set off toward Lucan at the same time, it was me who arrived by the side of Sealgaire HQ first. As I waited for Jonah, I noted that the usual hustle and bustle surrounding the house was absent. Apprehensively, I walked down the dirt track toward the motor home. A loud smash followed by a scream found me fast, and my senses zeroed in on the location. I catapulted over the fence and sped through the garden to the back of the main house. The silver components of the door didn't hold me back, for the entire door had been decimated. I rushed through the rectangular hole in the wall.

Shattered glass, playing cards, and one-cent pieces were scattered across the polished marble floor, where Gabriel was struggling to fend off a Vampire. Iona was clutching a silver blade, pinned in the far corner by the knocked-over table.

The demon straddled Gabriel, cracking its fangs. I flung myself at the Vampire, taking him with me through the brick wall behind us. We were both on our feet in less than a second, but for just a fraction, I hesitated, distracted by the arrival of Ruadhan. It was all the time the Vampire needed to throw himself back at Gabriel.

Ruadhan surged forward, but from his position he hadn't

seen Iona launching herself over the table, raising the blade above her head.

"Watch out!" I yelled.

Ruadhan's trench coat flew in the air as he flipped backward on the spot. As he somersaulted, Iona's knife nicked him in the arm and she fell to the floor with a thump.

The Vampire had Gabriel by the throat, and I recognized the black gloves from two nights ago. But the demon was scarred beyond just the slice over his lip and cheek; the right side of his face almost matched the mosaic tiles. The damage from William's silver arrow had left his skin discolored and cracked like graying ground in a drought.

"Psst!" I hissed, and the Vampire craned his neck in my direction, his green eyes becoming blood-red in response to the balls of pure white light rising in my palms. Gabriel was my soul mate, but Ruadhan was the closest thing I had to a father, and he was vulnerably positioned just outside the door frame. I had one second, and all I could do with it was offer the Vampire a choice—his existence for Gabriel's.

Misreading the situation, Iona must have thought I was creating a diversion. She slid the blade across the polished tiles to Gabriel's waiting hand. Twisting his grasp around the handle, he drove it toward the Vampire's neck, but the Vampire was faster, catching Gabriel by the wrist. The knifepoint was a whisper from pricking the demon's sallow skin, but his stare remained fixed on me. With a howl, he said, "She was mine."

I willed my light to weave through my fingers. "Get out," I said in a final warning.

The Vampire disappeared, and the blade that had been at his throat plinked to the floor. Panting, Gabriel stood, quick to pull Iona to her feet. I called Ruadhan's name twice, and he appeared.

"I'm okay, little love," he said.

Gabriel and Iona held on to each other's shoulders, supporting each other's weight. They bowed their heads, and their temples met. The way they held each other made me feel as though I was intruding on a private moment. But then Gabriel scowled; his whole body quivered and he pushed Iona away.

Gabriel glanced to me, and Iona followed his gaze, her lips pulling in a fragile frown. Taking a breath, she turned away.

"*No*," I said, a wobble in my voice. "Gabriel, I think it's time we talked."

AFTER LEAVING IONA IN RUADHAN'S CARE, Gabriel and I were alone together in the kitchen of the main house. Gabriel pinched the collar of his plain black polo shirt, shaking away tiny shards of glass. I remembered him mostly in white, but now his clothes were dark, as though he didn't want to be seen.

The remains of the glass tabletop crunched underneath my ankle boots as I strode closer to Gabriel. Inwardly, I prepared for the pain that this conversation was going to cause us both. With no easy way to begin, I simply said, "She loves you."

"I know," he said, reaching for my elbow.

I was in love with Jonah, but a part of me would always love Gabriel, and his life and happiness were still of paramount importance to me. No matter how many times my soul had changed shape, his mark on me remained, though it had faded over time, which was a good thing; he was better off without me.

"You and I are meant to be together," Gabriel whispered in my ear.

His quick breath at the nape of my neck was familiar but different at the same time. Now it was cold against my skin. "I know it feels like that. We were designed to fit together, but that doesn't mean we have to remain a Pair." I turned to face him. "Inevitability, remember? Your happiness doesn't have to be dictated by it, not when there's choice, and both of us have a choice, Gabriel."

Gabriel's wavy blond hair fell over his forehead as he bowed his chin and asked plainly, "And your choice is him?"

"Yes."

He blinked slowly. "That's your decision, but it doesn't change how I feel about you—that you are my purpose."

Created as Angel Pairs, Gabriel and I were fated to each other. In the past, he had claimed that his love for me was his choice, but how much of it really stemmed from the way our connection made him feel? How I felt about Jonah had not been preprogrammed. I had fallen in love slowly, my feelings for him culminating in that laughter that had escaped his lips under the Christmas tree in the barn in Neylis. Gabriel felt something toward Iona; I had been sure of it when he kissed her at Sir Montmorency's soiree. And they were new feelings, born from within him, not ones that had already existed the day he was born.

And though Gabriel had once spoken of choice, of free will, he, too, had a faith and he chose to place his in destiny—in "meant to be."

I cupped his cheek and sighed. "Gabriel . . ." I searched for something that would make sense to him, and I remembered what Darwin had said to me when I had debated the meaning of life with him at his father's party. "Maybe it doesn't make sense now, but one day it might. Perhaps, at the end, we'll find order in the entropy of infinity." I tucked his hair behind his ear. "You and Jonah might both be right. There might be meaning behind all this chaos. There were signs pointing to Jonah, but I couldn't see him because I was blinded by you, by us, by a past that consumed my present, that consumes yours still. But I heard him, Gabriel. The pound of the drum, the sound of his heartbeat." I paused. "Perhaps you should stop looking and start listening instead."

Gabriel's tired, gray-blue eyes met mine. "I can't let you go."

"But you don't have to. The me you loved will never leave." I took his hands in mine and brought them to his chest. "She'll always be with you—in here."

Gabriel kissed me—very gently. He lingered at my lips

and then brought me in close by the small of my back. More forceful, more full of pain, he kissed me a second time, but then he pulled away, his brow dipping.

I nodded to him. "There's nothing there, I know. Because you're kissing a ghost."

Gabriel gripped the hem of my shirt. Finally, he understood.

I withdrew, and my mask nearly peeled away. I pressed it in place. "We should talk about Iona—"

Gabriel shook his head as though it were far too soon for such a conversation. At the party in Chelsea, I had witnessed Gabriel glow at her touch. There was something between them, however much he denied it. For him, ultimately what would define the end of our relationship was the beginning of another. Only then would he truly move on. But he needed to open himself up to the idea of it, and fast, before it was too late. I didn't know how long I had left here. Once I was gone, I wouldn't be able to protect him, and he'd be left here fallen, with no abilities. This attack I was lucky enough to have stopped proved that couldn't be allowed to happen. He needed to regain his light to save himself, to save her, and to find the happily-ever-after his story deserved.

"You love her," I said, "but not in the way you should. Not in the way you need to."

Gabriel stepped back from me, and his gaze fell to the floor. "Let's not do this, not now, please—" he said quietly.

With daylight dwindling outside, and the darkness descending on the doorway, our time together was coming to an end, and with a subject not to be rushed, I relented and turned my attention away from matters of the heart. "Do you want to tell me why that demon keeps trying to kill you? Do you know what he meant by 'She was mine'?"

Gabriel stroked his neck as though he'd just shaved. "That Vampire was Hanora's . . . well, I'm not sure what you'd call him."

"You mean he was connected to her through blood? He was her *mate*?"

"The word *mate* doesn't seem right. It would imply some sort of affection. I told you before, Vampires don't survive long when they begin to feed off each other. One is always destroyed." As despondent as Gabriel appeared, he seemed to welcome a diversion from the subject of Iona. "How much do you really know about Hanora?" He turned and opened a cupboard, pulling out a wooden broom.

Not much, I realized, as I answered. "Ruadhan told me she traveled with you for the better part of a century. That she was the first Vampire you freed from a Pureblood Master."

"That's right. After your death, *your first death*, I left for the first dimension to seek out your essence in the in-between. Of course, it wasn't there, because you weren't really dead." He trailed off, recalling the injustice of it all—the "what could have been." He continued, "After consulting with Orifiel, I returned to Earth through the fixed gateway, emerging here, in Lucan. This is where I first met Malachi, and it's also where I found Hanora."

"Okay," I said as I flipped on a light switch for Gabriel's benefit.

He leaned his weight against the broomstick. "The first time I came across her, she and her clan were attacking some of the locals boarding a train for Dublin. But, hidden from view, I watched as she spared a mother and her baby. The second time I saw her, she was protecting some children caught in an air raid. I had never met a Vampire like Hanora. She was the first I'd ever witnessed with that spark, that *recollection* of their once-human self." He tipped his weight back. "She was impossible. She gave me hope when I had none. And so the night I left for London, I took her with me. And this Vampire who seems hell-bent on trying to kill me was left behind—unhappily, I am sure you can guess."

"So, what? He's been trying to kill you ever since?"

"No, to seek me out would have meant leaving Lucan, and disbanding from his Master and clan. I expect he was able to sense her end through their blood connection."

Gabriel rubbed the back of his neck, and I cut in, saving him from voicing the truth of it, from having to say that he'd murdered her. "So he's upset that she's dead?"

He shook his head. "She'd spared the lives of the innocent instead of taking them. She disbanded from her Master. *She was shamed.*" He paused and then said, "He's only upset that I killed her before he could."

"Lovely."

Gabriel began to sweep up the broken glass. "This is where

his clan is based. It was only a matter of time before he saw me."

"So why did you come here? Why take the risk?"

"You," he said. "The fixed gateway opens out here, so without a crystal to command a rift, this is the only spot in the world you could have potentially jumped dimension and ended up." Gabriel swept the broken splinters away from my feet.

"Gabriel, stop," I said, reaching for him. "Why not pick another town nearby? Why not hide?" It was as though I was pleading, as if three years hadn't passed and I might persuade him to reconsider his decisions.

Gabriel's shoulders hunched, as though he was only now realizing the answer. "Iona?" he said, a question for himself.

"Yes?" Iona's voice was unsure as she approached the doorway. Ruadhan trailed behind her, keeping watch. Seeing Gabriel wielding a cleaning implement seemed to get a stronger reaction out of Iona than the way her kin wielded their weapons of silver. "Oh, no, I'll do that!" Iona's polka-dot dress caught between her legs, sticking to her knitted tights as she rushed over. It still amazed me in this modern time that Iona was so traditional in her ways, so much so that she wouldn't even let Gabriel clean up a floor. Gabriel was nothing but chivalrous, so I was sure the only reason he was letting her take the broom was because he knew it would make her feel uncomfortable if he didn't.

I found it awkward watching Iona play such an out-of-date

role, so I stepped in. "Why don't you let me—" I gestured for Gabriel and Iona to stand in the garden. Though my right eye was tired, I was able to identify each fragment of glass littering the tiles. I bent my head toward the floor and blew a steady but powerful stream of air. The broken bits levitated to eye level.

I created a galaxy.

I willed the pieces to spin like planets in a solar system. Round and round they twirled, gaining momentum. The golden glow from the ceiling light acted as the sun, causing a blinding gleam to bounce off the clear shards. I clapped my hands together, and my galaxy folded in on itself, the glass pulverizing back to silt. Like in an hourglass, the sand poured from the top down, collecting into a pile on the floor.

Just as a satisfied smile crossed my face, Iona appeared, her mouth open in wonder at what she must have witnessed. "Might need a dustpan," I said. "A big one."

Ruadhan remained in the garden with Gabriel, giving me time alone with Iona. While I couldn't rush Gabriel to face his feelings, I worried he would take too long to realize what I had—that he should be with Iona and that she would save him. Maybe the best way to get to Gabriel was through her.

Iona came inside, and as she swept, I whizzed around the room, cleaning up the mess from the demon's attack. "Where is everyone?" I asked.

"Out on patrol, the lot of 'em. The sun's setting. They'll be back soon."

I'd arrived back half an hour ago, but as yet Jonah hadn't made an appearance. At least he'd not shown up here at the house. I couldn't sense him, so he couldn't be injured or in trouble. "When you were with Ruadhan just now, you didn't happen to see Jonah, did you?"

Iona nodded as she opened a garbage bag.

"Aye, saw him walking to the motor home," she said, filling the black bag. Its weight clearly heavy, I took it from her and slung it out of her way. "Thank you," she said.

I then collected the pack of playing cards. "You were playing with Gabriel when the Vampire broke in?"

"Um-hum."

"We used to play chess," I mused. "Did Gabriel finish teaching you?" He'd been giving Iona a lesson at the Henley house. I remember how upset I'd been to see him smiling at her across the board that he'd once gifted to me.

"Nay," she said. "He brought the set with him, but he keeps it under a floorboard. Said it's superspecial, it's not really for playing with, like."

"It was a gift he gave me, a long, long time ago." I smiled, shuffling the cards and then placing them down. "I'd like you to have it."

"Oh, no, I couldn't—"

"Please. Gabriel's a good teacher. I'm sure it'll make for some wonderful memories." Whereas I couldn't before, now I could let go of it, and somehow that brought me great relief.

I stacked the one-cent pieces into towers on the counter before Iona knew what was happening. "You were betting?" I asked.

She shrugged. "Not for anything serious. But makes for a better game. My family's always done. But could be with anything—pennies, sometimes matchsticks, whatever's knocking about."

"Matchsticks?" I repeated.

"Aye."

The worn deck belonging to Brooke's invisible friend had also been accompanied by a pack of matches. Absentmindedly, I began to fiddle with the cards, and flicking the corners, I noted another detail. "Huh," I muttered.

"What?"

"Nothing, must just be an Irish thing."

"What must?"

I offered her the perfectly sorted deck. "There's fifty-four cards in your pack, which means you play with the jokers. In the pubs where I worked, we always removed them."

Iona laughed softly. "He made us use 'em as wild cards, no matter the game." I stared at her, puzzled. "It's not an Irish thing." She looked up to the heavens, then back at me, before finishing that sentence. "It was a—"

I RACED TOWARD LITTLE BLUE, almost knocking over the first batch of Sealgaire troops returning from duty in my haste to find Brooke. Swinging the door open, I barged into the small living area where she sat with her legs up on the sofa, magazine in hand.

"Lailah!" she said, springing to her feet.

"Don't 'Lailah' me. You heard me coming."

"Jeez, what's eating you? Chill your boots, why don't you," she said, cool as milk.

I pinched the spine of her fashion magazine and held it in the air. Turning it over, I handed it back, and said, "Difficult to read upside down, even for the likes of us."

Her jaw unhinged. I began to roam the Winnebago, and she zoomed to the table, trying to snatch a roll-up and a pack of Rizla. I caught her wrist midgrab. "Since when do you smoke?"

She hesitated and I thought she was considering coming clean, but then she pushed me away. "You've been gone awhile. Stuff changes, people change."

"Really?" I said with sarcasm. "Just yesterday you told Phelan off for lighting up in the motor home."

Her mouth snapped shut. "I don't have to answer you."

"No, you don't, but I'd like you to."

I wanted her to be the one to say it, not me, and so I waited.

Finally, with a scowl, she said, "You've destroyed my masterpiece, I see."

Clearly, I'd be waiting a long time.

"I think it's probably more wearable without the add-ons."

She huffed. "If it's easy, it's not fashion."

We continued to stare each other down in stone-cold silence, until finally I said, "Bring him out, Brooke."

Her gaze fell to the floor. "Who?"

"The joker in your pack."

To my right, the linen curtain twitched. The second he stepped out, Brooke started, "Lailah, it's complicated, it's just . . . it's a—"

I finished both Iona's and Brooke's sentences. "A Fergal thing." I turned to him. "Yeah, I know."

NINETEEN

JUST WHEN I THOUGHT that nothing could surprise me . . .
"You're a Vampire?" I said.

I was expecting Fergal but not quite like this.

Fergal unfastened his navy gilet and played with the zipper. "Aye."

I had once thought Angels and demons to be the very antithesis of one another. Of course, I knew better than that now. The Purebloods had once been Arch Angels, and the scavengers were once fallen Angel Descendants, beings made from light who had later been changed by a dreadful darkness. Fergal had been born to a fallen Angel, making him Of Elfi, and so his features had always appeared Angelic. And now, though he'd somehow been infected with venom, his looks didn't differ all that much. His skin remained fair, his ruffled hair still white blond, but where his gray-blue eyes had once been calm and inviting, now they glowed red in warning.

"How did this happen?" I didn't trust Fergal and so I kept my focus fixed on him.

"I changed him," Brooke answered abruptly.

"Not possible. You're a Third Generation, you shouldn't be able to turn humans into Vampires." I scanned Fergal, checking that he wasn't carrying anything he shouldn't be.

"Yeah, and Jonah's a Second Generation. He shouldn't have been able to turn me into one, either," she reminded me, with a lick of sarcasm.

I took a deep breath, my mind whirling. "Even if I believed you, Fergal here made some bad choices, and because of them, his soul was dark when Padraig attacked him. Only light souls can be changed, Brooke."

Fergal shifted his weight ever so slightly and I threw up my hand, looping stringy white light around my fingers like thread. "Fool me once, shame on you. Fool me twice, you won't be around to have a crack at the hat trick. Am I making myself clear? Keep your distance," I warned, and as he drifted toward Brooke, I added, "From her, too."

Brooke flailed dramatically. "Ugh! Do you gotta be so freakin' rude? He's sorry, all right? Tell her, Fergal."

Sensibly, he edged away from me. "Padraig was my brother, and he was my best friend, but what I did was wrong. It's for the Lord to decide who lives and who dies, not me. I am sorry,

Lailah." Fergal's pitch was even, and his stare never wavered from meeting mine.

"*See*," Brooke sneered.

"Right, and did the Lord decide to turn you into a demon? Because I thought it was little Miss Thing here."

"He moves in mysterious ways. . . ." Brooke tipped her chin to Fergal, and he nodded back as though she had given the exact right answer.

I huffed, but however ridiculous it was, Brooke actually believed what she was saying. "Why would the Lord give Fergal another shot at life by having you turn him into a demon, which, let's face it, is kind of a dressed-up version of being dead?" I asked. Brooke wriggled her nose, thinking. When she didn't reply, I continued, "If he was seen by Phelan, by the Sealgaire, it would completely undermine their faith. They don't believe Vampires were ever human." I paused, then added, "Not sure your Lord has entirely thought this through."

Though Brooke was still searching, she didn't have a comeback. Fergal, however, always did. "It might seem unclear now, but the Lord has a purpose for me."

More talk of purpose and of meaning, but I knew things about the dimensions that the Sealgaire and even Ruadhan and Brooke didn't. But as Darwin had once suggested, the universe was infinite. It was conceivable that there was something greater going on beyond even what I knew. And, inwardly, I couldn't ignore that I was starting to believe in signs. Maybe there was a higher being redrafting an ever-expanding design, but for what end I doubted any of us would ever know. The Sealgaire—men of the Christian faith—called him "Lord," and Darwin—a man of science—referred to him as "the man wearing the jacket." And, though they were dressed differently, perhaps underneath they were one and the same.

"But you were dying," I said, sitting down.

"He was hurt, real bad," Brooke said. "But right at the end . . ." She stopped, choked up by the memory.

Slowly, Fergal sat down on the sofa and, facing me, finished on her behalf. "I repented, and the Lord forgave me. My soul was saved, but my body was broken. Brooke did something to me, and I became like her."

Somehow repenting his sins had caused Fergal's soul to shift back to light. I remembered Ruadhan saying that while in some cases it could take a long time for a light soul to turn dark, in others one single, bad decision could be an immediate catalyst. A person's energy was interchangeable, he'd said. And clearly it worked both ways. Whatever the mechanics, Fergal's energy had reverted back to light, and somehow Brooke had been able to infect him with venom before he died.

I shook my head, utterly bemused. "Bet you believe demons were human once now."

FERGAL SAT UP FRONT in the driver's seat while Brooke repaired my butterfly mask. It didn't take a lot of effort to peel it from my skin. I was surprised it had lasted as long as it had, given the events of the last couple of days. After touching up the chipped paint, she carefully set the mask down to dry while she created more 3-D butterflies.

I sat across from her, fiddling with my hair. "Is he drinking from—"

"Humans? Yes, he's able to now. At first, it was the same for him as it was for me. But he doesn't rely on my blood or my energy anymore. He can get it himself from a mortal," she answered.

I crossed my legs, watching her work. Jonah was Brooke's maker, so she would never be as strong as him. Was it the same for Fergal? Would he never be as strong as Brooke? It seemed with every impossible "next generation," the attributes that made them supernatural were diluted. I wondered if the same could be said of the mind as of the body. "Brooke. Do you . . . ?"

"Love him? Yes." I opened my mouth, but she anticipated my question. "I don't feel that way because we are connected by blood. I felt it before that, before he was like me."

"There was a time when you said you loved Jonah," I challenged.

"I still do. But I know now that loving someone is different from being in love with someone. I was never in love with Jonah." She went back to shaping her butterfly.

"Are you sure it's not just because you don't want to be alone?" I was thinking of Jonah, of course, and I regretted my question as soon as I'd said it. It was a self-indulgent one.

"Nope. Definitely the big *L*." And then, as if she were

educating me, she added, "You just know when you know." She asked me, "You mind if I camp out here tonight? Can't exactly stay in the motor home, at least not with Fergal."

"Why haven't you told them about him?"

"He'd prefer his family to think he died that day."

"Why? Is it because he's ashamed of what he's become, or because he doesn't want to shatter their belief system?" If the Sealgaire saw him now, there would be no denying that the Vampires they slaughtered daily had once been human beings. That something they believed so vehemently was actually wrong.

Brooke didn't give me a direct answer. "The Lord has a purpose for Fergal. We'll know what that purpose is when we're meant to. Until then, we wait."

I could think of no plausible purpose for Fergal being turned into a Vampire—he and Brooke might find themselves waiting a very long time to get the sign they were so obviously expecting.

"What about Gabriel? Ruadhan?" I asked.

"He doesn't want *anyone* to know. Not yet," she said, and I realized that she wasn't just answering my question; she was asking me to keep their secret.

Dropping the last linen butterfly onto the small pile, Brooke collected the painted mask.

"They need to know, Brooke. It's important. What if the Purebloods find out this can be done?" A sickening, sinking feeling pulled in my chest. If what Riley had told me in the pub was accurate, then in the time Jonah and I had been in the third, the world's population had decreased drastically. We put it down to the Purebloods' feeding more from the dark-souled mortals, and that still rang true. But as for the light-souled mortals that were being "stolen" by the Purebloods' Second Generations . . . what if they weren't stealing them, what if they weren't taking them to be changed by a Pure-blood? What if the Second Generation Vampires were doing what Jonah had done and were creating new Vampires them-selves? And what if those Vampires were in turn creating even more, the way Brooke had done with Fergal? That would be a far more efficient way to increase their armies. Then again, if each generation were weaker than the last, they'd be produc-ing quantity over quality. The idea didn't sit well with me. I was missing something, but I wasn't sure what. I needed a clear head, and I wasn't going to find that here.

"I'll sleep in the motor home," I said. "You can take Little Blue."

Brooke thanked me as she continued gluing the intricately detailed butterflies around the edge of the mask, spreading three smaller ones just below the eye slit. Again, their antennas pointed outward as though they were flying free. She reapplied the resin before affixing the mask back onto my damaged skin. Without asking, she picked up the hand mirror, holding it out so I could fully appreciate her talents. My bloodshot right eye was the only thing I noticed.

"There." Brushing my hair behind my ear, she paused. "Where's the hairpin?" Before I had a chance to think, Brooke squealed, "More importantly, where the feck is my coat?"

"I must have left it behind," I murmured, angry with myself for being so careless.

"My coat or the hairpin?" she demanded.

"Both," I confessed. I calmed myself: I may have done a disappearing act on Darwin, but it certainly wasn't the first time. The coat and hairpin would be safe with him, but right now I needed to rest my eye.

I SHUT MYSELF AWAY in the confines of a single room in the motor home. There'd still been no sign of Jonah when I'd arrived, and Gabriel and Ruadhan were still immersed in quiet conversation, same as they were when I'd sped by them in the garden en route to Little Blue. Ruadhan had worn a troubled expression, which I'd assumed was due to the attack on Gabriel. I hadn't realized at the time that his concern was for Jonah.

I allowed my eyelids to close, and I dozed lightly at first, but soon I was drifting in the darkness.

A sudden flash, and my mind soaked red.

Burnt orange filtered from the corner of my consciousness like smoke, twirling against the crimson backdrop.

Another flash, and my mind turned white.

A green glow appeared at the center of a horizon, and

speeding forward, the white page of my mind folded into a point. The green bled, painting the sheet, and then bent into the shape of an upside-down triangle.

Seeing double, I was now looking at two of them spaced side by side.

But then, like rose petals being tossed over a grave, blue butterflies burst forth.

An explosion erupted, and they dispersed, flying free.

I woke with a start. Ruadhan was banging on the bedroom door. "Little love," he called. "Are you awake?"

Opening my eyes, I said, "Yes. I am now."

He let himself in and sat at the bottom of the bed, holding out a small pile of clothes. "It's Sunday. Mass starts in an hour. Phelan will expect you to attend, to be seen by the wider community." Ruadhan was already dressed in a smart shirt and trousers, and he'd shined his leather oxfords. "Here," he said, handing me a preselected outfit.

I fingered the fabric. "Phelan pick this out, perchance?"

"Aye."

"Perhaps if he gets bored of slaying demons, he might consider a new job as a stylist."

Ruadhan laughed, that lovely, hearty, wonderful laugh of his, and I cracked a smile. "I don't suppose Jonah will be joining us? Where is he anyway?"

"He's already off out."

"Lucky him," I said, thinking he'd gotten wind of the morning's arrangements.

With my lack of enthusiasm about attending church so easy to read, Ruadhan pulled me up before I had a chance to really protest. "Now, I know it's not the same, but let me get you a cup of tea, sweetheart."

I stretched my arms around his waist and flattened my right cheek to his chest in a bear hug. "What would I do without you?"

PHELAN MIGHT WANT HIS PEOPLE to believe I was a biblical savior, but I didn't fancy wearing the traditional skirt he thought gave the look of one. I stayed in my jeans and ankle boots, selecting only the lace-trimmed, sleeveless blouse to change into from the pile of clothes. Though the sun was partially hidden behind a cloud, I met it nonetheless, and I couldn't help but notice that Gabriel watched from the window of the motor home. He must surely long for the heat of a thousand summers kissing his skin again. I hoped it wouldn't be long before he was able to experience the vitality of the sun the way he had before. It was like gravity; once you were aware it existed, to lose it would leave you out to drift.

We met Phelan at the front of the house. Riley and Claire were already there, trying to quiet their little girl, who flailed in her mother's arms.

"I'll fetch it," Ruadhan said to Claire as he ruffled the little girl's dark hair.

I looked to Claire with a quizzical expression.

"Her favorite storybook," she explained. "She doesn't quite

understand the message yet, but she likes the colorful pictures of the animals."

Ruadhan returned at superspeed, passing a board book into the two-year-old's sticky fingers. "After mass, sweetheart."

I found it astonishing that Claire, a member of the Sealgaire, would allow a "demon" to read to her child. I must have worn the surprise on my face, as Claire said, "Iris is very fond of Ruadhan. She won't have anyone else read to her."

Ruadhan strolled beside Claire, and I followed behind with Iona. Though it was nearly midday, it felt much later on account of the gray sky and damp, wet weather. Phelan's men hurried along the families they were escorting from their homes to mass. They all slowed when they passed us by, gaping and whispering. Iona didn't notice. She was wittering on about the reading she was due to give, but I barely heard her. I was too busy sticking my tongue out at Iris, who, positioned like a koala bear over her mother's shoulder, blew bubbles at me.

The gates were open wide, welcoming the townspeople, and as we strode up the long path leading to the church doors, something—*someone*—caught my eye at the side of the building.

I sidestepped, veering away from the men, and Iona trotted beside me, still chatting away. ". . . it's always very popular."

Up ahead, the darkly dressed figure turned and began to walk away.

"Sorry?" I said absently to Iona.

"Psalm 23," Iona repeated.

"Lailah," Phelan shouted, eyebrows raised as if I were holding them up. When I didn't respond, he whistled in that infuriating way of his.

"Go greet your flock," I snapped. Surely by now Phelan had gathered that I didn't like being told what to do.

Ruadhan patted Phelan's back, encouraging him inside with an "I'll go and get her this time" kind of look.

"Who is that?" I asked Iona, pointing to the figure now disappearing into the depths of the graveyard.

Like a meerkat, she angled her face and peered up. "Oh, that's just Malachi, the caretaker." She smiled as Ruadhan arrived at her side.

Malachi.

"Sweetheart—" Ruadhan began, coming between us. Iona took his extended arm.

"You go on ahead," I said, my eyes following Malachi—the fallen Angel I'd met long ago. "I'll be right there."

I thought myself to the bottom of the graveyard and scanned the surrounding land. To my left, the autumn aurora continued to seep into the sky, painting the backdrop for death and destruction. The hill was still, with no sign of any Pure-bloods, and I wondered if Zherneboh was now satisfied with the number of demons he had collected in his jar. I cleared my consciousness, searching for Zherneboh's presence in the darkest recesses of my being. I couldn't feel him. Wherever he now was, he wasn't close. But that didn't mean there weren't others.

I would have to keep my wits about me. My supersenses picked up on a twitch from within the orchard, and I arrived at the center of a cluster of apple trees a moment later.

With his back to me, he hung his head, turning only when I called his name. "Malachi."

"Lailah," he replied. "Good to see you again."

"Is it? The fact that I'm standing in front of you now means I failed to deliver on your request to end the worlds."

"I never said that to end those worlds, you would be ended there, too." He removed a hand from the pocket of his overcoat and took off his hat, straightening his ash-blond hair underneath. "Come. Take a walk with me."

Fruit trees with bowing branches surrounded us, and despite being fall, the leaves here were green and fresh. This morning, the sun had taken a back seat to the cover of cloud, but somehow, here in the orchard, a sticky, Mediterranean-style heat hung in the air.

"Did you come to Lucan to try to find me?" I asked. "To hand out more orders?" Though this meeting was an impromptu one, I was quickly forming my own agenda. Malachi was old and wise; the knowledge he possessed might help me formulate a plan to save humanity.

"No. Lucan is home to my more permanent residence. I have been the caretaker of this land for millennia."

I ducked under a wayward branch. "I thought you were stateside when Gabriel came looking for you?"

His answer was easy. "On such occasions that business calls me away, I have a deputy."

"Right," I said. "And what exactly are you taking care of?"

As always, Malachi's expression was unreadable. "Why waste time asking questions you already know the answer to?"

"So, what? You care for the land, home to the doorways to the first and the third dimensions? Is that not a dangerous vocation for a fallen Angel?"

"You would think so, wouldn't you?" He pressed his hand into the small of my back, redirecting me through the thicket. "Unlike any other, I possess a certain set of skills."

"You called yourself the Ethiccart?" The last time Malachi and I had met, he had told me that Orifiel had bestowed the job title of the Ethiccart upon him, and from what he had implied his role had somehow involved a redesign of Styclar-Plena after the day the darkness fell—the specifics of which he hadn't shared, insisting instead that I must see it for myself.

"Yes. When you passed into the third, you witnessed my work firsthand."

I slowed my pace. "The structures, the sea of souls, that was you?"

"My design, Zherneboh's hand. Though I have never seen it with my own eyes, on account of the nature of the world."

"On account of the fact that if you passed through, you would become one of his scavengers, you mean. Like the other fallen Angels."

"Ah, you were able to see through the creatures?" For the first time during this exchange, Malachi's elevated tone gave something away. It sounded almost like hope.

"Yes. Why would you ask me to end the Purebloods when you designed them a sustainable system? You told me before to bring both the third and the first dimensions to an end." I stopped. "*Whose side are you actually on?*" I demanded. I had gathered from our previous conversation that Malachi acted as a sort of middleman, offering his services to the highest bidder. The fact that he had no allegiance to anyone but himself made me uneasy.

I spun around, checking there was nothing untoward behind me.

"Calm down, child. I told you before that I am with you, not against you." He waited patiently for me to accept what he said.

With caution, I continued to follow him through the dense orchard.

"It was a necessary evil," he said. "The sea of souls, as you put it, is fueled organically through natural selection; the scavengers collect the dark matter of the dead, they don't kill for it. Overall, far more lives would be lost if it didn't exist at all."

My mind whirled. "Was Pandora's box up there your design, too?"

Malachi's eyebrows arched. "Yes. It seemed sensible to keep the gateway to the third hidden. When it first appeared, it was on full display above the land. In the beginning it was easier to conceal, but with the advancement of technology, it's become increasingly more difficult to disguise." Malachi slowed beside a small allotment plot. "These men with the infernal gadgets," he grumbled.

I thought of Darwin and his team as Malachi directed me around the vegetables. "But it doesn't just hide the gateway. Zherneboh's been depositing Vampires—"

"Into a chamber—yes, child, I know my own design. An add-on Zherneboh desired. He is collecting the strongest of his demons to slay the inhabitants of Styclar-Plena when they are flushed out of the first, you see."

"You are both sure that I will do as you ask, but you are both wrong. I told you before that I've no intention of passing through to the first. Ending that world will not save this one."

"On the contrary, if you don't end Styclar-Plena, this world will be the first to die."

I dug my heels into the ground. "Without me he can't."

"If you won't, there are other means to his end. A new discovery—"

"What new discovery?"

"The crystal in Styclar-Plena is fueled by the light energy released from a mortal in death. Without humankind, there would be no light to transport. It wasn't possible before; even with the might of the Purebloods, still there were not nearly enough . . ." He paused, waiting to see if I could put together the pieces.

"Zherneboh knows." I gasped. "His Vampires can create

more Vampires." My mind tumbled. The Vampires that had descended upon us as we walked back from the pub were not like ordinary Second Generation Vampires—they had appeared weak and frail. It was only Hanora's mate and the Vampire who had taken Cameron that were strong. "Zherneboh doesn't care that they are weaker, because their purpose is not to fight."

Malachi nodded. "No light souls, no energy. No energy, no way to sustain the Angels' world. Orifiel will either perish in the darkness of his dying Styclar-Plena, or he will do what he hasn't since the day he betrayed his brother. He will pass through the gateway and face him." Malachi held his hat to his chest. "You must deliver Orifiel to Zherneboh first, Lailah, or there will be no souls on Earth left to save." Malachi placed his hat on his head. "Step forward, would you?" I did as he asked, and from nowhere, a cottage built of stone stood before me. Strobes of light cascaded over the dwelling in twinkling waves of white and gold.

I did a double take. "How did I not see that before?"

"By manipulating light, you can cloak just about anything, if you know how," he replied.

A tree towered high above the red slate roof. Its branches drooped with an abundance of tempting apples. Malachi reached out in front of me and pushed back the tangled branches to reveal a luminous streak of brilliant white light.

"The gateway to the first," I said slowly, entranced by the extraordinary sight.

"A door you must walk through to save a world you and I have both come to call home."

I contemplated his request, the fresh burden he had placed on my shoulders already weighing me down. If I didn't bring an end to Styclar-Plena, then the inhabitants of Earth would be the ones to pay. "I understand, but—"

"But what?" he asked quickly.

"Once Zherneboh takes his revenge, what then?"

"Once you bring about the end of the first dimension, the end of the third will follow. And then you must kill them all."

"You want me to kill every single Pureblood, every single generation of Vampire on this planet? *On my own?*" I hoped that if I put it like that, he'd have something more useful to say.

"Kill Zherneboh, and his house of cards will fall with him."

Malachi stretched the branch back farther, encouraging me to step through the gateway. But then, from the lapel of his overcoat, a bright spark flickered. It was coming from a golden pin shaped like a leaf. "Phelan lent me a hairpin that looked just like that."

"The leaf is a symbol of the fallen. The fallen Angels wear them as a promise to me."

I took a step back. "I don't understand."

Gently, Malachi let the branch spring back. "By Earth's time, Zherneboh emerged from the third thousands of years ago, after which he sought out the Arch Angels who were visiting Earth and collecting the light energy to fuel the crystal."

Malachi ran his finger over the rim of his hat in quiet contemplation. "Zherneboh took thirteen before Orifiel realized. Back then, several millennia ago, the Arch Angels worked alongside the first of the Angel Descendants, ferrying the souls from one plane to the next, and so to protect the Arch Angels that remained, the Descendants alone were purposed with the task of moving the souls."

"These were the Angels that were not paired to one another?"

"Yes, Angel Descendants Mark 1. A defective batch by all accounts. One by one, their lights dulled, and when they fell, they passed through the fixed gateway from the first to here." Malachi's tone became deep and dark. "But Zherneboh and his kind were waiting."

I gulped, hard.

"Orifiel had removed the Descendants' crystals, thus stripping the Descendants of their gifts and rendering them defenseless for the rest of their extended existence—ripe for the picking. They were taken into the third."

Gabriel's face appeared in my consciousness, along with the most terrible realization. If he were pulled into the third, he, too, would become a scavenger. "It's unthinkable," I said.

"With the Purebloods' sustainable system in place and their scavenger servants at work, the Purebloods dispersed and set about building their armies, which would both hunt for them and of course one day fight for them. Not all of the fallen were lost. I was able to save a good many before the Purebloods were able to snatch them for the third, delivering them instead to the only place they would truly be safe."

"The sea," I murmured, and Malachi nodded.

"But what could they have possibly promised you in exchange for their lives?"

"To fight for me when the day came."

"What day?"

Malachi took my hands in his, and as our skin met, the image of the painting on Darwin's landing filled my mind.

It was as though I were inside it.

Suddenly, and all at once, bright-green upside-down triangles glowed.

The ground quaked under my feet.

The wind whipped at my ears.

The butterflies took flight.

The strobe of light shot up, disappearing with a whoosh, and the leaves on the ground scattered. As they did, one lone leaf lifted. Smudged in black charcoal, his name had been concealed in the bottom right corner all along: *Malachi*.

I jolted, snatching my hands out of his grip. "You were the seer?"

"I couldn't be certain, but looking at you now . . ." he mumbled, staring at my butterfly mask.

"You had a vision of the future?"

"Being created in Styclar-Plena means our very makeup contains the means to travel through the fabric of the universe. It allows us to jump from one world to another, but doing so creates a bend in the linear line of time. The curves allow us to peek around the corner before we travel down the road." Calmly, Malachi put his hands back in his pockets.

"You saw a robot kill me?" I said.

He shook his head. "The vision was unclear. I painted what I perceived."

Edging backward, the cottage disappeared from in front of me. The second it did, distorted raised voices echoed all around, distracting me from the conversation, but Malachi saying "The fallen are gathering" brought my attention right back to him.

My gaze fell to the pin on his lapel. "Wait, the jewelry, the leaves you gave them—"

"Devices." He cut me off. "A kind of homing beacon. The fallen Angels will fight with you, Lailah. They are already on their way."

"On their way—" I didn't get a chance to finish because a crash sounded from within the garden. I recognized a voice. "Darwin."

TWENTY

LEAVING MALACHI BEHIND, I thought myself to the edge of the garden that separated the two gateways just in time to see Darwin get knocked to the ground by a Second Generation Vampire.

I reacted instinctively.

I charged forward and collided with the Vampire. I wrapped my hands around the demon's throat and broke his neck before he had a chance to shriek.

I sensed another coming up behind me and sprang from the chest of the dead demon, landing atop the Vampire's shoulders. He hissed, bringing his hands up above his head, but I'd already willed my light, and my red-hot hands seared his skin. I twisted and snapped his neck, ripping his head from his torso. Instantly, it disintegrated from the heat of my hands.

A sudden, violent vibration shook the garden, and Darwin slipped as he scrambled to his feet. I knew what was coming.

"Darwin!" I shouted. "Run!"

Still in a daze, he mouthed, "Cessie?"

And then the demons descended. A swarm came down from the hilltop. Darwin remained rooted in place as I willed golden globes to form in the palms of my hands. As the Vampires charged down the hillside, they momentarily disappeared from view as they passed through the foliage bordering the garden.

I took a defensive stance next to Darwin. As the first Vampire broke through the tree line, I focused on the buttons below his collar and took aim, releasing my charged white light. The Vampire shrieked but his insides bursting through his rib cage drowned out the noise.

I could tell where each demon was about to emerge by the break in the brambles as they careened over them. I shot out fireball after fireball, knocking the Vampires down like bowling pins. A large demon fought his way through the pack; he was only meters from my face when I struck him in the chest. He ricocheted off another demon, and with a deafening clatter, they both smashed to pieces.

One at a time, I picked them off with ease. Some merely melted; others left this world more dramatically, exploding like fireworks.

One thing they all did was cry.

When all that was left was the smoking remains, I turned back to Darwin. He still lay on the ground, frozen in fear.

"Are you hurt?" I asked quickly.

"No," he said nervously. He felt the grass around him until his palm landed on the crystal hairpin. It glowed beside him, flashing the same way Malachi's pin had. Darwin must have found it and followed the signal it was emitting. His satchel had fallen open, and its contents—a silver dagger and the wooden box containing the crystal syringes—lay beyond his grasp. His eyes widened, staring at them.

Suddenly, Ruadhan and Gabriel appeared.

Ruadhan reached me first. "Lailah?"

Darwin knew me as Cessie, and snapping his attention back to me, he repeated my real name under his breath. I would have to explain that later. . . .

Just as Gabriel neared, a dark blur zoomed past. A blur that turned out to be Jonah.

The rumble of a second swarm sounded, and I leaped through the air, putting distance between me and everyone else. This time, I willed my light in a white sheet. Pushing it out from my chest, I sent it cascading toward the boundary to the left of the garden, and it drew over the land slowly like sunlight on a dark winter's morning. A roar rose up as my white light crashed between the tree trunks like a wave, meeting a mass of demons heading in our direction.

Confident I had ended them all, I went to retrieve the

satchel and its contents, fearing that if I didn't return them to Darwin, he would risk coming back for them later. But then a half dozen more demons descended.

I was starting to lose my patience.

"Stay back," I instructed Ruadhan, who was pulling Darwin to his feet behind me.

All six demons charged. I anticipated the two who flanked me first. Extending my arms, I shot white lightning from my fingertips. Both jumped at the last second, and though I struck one of the demons, causing him to disintegrate in midair, I came just shy of hitting the other on my left. As the Vampire plummeted, I threw my hand above my face, and the demon stopped, suspended only inches above me. I opened my palm and thrust it against his forehead. A rush of current passed through him like volts. His veins bulged as I heated the dark matter circulating through his body, and he was set alight. His bones crumbled and his skin melted as his body fell and turned to mush at my feet.

As the final four dove toward me, I leaped and willed my light. As they swiped for my legs and ankles, they met the golden glow, and below me they burst into flame.

Vampire ash fell like a blizzard as I made my way to the satchel. But at the center of the dissipating smoke, another demon appeared. Stooped down, he faced away from me. I halted and readied myself to strike.

Just before he turned around, I noticed two things: the silver blade in his hand and the familiar fabric of his checked shirt.

The demon looked up.

"Cameron," I whispered. The freckles that had once dusted his nose had disappeared below milky skin, and his rounded cheeks had given way to far sharper angles. Still, I saw the childlike expression of the young boy staring back at me.

Though a snarl reverberated in his throat as he slunk toward me with Darwin's dagger raised, all I heard was the wistful sigh of the timid fourteen-year-old lad who had clutched his weapon with inexperience and fear.

And though his fangs hung over his lower lip and his eyes were filled with crimson, all I saw was the flush of his skin after he'd pecked me sweetly, thanking me for the advice that I believed resulted in his death.

"Stop," I commanded, and he listened, halting three feet away. "Cameron," I said, calling him by his name softly. His lips pulled in a tight and tentative line. For a flicker of a second, I thought he recognized me. "It's me, *Lailah*."

"Lailah," he rasped.

"Yes." I extended my hand. "Come with me, please, Cameron."

I thought he was lifting his heel to step toward me.

I thought the curve of his lip was a smile.

I thought his grip shifted around the dagger to drop it.

I was wrong.

His step was a leap.

His smile was a snarl.

His drop was deadly.

I had to fight my instinct to light up. I had killed Cameron once; I couldn't do it again.

Suddenly, everything moved in slow motion.

A glint from the sun hit the curve of the knife's edge, causing a white star to blindingly stretch across my vision.

Ruadhan's trench coat eclipsed the light as he vaulted between Cameron and me.

The dirt below the grass bounced higher than my makeshift father as he pulled Cameron down to the ground with him.

Cameron bounced back up. Ruadhan did not.

With a shrill hiss, Cameron took off.

"Ruadhan, no," I whispered, helping him to his knees.

Ruadhan swallowed hard, his hand pressing just below the silver blade that stuck out from his chest. As he tipped his face to me, black ink blotted his fair skin. But he didn't flinch as his skin began to sizzle.

There was nothing I could do to stop the black lashes growing up his neck. Ruadhan struggled to keep his stare fixed on my own as he burned. Shaking, I gripped the handle of the blade and considered pulling it out, but it had pierced his heart. If I removed it, he would only die more quickly.

I clasped my hands in a prayer shape at the tip of my nose, my mind tumbling trying to take in what was happening while simultaneously looking for a way out, a way to stop this.

There was nothing.

"I don't know how to save you," I said. "Someone help

me!" I twisted around, watching as Gabriel approached with a pained expression on his face.

"Sweetheart . . ." Reaching forward, Ruadhan placed his hand to my cheek and said, "Save me with your light. Let me find peace in your glow."

I was winded.

A bloodied tear formed at the corner of Ruadhan's eye as the deadly light from the silver spread out from his heart through his veins. As his insides lit up, it was as though the rising heat spread over me, stifling and paralyzing me.

Gabriel had promised Ruadhan's final moment would be one filled with light, but Gabriel was fallen now. He wasn't able to grace Ruadhan with what Ruadhan thought to be a gift. The enormity of what he asked of me was too much; Ruadhan didn't want his final moment to belong to the darkness or the devil; he wanted me to end him with my light.

"I can't," I said weakly.

I cupped my hand on top of his at my cheek and pressed down in silent desperation.

"Sweet—"

As his plea, his last word, broke apart, I met the eyes of the man who had become my father. A single, bloodied tear fell, hitting the grass between us as his form dissolved in front of me.

Particles of ash replaced his body, and as they hung in the air, for a moment the shape of his face remaining, his lips formed the word "—heart." Horrified, I tipped my weight forward, but the ash broke apart and he scattered with the breeze before I could reach him.

The silver blade fell through thin air.

It was so quiet.

It was so still.

My eyelashes fluttered uncontrollably, but the rest of my body was stiff, a cold numbness filled me.

I sat there, waiting.

Slowly, I lifted my palm away from my cheek, but Ruadhan's hand was no longer beneath my own. Like sand through an hourglass, the last of his remains had slipped through my fingers.

He was out of time.

The person who had always picked me up was no longer here to do so, and so even though I wasn't ready, I stood on my own.

"Lailah." Gabriel's tone was low.

He was gone.

Ruadhan was gone.

I gasped. "He died in darkness." I realized what I'd done, because of what I'd been unable to do. I grabbed fistfuls of air, trying to catch a single ember that was still fizzing.

Gabriel's hand pressed down on my shoulder. "Lailah," he repeated.

"No!" I snapped, and pushed him away.

My grief transitioned to anger. "No!"

Rage rose through my body, and I itched underneath my skin. Like a snake, ink wrapped over my wrists, traveling up my hands, arms, and neck. Bringing my forearms out in front of me, I saw that the markings the girl in shadow had worn stained my skin. Though she was gone, expelled on the mountaintop, the darkness she represented still resided in the makeup of my soul. But it was mine to control.

Looking at each of them with watering eyes, I held my hands up, begging Gabriel, begging Jonah, and begging Darwin to keep back.

The wind picked up, howling in my ears. I smashed my balled fists into the hard ground. Massive cracks formed, traveling down to the edge of the garden, and the land began to break apart.

I was the earthquake.

My fangs cracked, and as I looked back up, Gabriel, Jonah, and Darwin were painted red as my eyes bled. I roared like an animal, and taking a breath, I blew down the trees that separated the garden and the orchard.

I was the cyclone.

I spun, and looked beyond the graveyard to the back of the church, where I fixed my attention on the depiction of Jesus nailed to the cross on the tall stained-glass window. Ruadhan was a man of faith. He'd believed in such stories, and where had it gotten him? He died a demon. He deserved everything, but death afforded him nothing.

With my focus zoomed in on the central red plane, I smacked my hands into a prayer shape. I clapped, slowly at first, and the glass vibrated.

Once.

Twice.

Three times.

The stained-glass window cracked as I clapped over and over.

I dissolved into madness.

I looked to the heavens and I screamed.

The image of Jesus on the cross erupted, exploding through the nave, from which, even at this distance, the cry of the congregation could be heard. The world would mourn for my Ruadhan.

I was the volcano.

It was as though the world responded to my inner rage—the final curtain had fallen on Ruadhan's life, and with it day turned to night.

Above me the stars and planets lit up, dressing the dark veil like sequins.

I grew more incensed, and Gabriel fought to penetrate the protective globe I had projected around myself. Meanwhile, Jonah ran round my side, coming into my line of sight. Though his mouth moved, from within my bubble, I couldn't hear what he was shouting.

The moon appeared, spinning like a ten-pence piece.

I didn't have a lasso to tether the moon, but I didn't need one. Using all my will, I dragged it toward me. And as it came closer, growing larger, the whole world trembled. The land suddenly tipped by ninety degrees, sending everything and everyone sliding.

As the moon drew closer, it became a mirror, and the girl in the shadow stared back at me.

Her image shocked me and my shield fell.

Jonah immediately grabbed my elbows, trying to restrain me against his chest. "Lailah, stop," he pleaded.

I shoved him away, and over his shoulder, the moon increased in size, emulating my widening eyes. The black spots in the blue of my irises spilled into my pupils, creating big black holes. Just as I thought about swallowing the world up inside them, everything froze.

The moon stopped moving.

The ground stopped shaking.

The screams stopped sounding.

A voice cut through the absolute silence.

I willed my limbs to move, but they refused me. My breath caught in the back of my throat as a figure appeared beside me, beaming so brightly that I was forced to squint. After a moment, the being, ghostlike in his transparency, floated toward me. His figure rippled as though he were a reflection in water.

He wore a dark-navy jacket that shone as though it were covered entirely with glass. Polished buttons, captivating in their eclectic designs, fastened the fabric. A derby hat sat crooked on his head, revealing his white hair, and a crystal topped the staff in his hand, showing his age.

He lifted his chin.

Black roman numerals drew around his pupils, detailing a clockface.

He came forward, observing me as though he were waiting for me to speak. He then shook his head, and said, "Of course. Pardon me." With a twirl of his cane, my muscles relaxed and I was once again able to move.

"Who are you?" I asked. Reining in my emotions, I observed the devastation I had caused. Jonah, Gabriel, even Darwin, who cowered twenty feet away, were motionless— paralyzed as I had been.

The world was standing still.

The man's smile dazzled as diamonds dotted his lips. "My name is Emit." He paused, and then, carefully adjusting his blazer, said, "The man wearing the jacket."

God?

Up until recently, with the appearance of the signs I'd been seeing, the only time I had really considered that God might exist was when Darwin, a man of science, had used the "man in the jacket" image to explain his belief system. Perhaps that was why God was choosing to present himself to me in this way. But now that I was face-to-face with such an entity, the most important questions escaped me.

"How are you doing this?" I demanded.

"I am not *doing* anything. I *am* this."

"You've stopped time?"

"I am time," he replied.

He tapped his pocket and then, raising his staff, directed me to the moon that I had pulled out of the sky. He did not look amused.

"You took him away from me," I both explained and accused.

He pointed the crystal handle of his cane at me. "You took him from yourself. You made a choice."

"My choice was Cameron over me. Not Cameron over Ruadhan," I growled.

"You made your choice, as did he. Action and reaction—it is the nature of free will." He shrugged. "Your choices become the lines of chalk you travel on, and they cross over, travel next to, and join up with one another. Some lines are long, some are short, but you are all connected. You are all part of the same design."

"He's in the nowhere."

"There's no such thing as nowhere. Until your pattern is ready to be stitched, I keep a watchful eye." He blinked, and when his eyes opened, numbers appeared around his irises, and at the center of his pupils was the image of me, jumping from the ledge of the grandfather clock.

Like a chameleon's, Emit's skin shifted: His cheeks glowed blue and a sprinkle of white crystals freckled his nose, creating a nebula.

"My free will was taken when I bartered away my existence," I said, "so I shouldn't have had a choice. Take it back. *Bring him back*. And claim what you're owed."

"The fabric of the universe is being torn apart," he replied. "You will fasten it back together. That will be your payment."

With a fleeting glance, he assessed the moon. "Some things, however, are more easily fixed than others." A mirrored button hung loose from his pocket, dangling from a frayed seam. He pinched it between his fingers, and as he tugged the thread from the inside of the lining, the moon retracted and wobbled at the same time as he tied a small knot. "That should do for now."

As the Earth righted itself back into place, Emit brought his hand to my left cheek. Without a word, he brushed my mask. Touched by time, one by one the 3-D butterflies came to life. I was dizzy as I watched them fly away, my mind whirling, trying to comprehend.

The nebula on Emit's skin rose and fell with his quick smile, and above us, three shooting stars streaked.

I whispered, "Why?"

He stopped abruptly, and the sparkle from his jacket was blinding. "There will come a moment when you will know, and I look forward to it, Lailah, because the one that follows will see you become the most exquisite button upon my jacket." He looked me in the eye, and hidden in his pupils, Ruadhan was sleeping. "I will keep him for you until then."

TWENTY-ONE

GREEN TRIANGULAR EYES FLASHED.

I woke abruptly and sat up. Daylight streamed through the small window above my head as though it were growing the freesias on the wallpaper. I took a deep breath, inhaling the smell of the bed linen, just as fresh as the flowers looked. Gabriel was hunched over a chair beside the bed, asleep, with his head in his arms.

"Gabriel?" I said, nudging him with my elbow.

He lifted his chin. "Lailah."

He stared at me, his blue eyes wide and weary, and it took me a moment to realize why they were sad.

"Ruadhan," I said with a heavy breath.

"It's okay," he began.

The memory of Ruadhan's death flooded me, and my

entire body ached. The events I had been responsible for came to me. I turned my arms over, looking for the tattoos that had belonged to the girl in shadow.

"They're gone," he said. "They disappeared last night."

"I pulled the moon out of the sky," I said.

Gabriel looked at me, confused. "You must have been dreaming."

Dreaming? Nothing about what happened had felt like a dream. The way the Earth shook, the way the wind whipped and the screams . . . Then, his arrival. Emit, the man wearing the jacket. Had he wound back the clock, reversing the destruction I had caused?

"What happened?" I asked.

"After he . . ." Gabriel stopped, collecting himself. "You were upset. The markings began to stain up your arms, and when they became set, you collapsed. I brought you back here; you've been asleep for seven days since."

Emit must have rewound to the moment before I caused the earthquake, erasing it from everyone's memory but mine. I recalled the image of Ruadhan sleeping inside Emit's eye, and it brought me some comfort to think he hadn't faded into nothing. His soul was safe.

"Jonah?" I said. "Darwin?"

"Darwin is fine. He didn't say much after. He gathered his things and left."

"The hairpin—" I started.

"Returned to its rightful owner." Gabriel answered my question before I had finished it.

I pushed the duvet away and dangled my legs over the side of the bed. "Where's Jonah?"

Before Gabriel could respond, I heard a child's cry. I charged into the living area. Iona did a double take when she saw me. Iris, however, wasn't startled by my sudden arrival. Instead, she stopped wailing and reached her hand out into the air, leaning her weight forward.

"I heard her cry," I said, smiling at the little girl.

Iona hesitated, staring at me with a strange expression. "Erm—I was trying to read her the picture book Ruadhan gave her. It's her favorite," she explained. "But she's asking for *him*."

Iris jumped off Iona's lap and, with a wobble, began to run over to me. She opened her arms wide as she approached, and I reached for her as she steadied herself, hugging my leg. "Uta-flies!" she exclaimed.

"Lailah." Gabriel was behind me, a mirror in his hand.

He picked up Iris and then handed me the mirror. Before raising it to my face, I felt my cheek: The 3-D butterflies were gone. Emit's touch had set them free.

When I looked, my reflection startled me.

Still, I wore Brooke's beautiful butterflies, but they were no longer painted onto a mask. It was as though they had seeped below the prosthetics, tattooing my cheek. Like the galaxies that had swirled and moved across Emit's skin, the creatures fluttered their wings as though they were alive.

"It's like you've walked in front of a projector," Iona said, waving her hand up in front of my face as if somehow that's exactly what was happening and she was trying to find the proof.

"Utaflies! Utaflies! Utaflies!" Iris chanted as she squirmed in Gabriel's arms, reaching for my face.

Gabriel withdrew, but I said, "It's okay, let her."

Iris placed her palm on my cheek and my skin tingled. The butterfly wings tickled her and she giggled, utterly entranced. "Read me!" she squealed finally.

I picked up the picture book from off the floor.

"Unky Ruadhan!" She smacked her leg with her hand.

But Unky Ruadhan was gone.

I took a seat on the sofa, and Gabriel placed Iris in my lap. There was much to do, but before I started, there was someone I needed to speak with. "I'll read to her. In the meantime, could you fetch Phelan for me?" I asked Gabriel. "He and I need to talk."

I glanced down at the book. The cover image was of a rainbow arcing over animals, and I read the title. *"Noah's Ark."*

Eagerly, Iris ran her tiny fingers between the pages as she shouted, "Ankaroo!"

"She means 'kangaroo,'" Iona translated. "Cup of tea?" she

asked tentatively, and even though I had no desire to drink one, there was nothing I wanted more.

"Please," I said, thinking of Ruadhan.

" . . . The rainbow will remind you," I said, finishing the story for the third time, and then, finally happy, Iris sat and began to play.

"I wonder what's taking so long," I said.

"Sunday mass will be finishing about now," Iona said. "Phelan will be at the church."

Iris made clip-clop noises as she bounced a pony in the air, and the very fact that she was still here in Lucan, at the heart of the danger despite my warnings, filled me with contempt. "Iona, I'm leaving tomorrow."

"Tomorrow?" she repeated.

"Yes. And when I return, the very worst of Hell will be unleashed right here on your doorstep. There will be no escaping it. You need to make certain Claire gets Iris to the sea."

Iona fiddled with a button on her cardigan, but then, stroking Iris's auburn hair, said, "Aye."

I heard Gabriel's and Phelan's footsteps before the door of the motor home swung open.

Iona picked up Iris and headed for the door. "I'll take her back to Claire."

Though Phelan had guards patrolling the grounds,

Gabriel glanced between Iona and me, conflicted. "Go with her," I encouraged.

He nodded and then escorted them outside.

Phelan took one look at my face and said, "Neat trick."

Taking a packet of Golden Leaf from his back pocket, he slid out a pre-rolled cigarette and lit up.

"Ruadhan is dead," I said flatly.

"Aye." He tugged on his roll-up. "Sounds as though you're suffering." His tone was devoid of sympathy. It was as though he was seeking confirmation so that he could go ahead and tick *suffering* off my application for his vacancy of "Savior."

"You told me Cameron was dead."

"Aye. What's that got to do with the price of milk?"

"He killed Ruadhan."

Phelan's reply was immediate. "Not possible. Cameron was killed by that demon. I saw it myself."

I studied Phelan's aura, and still his form had a subtle golden hue framing his body. Nothing about his physical reaction to my accusation suggested he was lying.

"You may have thought that's what you saw, but you were wrong. He wasn't killed. They changed him."

"Changed him how?" Phelan shot back.

"They turned him into a Vampire."

Phelan scratched the back of his head with irritation. "Not gonna have this argument with you again, Lailah. *Demons were never human.*"

"I'm telling you that you are wrong."

Phelan blew smoke from his nose, shaking his head as though I were a broken record. He and I now shared something in common that we hadn't this morning. After Emit had presented himself to me, no longer would I question whether there was a force out there greater than what we knew. Now, we both believed in God, even if we called him by a different name. Where we differed was that Phelan had a religion, one that was ignorant to the truth of things, and one that would put him and his men at risk. And no matter how many times I tried to tell him that his teachings were wrong, he wouldn't hear me. He was going to have to see it for himself. Fergal said the Lord had a purpose for him, and maybe he was right: His purpose would be to prove my point.

"Come with me," I said.

Time to set Phelan straight.

We made our way over to Little Blue, and though I expected that I would have to force Fergal to reveal himself to his cousin, once again I was surprised. He was in the living area when we walked in.

"Fergal," I said.

Phelan glanced at me, his brow rising.

Fergal stood up from the chair, threw down his cards, and removed his beanie. Ruffling his white-blond hair, he turned to us. "Lailah."

I almost tripped over myself.

No, it couldn't be . . .

Fergal was standing before me, human.

"*What?*" I said. "You're—"

"Alive?" he said. "I know. I got back a few days ago. It's good to see you." He smiled.

"What did you want to show me then?" Phelan pushed, searching the small space as if he were missing something.

For a split second I doubted myself.

I doubted the destruction I had caused in the garden. I doubted the meeting with Emit. I doubted all the things that had come before it.

Perhaps I was going mad.

The snap of a can of pop being opened caught my attention. I stormed past Fergal, who was subtly wiping beads of sweat off his forehead. Behind the curtain, Brooke hovered tentatively, a cold can of diet soda clutched in her right hand and a bag of chips in her left. If I didn't know better, it would seem as though she and Fergal were playing a game of cards, and she'd gone up front to fetch snacks.

Everything about Brooke was off. Her red hair was messily pinned back, she was wearing her designer shades inside, and as I took a fresh breath, I realized that she smelled different.

"Brooke?" She bowed her head, and I whispered, "You're human."

"Shhh," she snapped, lunging forward. Clumsily she fell into my shoulder, and I moved to steady her.

"What's going on?" I demanded.

The door creaked and Jonah said Phelan's and Fergal's names as he entered. Maybe he would offer me a more straightforward answer to what had happened while I had been unconscious.

Jonah was pulling down his hood and straightening his leather jacket when I returned to the living area.

"Lailah," he said, surprised, as if he hadn't been able to tell I was in the next room. And then I realized why.

It was as though the world had stopped spinning again.

But this time, it was just me that was out of kilter.

Lost for words, I stumbled outside. Phelan and Jonah followed.

"You gonna explain what it is you think I need to see?" Phelan demanded.

It was not Phelan's faith in God that was misplaced; it was his belief in a man-made religion. My plan had backfired. Phelan's ideology would have been destroyed if he had seen Fergal as a Vampire; instead, Fergal was safe, well, and still human. He was a miracle. If the Lord, if *Emit*, had a purpose for Fergal as Fergal had insisted, evidently it was to reinforce Phelan's belief.

With my back to both of them, I first heard the jangle of Iona's bracelet before seeing her and Gabriel approaching. Though they were thirty feet away, I detected the tension in Gabriel's body.

I shifted in place and answered Phelan. "Nothing. I must have gotten the wrong end of the stick." There was no point in trying to convince him that the last time I had seen his cousin, he had been a demon. He simply wouldn't believe me.

And I was starting to think that maybe, just maybe, Phelan was not *meant* to know.

Gabriel's eyes met mine as he and Iona approached, and seeing the Winnebago door ajar, Iona bounced happily to my side. "Oh! You know!" She beamed. "The good Lord has delivered Fergal back to us!"

I moved so that Gabriel, Iona, Phelan, Jonah, and I were positioned in a disjointed circle, and I scrutinized each of their expressions, trying to assess who knew what.

Gabriel came forward first. "Brooke thought Fergal had passed. She was mistaken." Gabriel shot me a knowing look, one that told me that what he was saying was for Phelan's and Iona's benefit. Clearly Gabriel had manufactured a story, and based on both Phelan's and Iona's reactions, it was one they believed.

"He lost his memory, didn't know who he was even, but then one morning he woke up and he remembered!" Iona exclaimed.

There was a slight twitch in Phelan's steadfast stare, and I knew him well enough to know that it would be in his nature to be highly suspicious of such a story, but it tied in nicely with their scriptures, so at least on the face of things, he was choosing to accept it. Though I wondered how much, and how far he would question it internally.

"I'm so glad you had a chance to see him again before you left," Iona added. Her skin glowed.

"Before you left?" Gabriel repeated, before anyone else had the chance.

I cleared my throat in an attempt to compose myself. "Yes. And when I come back, that will be the day Zherneboh will unleash Pandora's box." I tucked my hair behind my right ear, carefully considering how best to phrase my instructions. "I intend to bring Orifiel back with me, and when I do, Zherneboh, his Purebloods, and the strongest of his armies will be waiting." Directing myself to Phelan, I continued, "This may be the only opportunity we have where the Devil and his servants will all be gathered in the same place at the same time. It's the best—maybe the only—chance we have of eradicating them from this world. Do you understand?"

Phelan lit another cigarette; he did his best thinking when he smoked. "When?"

"I'll leave tomorrow, just after sunrise." I would need to refuel, and so tonight I would drink blood, and tomorrow I would meet with the sun before entering the first dimension. "I don't know when I'll be back." And I didn't. The first dimension, like the third, traveled at a slower speed than Earth. An hour there was around a year here. I would have to get in and out as quickly as possible. "If you insist on being part of this fight, then aim your weapons at the Second Generation Vampires. Keep clear of the demons like the one you saw in Henley. I'm the only one who stands a chance of defeating them."

Jonah fidgeted uncomfortably where he stood.

"You'll have help," I added.

"What help?" Phelan took a drag on his smoke, the reek of burning paper offending my sense of smell.

"Speak with your caretaker," I said to Phelan before turning to Gabriel. "Speak to Malachi. He is readying another force."

The circle went quiet, and I could feel Gabriel's impatience to speak with me alone, to fully understand what it was I was planning to do in Styclar-Plena. But it was Jonah who got to me first, taking me by the elbow. His breath tickled my neck as he leaned in and whispered, "Please—"

I nodded, and he followed me as I walked behind the Winnebago, stopping in a secluded spot nestled underneath a tall tree.

"How?" I asked finally.

I had never seen Jonah's cheeks flush before, but they were flushing now. "I'm not sure."

"Brooke? Fergal? And . . . and you? All three of you are human," I said. "What about the rest?" Had something happened while I had been sleeping that had somehow caused every generation of Vampire to revert to their human self?

"It's only us, near as I can tell. The kid farmers shot at a Vampire just this morning behind the graveyard." Jonah rubbed his hands together, and I realized he was feeling the chill of the autumn day. I cupped my hands around his, and bringing them to my lips, I blew into the center, warming him.

"All at once? One at a time? What?" I asked, trying to make sense of what I had once thought to be impossible.

"One by one. I only found out about Fergal after he'd changed back."

My mind was spinning trying to put together the pieces. "The reason you were slower than me . . . the reason you tripped on the landing . . . the reason you were hurt that night we came back here . . ."

Jonah nodded slightly. "I felt different after we came out of the third. I started to change back, but it was a gradual process. I wasn't sure what was happening. But after me, Brooke's change was immediate. She had no warning. And then, Brooke said that Fergal transitioned back just as fast as she did."

I became distracted as I watched the curve of Jonah's lips; they were ever so slightly thinner than they had been before. I didn't mean to stare, but I couldn't help it. Jonah pushed his hand through his dark messy hair in response, and I realized then that it was a nervous compulsion.

Without meaning to, I was recataloging Jonah's every feature. He'd returned to the Jonah he was before the venom changed him—inside and out. His milky skin was almost tan, courtesy of the Floridian sun. He now had subtle laugh lines and a scar running over his chin. I recalled the story he'd told me on the journey back to Lucan of how he'd had to go to the hospital and get stitches after he'd collided with another player in a soccer match.

When I was through absorbing every detail of his flawless imperfection, I met his warm hazel eyes.

"I seem different to you now?" He brought his thumb near to my cheek, and one of the butterflies fluttered its wings, reminding me of what was woven into my skin. He stepped back as I grimaced. I didn't realize at the time that he thought my expression was my answer to his question.

The reality of what this change meant hit me fast and hard.

He was human—flesh and blood.

He wasn't trapped, alone in the darkness anymore.

He didn't need me.

I was hollow. I knew then that despite myself I had allowed him to get under my skin, but now he had left. The things he'd said, the promises he'd made, no longer stood. I shouldn't have let him in. I shouldn't have indulged in the idea of him and I together for even a second, in some form of fictitious, fairy-tale future.

"I have to go." I turned away.

He grabbed my arm. "What's wrong?"

Snapping back, I looked him dead in the eye. "You. You're what's wrong. One night with you, and you changed things. Ruadhan told me death is only something to be feared when you have someone to live for. You made it your business to be that someone."

Why? Why couldn't he have listened to me and stayed away?

"You've made me weak when I need to be strong. You've made me want and wish for things that can never be. You said you never wanted me to regret anything about you, but I do. I regret *everything*," I said, my voice strained. "Because of you, I am afraid."

Jonah reached for my shaking arms, but now human, he couldn't keep up with me when I sped away.

TWENTY-TWO

I RETURNED FROM DUBLIN late in the evening. I'd fed from a dark-souled human and spent the rest of the day alone, staring out over the Irish Sea from the port in quiet reflection. I'd thought about Gabriel and Iona, how I hoped that he would allow himself to love her and that she would be able to save him in time. I'd thought about Brooke and Fergal, and how they now had a chance of living a normal life together. I'd thought about Phelan and his men, about Riley, Claire, and Iris, about the families like them all over the world, who, if I was able to defeat Zherneboh, could once again walk their streets when the sun went down. For a second I'd thought about my own mother, and feelings of regret had flooded me that I was about to leave without having found her. Where once I had wanted to seek her advice, now all I cared about was knowing that she was safe.

I hadn't wanted to think about Jonah. All that did was bring about self-pity. And now was not the time for that. As for Ruadhan, I'd struggled. I understood better now what Iona had said, how it was hard for her to picture the faces of the ones she'd loved and lost, as I, too, had found it difficult to see Ruadhan's face when I had tried.

The lights were off when I stepped inside Little Blue, but Brooke was awake, sitting on her own at the small table. I flipped the light switch.

"Hey," I said.

She turned. "Hey."

I eyed the candy wrappers strewn messily on the tabletop. "Not a bad way to celebrate getting your humanity back—having a midnight feast, I mean. Must be nice to be able to eat sweets again."

"Yeah, well, the Lord giveth and the Lord taketh," she said with a mocking tone. She lowered the sunglasses she was still wearing and blinked heavily. Her eyes were frosted over, and I couldn't discern her pupils from her irises. "Not sure I'd swap a sugar rush for my sight," she added, putting her shades back in place.

"Oh." My breath caught in my throat.

"Yeah, oh." She got up and made her way to the sofa, where she snuggled beneath the throw. I'd never seen Brooke wobble, not even in the highest of stilettos. I followed and sat down next to her, tugging the blanket gently. She gave up some of her warmth.

"How do you feel otherwise?" I asked.

"Not really got past the being-blind part quite yet." Her voice quivered, a sadness sounding through her sarcasm. "I already miss Fergal's smile. Jeez, it's only been a few days and I can't even imagine it, in my head I mean." Thinking once again of Ruadhan, I knew exactly how she felt. Bringing the blanket up to her ear, she curled into the fetal position, and though she tried to stifle it, she sobbed. "It's kinda cruel to get something back, then to have to lose it all over again." Once more, I knew exactly how she felt. "I mighta been a Vamp, but do you know what? I have never felt so in the dark as I do right now."

My heart broke for Brooke. From a strained, barely there relationship, through our ups and downs, we had become unlikely friends. No matter what she was, Vampire or human, I knew who she was. I knew the color of her soul. And right now, I didn't think it could get any bluer.

I didn't have to search hard to find a way to remedy Brooke's affliction. Not long after I had found Gabriel, he had tried to take away my scars. He'd said I had to remember for him to be able to remove them. I hadn't known at the time how he was able to do something like that, but now I was in possession of my own Angel abilities, and like the rest, it was second nature. I didn't need a tutorial.

I couldn't bring Ruadhan back, and I couldn't have a future with Jonah, but I could make it so that Brooke could see Fergal's smile again. I could give her back what she had lost. I could take away her scars.

"Brooke," I said, pulling her back into a seated position. "Let me help you."

BROOKE WAS ONCE AGAIN marveling at her butterflies on my cheek.

"I would never have believed it if I weren't able to see it with my own two eyes," she said.

"Well, know that now your wonderful work will dress my skin no matter where or when I am." I checked the small clock on the sideboard. "Speaking of, it's nearly time."

"You don't have to go." Brooke batted her lashes; her eyes were still adjusting to the light.

"You know I do." I got up and straightened the black, sleeveless jumpsuit Brooke had given me to wear. I hadn't protested. Paired with black sneakers, it seemed as appropriate as anything else for traveling to another dimension and onto a battlefield.

"Jonah spent all day looking for you. So did Gabriel."

I hesitated. "The only thing left to say is good-bye, and this is one I'd rather skip."

Brooke pulled me into a hug. "Thank you, Lailah."

"No need to thank me," I said, pushing her to release me. Being able to give Brooke her sight back had made me feel as though, for once, a member of my family had somehow benefited from having me around. "Enjoy your life, Brooke," I said, and squeezing out a tight smile, I left her behind.

Outside, the day began to dawn and I breathed in the fresh

dew hanging in the morning air, knowing that this would be the last time I would ever smell it. The sky was clear, and the sun was burnt orange, matching the autumn as it climbed higher. And as it rose, so did the microscopic crystals on my skin. They were like beads of ice as they twinkled with an opulent white light. And with an almighty surge, my energy was renewed.

I decided to stroll to the church, but I didn't get far before Gabriel was at my back. "Lailah—" he called. I stopped at the end of the dirt track, just short of the main road.

He came to my side and seemed ready to voice the thousand things he must have wanted to say. But he simply stared at me instead and, cupping my cheek, planted the lightest of kisses on my forehead. Then, without looking back, he walked away.

A lump formed in my throat. He'd finally accepted that our paths had diverged.

I watched his every step until he was safely inside the motor home, before continuing toward the church. As usual, the gates were locked, so I jumped over them in a single bound, making my way up the long path. There were sounds coming from inside, and the main door was slightly ajar; I wondered if Iona had broken her promise to me and come here alone again.

I was careful as I maneuvered around the silver, but inside, it wasn't Iona I found. It was Phelan.

He was on his knees at the foot of chancel, his gun beside him, his head bowed. I didn't want to disturb him, so

I turned to leave, but he called out, "Kinda rude not to say *slán*, it's not as though you'd have to go outta your way, like."

He was still facing forward when I joined him. "Sorry. *Good-bye*," I said.

Sliding his gun farther away, he beckoned for me to come in closer, and at first I stayed put. But he gestured again. Only this time, he accompanied it with his usual impatient expression.

I plonked myself down, sitting cross-legged beside him.

"Iona texted me, said you healed Brooke of her blindness."

"So you know Brooke's human again?" I said.

This time he didn't argue with me about the semantics, and I wondered if that was because he didn't want to waste his breath, or because he was starting to think I might be right. "Do you know who else healed the blind?" He stared up at the stained-glass window.

I followed his gaze to Jesus on the cross. "We both know I'm not the Savior, Phelan."

He scratched his stubble. "Christ healed a man born blind, and his disciples asked him about the cause of the blindness— whether it was because the man had sinned or his parents had. Christ told them that it was neither, and he said, 'This happened so that the works of God might be displayed in him.'" He paused and then, looking at me smugly, added, "John 9."

"Your point?" I said.

"So, 'this happened so that the works of God might be displayed in him,'" he repeated. "You're not the Savior we were waiting for, but I think the Lord has delivered us someone infinitely better."

From the minute I arrived in Lucan, Phelan and I had done nothing but bump heads. And now, he was showing me respect. And so I made the same promise to Phelan that I had to Ruadhan. "I will try."

"Let me say a prayer for you before you go on your way, like."

Accepting his gesture, I bowed my head and clasped my hands together.

"May the Lord bless you and keep you. May the Lord make his face shine on you and be gracious to you. May the Lord lift up his countenance on you and give you peace. Amen."

"Amen," I murmured.

I thought myself away before Phelan had a chance to say anything that might ruin the moment.

Arriving at the orchard, I pushed past the drooping branches of the apple trees that were, despite the time of year, in full bloom. The cold had been exchanged for a sticky heat that clung to me as I sought out Malachi. I found him beside the allotment, and he wasn't alone.

"Lailah." He turned away from the women he had been conversing with, removing his homburg hat in greeting as I approached.

"I'm ready," I said, focusing intently on the surrounding land, looking for the join in the invisible seam of the magic cloak.

"See beyond my design, Lailah, and you'll know what to do." He guided me ahead of him.

"Wait."

"Yes, child?" Malachi said.

"My mother, she was an Angel."

"Yes," he said, as though I were merely stating the obvious.

"She became fallen. . . . Is it possible that you may have helped her? Would you know if she is safe?"

"I have delivered a good many Angels to the sea. It is very possible she was among them. What was her name, child?"

"Aingeal," the fair-haired woman at Malachi's back said, stepping forward.

Malachi's brow dipped and he shook his head, confusion spreading across his face. But then the lines on his forehead ironed out, and as he regarded the fallen Angel coming around his side, he grunted to himself as if he had missed something that had been glaringly obvious all along. "My deputy," he said.

I stifled a breath. All the Angels I had met had a similar look about them, blond-haired and blue-eyed, but taking in the fallen Angel before me, I saw my once self staring back.

She approached me, offering a reassuring nod. Having parted with her crystal, she had lost her light a long time ago, but as she brought me into an embrace, it didn't stop an un-earthly warmth radiating from her to me.

This was the first time I would ever hug my mother, but it was also the last. Somehow, she knew it, too. With reluctance, she released me. Her smile fell away and her sadness showed with the quiver in her rosy lips. "My little girl," she whispered. "Did you have a good life?"

My mother was an Angel. When I was still in her womb and she here on Earth, Zherneboh had infected me with his venom. I had been born here, into human skin. It was only when I died at seventeen that I inherited my supernatural lineage, having woken immortal. I had the barest of memories of that existence—of my first life—but the glimpses were enough to let me know that I had lived the happiest life any person could hope for.

"Yes," I said. "And you?"

"I got to live," she replied, her body angled toward Malachi, and I realized that she had him to thank for that. "I couldn't be known to you, for fear the Purebloods would discover you through me," she explained. "I couldn't risk that happening."

"You sent the Sealgaire." I wanted her to know that I was aware of her efforts to look out for me from a distance.

"Yes. You have lived many lives, and I have always been on the fringes of them, where I was able." With a tremor, she said, *"I'm sorry."*

"What happened, what Zherneboh did, wasn't your fault.

You have nothing to apologize for." I assured her that I understood, that my feelings toward her were only loving. The wave of warmth I'd experienced when we embraced washed over me again and I wished that things could have been different, that I could have known her. But there was no point in wishing—things were what they were. Though life was a gift, it wasn't always one that was given in equal measure. And I was grateful that I had met her, even if it had been just once, before the end.

With one last look, I nodded and made my way forward. The red-roofed cottage appeared, as did the overhanging branches concealing the fixed gateway to the first dimension. I wasted no time pulling them back.

The shining silver and glowing golds were awe-inspiring, rippling with streaks of light like the sun beating down on waves. The very nature of it was inviting, offering a refreshing coolness in the humidity. I dipped my toe into the water. Submerged completely, I didn't hear Jonah calling my name at my back as I was pulled from this world and delivered to the next.

TWENTY-THREE

IT REALLY WAS LIKE walking toward a bright white light. This place was what Phelan and his men called the Kingdom of Heaven, and interestingly, their description of the transition between one world and the next was surprisingly accurate.

At first, on the other side of the gateway, there was simply luminous light.

I tuned in every sense, searching for signs of life, but found none.

As my sight adjusted, I found myself in a circular room with a diameter of no less than one hundred and fifty feet. The room was like a halo, with nothing at the center but a dead drop.

Forty thrones, each twice my height, were positioned along the edge of the outer ring. They were clear but had a sheen that made them look as if they'd been carved out of ice. On first glance, they were facing what appeared to be windows made from frosted glass. But as I pressed my palms to the curved window, it rippled at my touch. The entire sheet turned to liquid and then cascaded like a waterfall. Now there was nothing separating the inside from the outside.

The floor began to move.

The halo rotated, and I went with it. As it turned, I was offered a 360-degree bird's-eye view of the world, and I breathed in its sweet citrus scent.

Below me, the building misted with white cloud, which spiraled out into the land, transitioning from white, to blue, to orange, until the last ring circled red. The colorful clouds dispersed only when they reached the ocean.

And the ocean was just how Gabriel had once described it: iridescent blue, crystal clear, and unspoiled. The third dimension might have a sea of souls, but the sea that belonged to this world twinkled like a sea of stars, reflecting everything above it like a mirror. In the sky, the most beautiful galaxies in the universe converged. The new stars being born provided a backlight to the planets cast in shadow, and they popped in 3-D, their rings glowing green and yellow neon. Spiral galaxies bounced off one another as though an invisible hand were pushing them aside to make way for the birth of new wonders.

An infinite number of planets, moons, and stars scattered in the sky, layered on top of one another like glitter, so bright, so bedazzled, that this world's day was also its night.

It was as though I had a front-row seat to the greatest show there ever was or would ever be. And the stage was set to magnify every beauty Emit had created. This dimension was a looking glass.

And I had come here to shatter it.

The plate beneath my feet slowed and then came to an absolute stop, and what looked like a glass door manifested in front of me. As I stared at it, a green arrow pointing down flashed and the door opened.

An elevator.

If I was going to bring this world to an end, I would first need to locate the crystal being fueled by the light souls of humans and find a way to switch it off. With no sign of it here, I got inside the lift. The glass box dropped down an invisible shaft, and my view of the ocean disappeared as I descended into a white cloud.

The elevator bounced as it came to a stop, and with a ding, the doors opened and I was outside. The layer of white mist that hung in the air clouded my sight. As I adjusted to it, the building's steels grew like long arms from the ground, twisting upward until they spread like hands, holding the halo, which was now high above me.

The fast drum of a heartbeat echoed as something moved to my left. I closed my eyes, and splitting my soul in two, I willed the darkness. My eyes grew wide as the mist thinned, and finally, the creature it belonged to bounded ahead of me.

I gasped as a beautiful baby beast that resembled a snow

leopard ambled and fell on its new legs. It had a white fur coat and eyes of blue sapphire. Slowly, one by one, more appeared until there was a small litter of cubs playfully tumbling over one another as they passed by me.

The animals moved as though I weren't there, but then two shining blue eyes were on me, and the mama cat came forward. She sat on her back legs, watching me, and my heartbeat quickened. I had to restrain my darkness from seeping through my skin, but as I did, suddenly my shadow appeared.

The cat jumped back and rushed behind her cubs, nudging them forward in a bid to escape my presence. I hadn't meant to scare the creature. As her jaw dropped and as she whimpered, I realized she had no teeth.

Here in Styclar-Plena, there was only one tier to the food chain. The light from the crystal sustained the inhabitants entirely. The cat didn't have teeth because she didn't eat.

With no sign of the crystal or Orifiel, I looked to the dense woodland encircling the building's footings and made my way toward the two large trees that bowed over one another, creating an arch. With the frost on the trees and the snow on the ground, it could have been December, but it was warm.

It may have looked like winter, but it felt like summer.

A winding path led the way through the forest, and with every step I took down it, I began to feel strange. A sense of weightlessness washed over me until I could no longer discern my limbs from one another. I was simply floating.

As I drifted like a lost leaf washing downstream, more

creatures appeared, weaving and bobbing around the tree trunks on either side of me.

A bird that resembled a white peacock, but with long legs and a neck like a flamingo's, appeared on my right, skipping across my path as though it were jumping from pebble to pebble. As the bird stretched its elongated neck and fanned its feathers, glistening crystals speckled and then burst like a golden firework.

Beyond the bird, a pure white Arabian mare came into view. She was rubbing her mane against a tree trunk. As she turned and trotted away, the glow of her horn gleamed, and I realized she wasn't a horse at all, she was a unicorn.

Entranced by the creatures in the forest, I barely noticed that I was standing still. I'd reached the end of the woodland and was next to a river. Looking left to right, it ran all the way across, and on the other side, the mist returned, only it was now tinged blue. As I'd seen from atop the halo, the white inner circle had come to an end; I was at the junction where it spiraled into the first color.

The sapphire blue mist fogged at the riverbed, and even from here, the streaks of light against the color were obvious. The rifts opened like hairline cracks, and as they did, an almost operatic single note sounded.

Every minute here was far longer on Earth, which only gave Zherneboh more of an opportunity to put his plan B into effect. Quickly, I worked out a way to cross. I bent down, dipped my fingers into the clear water, and closed my eyes, willing my own body temperature to drop. I shuddered at the bitter sting of my blood running cold. I willed the freeze to leave my body, to transfer to the crystal-clear liquid, and the water began to freeze. Bit by bit, steam rose from the top of the river as it turned to dry ice. I whipped out my hands and clutched them together at my chest as I restored my body heat.

I sprang, one foot after the other, across the ice and pushed through the blue cloud. Once again my eyesight took a moment to adjust, and the mist dispersed around me. When it cleared, I found myself face-to-face with an Angel Descendant. Tall, blond, and blue-eyed, he had features similar to Gabriel's, but he wasn't nearly as beautiful as my Angel.

He stood on top of what appeared to be broken branches; in fact, the entire landscape appeared to be barren. It wasn't snowing here. I didn't understand the shift in weather, in setting, in the feeling this side of the river gave me.

The back of the Angel's neck was glowing, his crystal reacting to the fissure forming in the air, and as the Angel Descendant extended his hand toward me, his lips shaped a word that never reached me as he was pulled through the rift to Earth.

A hand clamped down on my shoulder, and I knew without looking whom it belonged to. "Orifiel," I said.

He didn't reply. As I turned, he stood back, staring at me in what I assumed to be a quiet, murderous contemplation. His expression was blank but his huge feathered wings rose up and out, stretching in a display of reckoning.

He exuded power.

"Come," he said, gesturing for me to follow him back the way I had traveled.

I willed my darkness, and in a display of my own, black smoke plumed in my palms. Orifiel nodded, acknowledging my authority. I shook the darkness away, and hastening for time, I joined him at a safe distance by his side. He waited until we were back in the thick of the forest before he spoke. "I've been expecting you, Lailah," he said. "Are we what you were expecting?" He brought his hand through the air as though he were presenting me with the beauty of the world and its inhabitants.

"You know why I'm here?" I said, answering his question with a question.

He did the same. "Tell me, what do you see?"

I shook my head, and as I did, a cross between a mink and a rabbit brushed my leg as it went by. Glancing down to my feet, the pathway was glowing blue as I traveled over it. "I don't understand what you mean."

"It's a well-kept secret and it's one I cannot ordinarily ask, but given your intent, I see no harm asking it of you." He spoke as though he was bringing me into a circle of trust, and he strode on as though he had no fear of me, of what I was here to do. When I didn't reply, he tried again. "You arrived through the gateway, you looked down upon my world from the observation deck, you saw the rainbow of color in my clouds?"

"Yes," I replied.

"Then you know that here, at the center of my rainbow, the light is most concentrated. The frequency of the crystal's light is such that what you see here is simply the manifestations created from your own mind." He paused. "It's therefore different for every being. What you are seeing now is being projected from your subconscious. It's what you expected to see."

I took a breath, and my lungs filled with a crisp citrus aroma. Still, I didn't answer his question. Instead, I kept my eye on him, only letting my focus slip ever so slightly as I listened for movement as we neared the clearing.

Another minklike animal scuttled past us, and Orifiel stopped briefly, allowing it to go by. "Every creature, every Angel, each and every one of Styclar-Plena's inhabitants, however, are very much real."

"You're telling me that my subconscious created a snow-filled forest?" I answered him now. Was this the "design" Malachi had told me to see past? "But not the snow leopard, not the unicorn? They are not manifestations?" There was a very large part of me that didn't want the confirmation—hearing it spoken aloud would only make what I had to do that much harder—but now I questioned what I was seeing.

"Coming from a life spent on Earth, do you really think you could even begin to imagine such wondrous creatures? Lives such as these?" he said, his tone nearing contempt. Then his voice lightened as he said, "A forest of snow, that's—"

"*Ordinary*. No, it isn't." I cast my mind back to Monts

d'Olmes, the mountain in Neylis where the snow had made the nighttime indistinguishable. In that spot it had been neither dark nor light. It was as though my soul had been turned inside out and used to paint the setting. And it had been where I had once again died. I wasn't surprised that a snow-filled forest had been painted from my subconscious. A combination of the past and the present, both becoming backdrops to my death.

I noticed as we continued on that the frost that had coated the branches of the trees was evaporating. It was as though Orifiel's telling me this place was not real made it so as it all just melted away.

"You understand, I don't *want* to kill this world," I said. "But your choices have led to my having no choice. Your actions have resulted in the loss of so much life on Earth. . . ." I paused and then repeated myself. "You know why I am here?" I whispered, stepping out of the forest. This time my question was a rhetorical one.

Ahead, clusters of beautiful creatures sat waiting. There were hundreds of them, beautiful and brilliant, and every one of them had eyes of sapphire blue. I remembered what Gabriel had told me once. That the light souls of mortals when brought here fueled the crystal and the crystal churned out that same light, using it to create the world and the creatures that inhabited it. The souls of these beings had once been human. In the eyes of a snow leopard cub, a young girl stared out. When I blinked, the image was gone, but I knew what I had seen. These beings were human souls reincarnated, brought to a higher dimension. What would become of them when I spread the darkness?

From behind the steels, Angels came forward, standing side by side with the creatures. They were smaller than Orifiel and had no wings. They were Descendants and something about them felt new. Their skin was paler than Gabriel's or mine; their eyes were wide and startled—it was as though they'd just been born.

I thought then that Orifiel had set this up, trying to appeal to my "light" side. Making me face the lives I was about to bring to an end. I hadn't realized that despite my thinking that I was standing at a safe distance from him, he had me exactly where he wanted me.

I peered up, and even with the loss of sight in my left eye, I could tell the Arch Angels had taken a seat at their thrones. But the more I focused, the more something didn't sit right. The galaxies swirling overhead were real. I could feel it as strongly as I could feel my own heartbeat resounding inside my chest. But every so often, it was as though I was missing a little piece of the image.

"You asked me a question before," Orifiel said easily as I continued to search, seeking the reason for the sensory disturbance.

After scanning the horizon in every direction, I focused

above me once more. This time, the gleam of light reflecting off glass for the smallest second was all I needed to uncover what was disguised.

We were in a dome.

The darkness that had once fallen, a darkness that was identical to the makeup of the third dimension, surrounded the land outside.

My gaze fell, and as it did, the white light bounced. Malachi had said you could conceal just about anything with light, if you knew how. As the setting became static once more, finally the crystal was revealed.

The steels were not just rising and holding up the weight of the halo-shaped observation deck; in between the twisting rods, the crystal sat huge and awesome. Its opulent glow filled me, and right then it was all I knew.

Somehow, it was as though it were speaking to me, but the message warbled and warped. And underneath the pre-programmed story that Gabriel and the rest had once heard, I uncovered the truth.

A series of images flashed through my mind, and I understood everything. How, after the day the darkness fell, this world that was once home to billions had begun to wilt and die. How the light souls Orifiel had brought across the planes had forced the glow to shine again, but it was weak, stretching no more than a hundred miles. That Orifiel had charged Malachi with the construction of the dome around the circumference of the light, trapping inside what remained of this dying world and keeping a line of separation between the light and the dark.

I understood that this was a small island now, and that the inhabitants didn't realize that beyond the ocean there was nothing more—that this was where their world ended.

A profound question came to me then. *How do you see light against light?*

And with it the purpose of the rainbow cloud was clear. The rifts needed a backdrop of color on which to be distinguished, and so the layers of the rainbow were ground zero for the Angel Descendants at work.

All of this to keep the ten-mile circumference of the purest white light, a place for rebirth, a place for dreams and imagination to be realized, and for the Arch Angels to continue to be able to sit on their thrones and gaze at the spectacle of the stars.

And maybe, just maybe, despite myself, feeling the sheer wonder of this world, I might have considered the possibility that it was worth it. *Maybe.*

But then, I heard it.

The cry.

The same cry that had begun to pass from Zherneboh to me but had been cut short.

One single, terrible note, and my eyes filled with tears.

I couldn't speak.

At the base of the crystal, the Angels and the creatures

stared at me, unable to hear what I could. The cry dipped and wobbled, like a radio stuttering between an AM and an FM frequency. The inhabitants of this place were tuned into the lie—into the frequency set by Malachi.

But I knew the truth.

The reason Orifiel had disposed of his brother, sending him to the third.

The reason he had Malachi engineer the sound waves and then sent him to the second.

The reason I was going to end the first.

The crystal was alive.

"Your question," Orifiel said for a final time.

The cry was still ricocheting around my head. The crystal was dying, but the light energy reaching it forced it to continue to breathe. And every breath was agonizing.

Unbeknownst to me, behind my back, the doorway to the in-between had opened. As Orifiel leaned into my ear, he answered me by returning the message I had once delivered to him. "No mercy."

TWENTY-FOUR

I ARRIVED IN THE IN-BETWEEN, a place Gabriel had once described as a prison. As I adjusted to yet another strange place, the crystal's cry reverberated through every inch of my being. I would carry the burden of that sound until I could do what I was now certain I must: kill the crystal and let the darkness spread over what remained of Styclar-Plena.

In my new surroundings, everywhere I looked my image reflected back. I expected to find the door Orifiel had pushed me through, I expected him to be watching from the other side of prison bars, but there was only my face.

A bulb of light flickered in the distance, and that one glimmer gave birth to hundreds and thousands more. Reflecting all around, they twisted ahead as though I were in a kaleidoscope.

With caution, I concentrated on my palm, and laces of light twisted around my fingers. The brightness shone and bounced through the tunnel, creating a nebula of strobes.

This was a prison, but it was one made entirely of mirrors.

Breaking out would be easy enough and then I would be right back beside the crystal. Why would Orifiel think this alone could contain someone like me?

I stomped my foot, and the mirror beneath me cracked. The fissures splintered, growing thinner as they raced forward.

Again and again I beat down my heel until the slits angled vertically and, finally, met with a wall.

I willed myself beside the almighty crack edging up the tall, seamless mirror. Pressing my fingers to my reflection, I pushed down. The first mirror blowing out caused the rest to fall like dominos. The ceiling followed, caving in and raining down shards containing my image, illuminated by the light show.

The last plane of glass crashed against my shoulder.

But there was no Orifiel.

There was no crystal.

I wasn't where I had been.

Instead, I was surrounded by green pastures that met a cloudless blue sky. For a second, I thought somehow I was back on Earth. But the two glowing orange suns told me different. The mirrored box had flattened and the shards had turned to green blades of grass in what resembled an English countryside.

I inhaled clean, fresh air, and concentrating intently, I listened for signs of life. There was nothing.

My mind raced, trying to solve the puzzle as to where I was. No doubt Orifiel would have had Malachi design the in-between. But if this was a prison, where was the cell door? Perhaps Malachi had hidden the building by cloaking it the same way he had the crystal—by manipulating light? Maybe the mirrored box and now these fields were a manifestation created from the depths of my subconscious, the same as the forest had been?

As I struggled to find another explanation, I tried to see through the design. I wondered if the knowledge that this setting wasn't real would cause it to disintegrate the way the forest had.

Nothing changed.

Eventually it was the sky that convinced me that my theory was wrong. The universe was not on show here; this environment was far closer in its nature to Earth than to Styclar-Plena, which meant I was somewhere else.

But if I wasn't in the first dimension, then where was I?

An image of the snow leopard cubs flashed through my mind, and my chest tightened. I was planning to commit genocide against an entire world. And just like the day I had killed Jonah's Pureblood Master, Emery, once again I had appointed myself judge, jury, and executioner. Malachi had told me that the inhabitants of Styclar-Plena were innocent, but it would be their lives that would pay for Orifiel's decision-making, for what I perceived as being his wrongdoing.

Malachi had said that what became of the Angel Descendants and the creatures was my decision, but it didn't feel as if I had any choice. There was no way I could end Styclar-Plena but still save its inhabitants. If I led them through the gateway to Earth, Zherneboh and his armies on the other side would slaughter them all.

My heart was heavy.

Ruadhan would have known what to do.

"I wish you were here," I said aloud, knowing that he was suspended from the game of life, waiting to be stitched back into the universe. I thought of Iona then, how she'd said she sometimes sang to bridge the gap between her and those she had loved most and lost. To connect with me, Ruadhan had often told me stories to help me understand the meaning in his message. But he no longer had a voice to tell me a tale.

My gaze fell back to the ground, and then the heavens opened. Despite the absence of cloud, I was caught in a downpour. As the wet drops soaked my skin, in the distance a double rainbow appeared.

The colors became bold stripes, and I once again recalled the Pairs of Angel Descendants holding hands and the eyes of the creatures I'd just seen in front of the crystal.

The rainbow and the image of Styclar-Plena's inhabitants

sparked another memory. As I tried to place it, in my subconscious, my inner voice was humming.

"The animals went two by two."

I couldn't help but smile at the memory of Iris's little voice squeaking *"the Ankeroo."*

The cover of Iris's favorite picture book, a gift from Ruadhan, flashed into thought, along with the title, *Noah's Ark*. And then I remembered the last line of the book: *"The rainbow will remind you."*

Ruadhan was still very much with me. The rainbow was his sign, reminding me of the message hidden within the story.

I spun around and spread my gray soul in the form of smoke.

Rushing over the land, through the haze, the white-silver flicker of a gateway appeared. Then came another, opposite it, that dribbled with black ink.

I was reminded of Gabriel's retelling of the day Orifiel had saved Styclar-Plena, the day the darkness came forward. The gateway to the second had become visible only against the black. And in the third, the dark gateway had been made visible only against the bright autumn arc of the aurora.

But whether a light or dark gateway, my gray gave them both a canvas upon which to be seen.

I recalled Darwin piling his coins on the bar top as he'd demonstrated how he believed the dimensions stacked one on top of the other.

The second dimension had access to both the first and the third dimensions.

And the first and the third dimensions had access to here—*a fourth dimension.*

The first and third were parallel to one another; the only difference between them was that the first dimension had become home to a crystal, a living being that had fallen out of the sky and created life with its light. Before that, the first had been a void, the same as the third. And the second dimension, Earth, had a sun, water, and breathable air; it was this world's parallel.

Orifiel must have discovered this fourth dimension, but unlike Earth, there was no life here—no light souls to steal. Still, he'd found a use for it. He'd built a prison directly on the other side of the fixed doorway from the first dimension to here, the fourth dimension.

But I had a far better use for this world.

Before the flood came, Noah piled the animals on board his ark, two by two. I was Noah, this dimension was my ship, and before the flood, I would rescue the inhabitants of Styclar-Plena.

Traveling through the gray fog, I arrived at the entrance to the first dimension. I concentrated and turned my palette from gray to black. Before I left, I glanced over my shoulder, and to the rainbow—to Ruadhan—I said, "I'll be home soon."

I emerged through the rift to discover that barely a second in Styclar-Plena had passed. Orifiel's back was turned;

he had only just begun to walk away. The fourth dimension, it seemed, ran at the same speed as Earth.

As the crystal's cry sounded once more, I willed a plume of black smoke to rise up and out, and it sped toward the crystal. The Angels and the creatures at the foot of the steels dispersed as the deadly black fog twisted up and around the crystal sphere.

Though the crystal appeared inanimate, it was very much a living entity; its cry broke apart as though it were taking its last breaths. My black fog swallowed the light energy brought here by the Angel Descendants that were being pulled toward it.

It was as though the crystal had been on life support, and I had just switched off the electricity.

"No!" Orifiel shouted, crashing an almighty, glittering wave down upon me. My barrier of black cloud shook, but it held, and I continued to pump the darkness over the crystal.

The cry was fading; the being so desperate to die was now able to.

A tremendous surge of light blasted from within the crystal like an exploding bomb, and it overcame my darkness. I fell to the ground, caught in the aftershock.

I struggled to see through the blinding white sheet, but then it dulled, and with one fierce final flash, the light was gone.

Though the crystal itself remained at the center of the steels, its life force had been released back into the universe.

The cry stopped.

The crystal was finally free.

Coldness came over me then, and the creatures came forward from out of the forest. Splinters in the dome overhead were already forming; I would have to act fast.

But first . . .

I hauled Orifiel off the ground. "If you try to move, I will grace you with an unthinkable end."

"You have condemned every soul here to the darkest of deaths," he said, and an unnatural emotion rang through his voice. Growing incensed, he shouted, "You're tainted! You're, you're . . . *the same as your father.*"

At the mention of Azrael, my hand clenched more tightly at Orifiel's robes, but before I could reply, feathered white wings beat above my head. One by one, the Arch Angels descended. They weren't trying to escape through the gateway to Earth. Afraid to go there, after so many of their kind had been lost to Zherneboh, they were smart enough to know what was waiting on the other side of the door.

The clear dome began to break apart, collapsing underneath the weight of the darkness that, with no light to oppose it, was rushing forth.

Creatures with white coats and wide sapphire blue eyes surrounded me. Hundreds upon hundreds of them appeared as they raced to the center of their world, fueled by an emotion they had never felt before: fear. The colored clouds dispersed, and the rifts became masked, invisible once again. Confused, the Angel Descendants arrived en masse, traveling by thought to this spot.

Keeping hold of Orifiel, I picked out the blue in the rainbow and willed the same to leave me. The silver slice in the air became prominent and inviting against the sapphire. It reminded me of Gabriel's eyes when he smiled.

In the fourth dimension, the Angel Descendants would no longer be tasked, their purpose no longer preordained. I would set them free. And I would save these beautiful and wondrous beings before me. As for the Arch Angels who had watched over this world and turned a blind eye to the terrible truth, I knew what I wanted to do. But I also knew what Ruadhan would do if their fates were in his hands. And so, in tribute to him, I offered them what he would have; I gave them forgiveness.

To Orifiel, I replied, "I am my father's daughter. His name was Ruadhan."

I encouraged the Angel Descendants through the gateway and as they went, two by two, they were drawn into and arrived safely in the fourth dimension. A whole new world fueled by a natural sun, the same as Earth; now it would be home to the crystal's creations.

As the final Descendant Pair and the last of the creatures left through the gateway, the darkness edged ever closer to the base of the steels. I gestured for the Arch Angels to follow the others through.

Not a single one of them regarded Orifiel as they passed by. And not a single one of them spoke. But the last to leave glanced over his shoulder and, surprising me, said, "Thank you."

Only Orifiel and I remained. We were leaving, too, but we were going somewhere else. With no time to waste, I dragged the squirming Orifiel to the elevator and bashed the glass with my fist until the door closed. As the darkness drew across the base of the building, the elevator jolted and the steels bowed beneath us. For a minute I wasn't sure we had enough time to make it out.

As the door opened, Orifiel dissolved into thin air. He might be able to make himself invisible, but I was stronger than he was, and I still had him by the scruff. Whether I could see him or not, I could still drag him the length of the halo. But even with my superspeed, I feared we were a fraction of a second too late to make it to the gateway. But then the observation deck buckled and tipped at a ninety-degree angle. Orifiel and I fell. I clung to his leg, and we slid as the halo snapped and dropped away.

We were propelled through the gateway. It rippled with luminosity for one last time, before, just like this world, it was lost forever.

TWENTY-FIVE

I clutched Orifiel's Robes as we fell face first back to earth. I yanked him to his feet, and he stretched his feathered wings out behind his back, a panicked expression slapped across his face. The gateway still shimmered silver, but it was decreasing in size. We emerged from the apple tree into Malachi's invisible bubble.

Malachi jumped up from the doorstep, and his homburg hat flew off his head as he rushed over. "Child!"

"Styclar-Plena is gone," I said flatly.

"Take your hands from me," Orifiel said, trying to shake me off.

I cast my gaze out through the orchard and adjoining lands, and straining with my impaired vision, I counted more than two hundred Second Generation Vampires scattered around the boundaries. Though the sight of Zherneboh's readying forces was troubling, it was not that which made me stifle a breath; it was the sky. The aurora had bled out from the third and spilled, soaking the entire scenery. Though the blood-red color was most concentrated where it splashed across the sky, particles of autumn orange hung low like a thin mist along the ground.

"How long was I gone?" I rushed.

"Calm yourself, child, only one year has passed. You have returned in time," he answered quickly.

"You sent her to Styclar-Plena?" Orifiel accused.

"Yes, brother, I did." Malachi removed his coat and sweater. Rolling his shoulders, he loosened his muscles, and great white-feathered wings sprang from between his shoulder blades. As his wings shimmied, the wrinkles on his forehead ironed out, and his blue eyes brightened. He simply shook away the years. I don't know why I was surprised. He was, after all, a master of disguise. He had said he was one of the first Angels created, but I had assumed he had meant that he was one of the first Descendants.

"You're an Arch Angel?" I said with a heavy breath.

"Yes. My throne was stationed next to Orifiel's, in fact. I acted as his right hand, until, of course, it no longer suited him."

"You knew about the crystal, and you masked the cry for Orifiel. . . ." I trailed off. Zherneboh had shown me his story. Without knowing he was doing so, Zherneboh had opposed Orifiel's regime, and so Orifiel had seen to it that Zherneboh was no longer in a position to do so. Malachi, on the other hand, knew the crystal was a living entity and had not only concealed the crystal itself from view but also covered the cry. So why, when Malachi had abided Orifiel's orders, had Orifiel sentenced Malachi to an existence on Earth?

"Yes, well," Malachi said, "after my work was done in the first, our great leader saw fit to station me here in the second to watch over the gateways and to monitor the activity from the third."

"You were meant only to watch, not act." Orifiel's top lip curled with contempt. "I did not instruct you to send the girl to our world and bring about its doom."

"No, you didn't, but you would have gladly let this world burn, and me with it, if I hadn't."

There was bad blood between these two, and their fractured back-and-forth only confirmed what I had already suspected of Malachi. He hadn't wanted to come to Earth, he'd had no choice, and so he'd had to find his own way. His survival was dependent on his ability to double-deal. His interests always lay with himself—even in the case of the fallen Angels whom he had rescued and delivered to the sea. He'd sent them there by securing their promise to return and fight when he called. He was not a character who could be easily trusted, but on this occasion, his agenda was aligned with my own, even if his motivations were selfish ones.

"Enough talk." Malachi gestured for me to leave the relative safety of the concealed cottage. "Zherneboh is waiting for him, child."

I hesitated, something niggling at me. "That's why Zherneboh never took you through the rift to the third. You promised to deliver Orifiel, didn't you? If he would spare you?"

Malachi's wings fluttered. "Zherneboh is not a *man*. He is a creature, and one who cannot be held to his word. Once his use for me as the Ethiccart was fulfilled, he would have pulled me through to the third—"

"And you'd have emerged a Pureblood," I concluded.

He nodded. "Not a fate that suited me, child. Luckily, there was one deal left to be struck." He looked again to Orifiel.

"And when Orifiel is gone," I said, "there will be no more deals to be made. Zherneboh will come for you, that's why you want me to end him, isn't it?"

"I can't deny that his end will spare my own existence, but so, too, will his end spare the entirety of the human race. Of course, I know your allegiance is with mankind; it just so happens that a by-product of your success in saving them will benefit me."

The light from the fixed gateway flickered behind me, and across the land, the Second Generations' attention pricked.

Malachi continued, "It is the light from the fixed gateway that I have manipulated in order to conceal us. Now that you have ended Styclar-Plena, all the fixed gateways will cease. Come, it won't be long before they will be closed for good. Better to present yourself to Zherneboh than to be uncovered."

Once again, Malachi encouraged me to move forward, but Orifiel resisted. I knew then that he feared facing Zherneboh. I wondered how long it had been since he'd had to fight, since he'd gotten his own hands dirty.

"Is there a problem, child?" Malachi pressed.

For a second I doubted myself. I thought of Ruadhan and what he might say if he were here, but I shook it off. There was one thing I absolutely believed was fair, and it did not stem from some dark side of my own self.

"No." Meeting Orifiel's eye, I said, "Your brother is due his revenge."

I whipped Orifiel up onto my shoulders and sped through the orchard. We arrived at the center of the garden. Restraining Orifiel by the edge of his magnificent wings, I called the Devil by his real name.

"Eden!" I shouted.

The air was still, and silence surrounded me.

Then the heavens opened, pouring with torrential rain.

Zherneboh appeared out of thin air. Several meters ahead of me he towered, and cracking his jaw, he released a shriek that made the hairs on my arm stand up. Before I could blink, a circle of Zherneboh's Pureblood Vampires wrapped around me. Hot dark matter oozed from their palms in liquid form. The substance looped from one Pureblood to the next, joining them in a deadly circle. Further rings spiraled out and up, stacking on top of one another until we were inside a familiar cone-shaped cage. But this time, the enclosure had not been created for my benefit; it was designed to hold Orifiel.

Through the gaps in the rings of dark matter, I saw the Sealgaire charge forth in the battering rain. But over Zherneboh's shoulder, the cliff shook, and the ground exploded. The oak tree wobbled as its roots were ripped from the dirt. The roar of hundreds of Second Generation Vampires sounded as they sprang out of the tomb.

Pandora's box was open and the demons were descending.

The Second Generation Vampires tore across the land, clashing with the Sealgaire. As the battle between man and demon commenced, I released Orifiel. Finally, he was forced to face the brother he had damned. As Zherneboh came forward, I stepped aside, and the Devil and the Arch Angel stood nose-to-nose regarding each other.

Orifiel's body language made him appear confident, but he could not disguise the quiver in his voice. "Once again, the river clashes with the rock. It has been a long time, my brother." But this being was not the brother Orifiel had once known. Eden had been lost to the darkness the day he had fallen into the third, and he had emerged as Zherneboh. And there was only one thing Zherneboh sought, the reason for everything that had come since the day Eden had died.

Vengeance.

Zherneboh snarled, baring his fangs, and his tattooed markings grew up his neck from beneath his cloak. Down at his sides, his hands plumed black smoke, and without hesitation, he commanded the darkness toward the Arch Angel.

Orifiel responded in kind, throwing up a protective white sheet.

The light and the dark collided for the first and the last time.

Zherneboh's and Orifiel's forces were equally matched and the light and the dark bounced off each other, sending the two beings sailing backward. Orifiel hit the ground so hard it broke beneath him, but he sprang back up in time to defend himself against the next spell of Zherneboh's darkness. The black smoke hit Orifiel's wings, which were enveloping his body in a protective shield.

Zherneboh's Purebloods hissed and growled, acting as the witnesses to Orifiel's pending execution. Both Zherneboh and Orifiel were beings of immense power, but one thing Zherneboh had that Orifiel didn't was strength in numbers. I wondered if Zherneboh might call upon his Purebloods to bring this battle to an end. But then, Orifiel's death belonged to Zherneboh; I doubted he would share it unless he had no other choice.

Orifiel jumped and then tumbled repeatedly through the air, following the curve of the inner circle and expelling bolts of white light as though they were throwing stars. I ducked as they whizzed by my head, and one by one they disappeared, dissolving into the darkness as they collided with the rings of hot dark matter.

Between the Purebloods' dark rings, Second Generation Vampires were pushing through Phelan's wall of men. Limbs were torn and blood sprayed as Zherneboh's demons slaughtered them with ease. Rounds of gunfire drummed as the Sealgaire tried to gain ground, and though a Vampire thudded just outside the cage, squealing before his head exploded, the Sealgaire were not faring well.

They needed help.

I cast my gaze around the circle of Purebloods and willed my soul of gray to manifest in a thick fog. I concentrated, imagining the stifling smoke as if it were wafting from a bonfire. Zherneboh thought he needed to imprison Orifiel to stop him from escaping, but there was no reason I couldn't do some damage to the Purebloods and still keep Orifiel contained.

While Zherneboh and Orifiel continued to fight fire with fire, I willed my gray soul to leave me, and the smoke bobbed and weaved among the Purebloods. Where it met the dark matter, it dissipated, but it was still able to cloud around the demons' throats, tightening like a noose around their necks. The smoke invaded them.

The Pureblood closest to me choked and, tipping forward, broke the chain. The ribbons of dark matter drooped and then fell away. Orifiel did not try to run. In fact, as I regained my balance, he and Zherneboh leaped and crashed into each other in midair. And it was the Arch Angel who came out on top as they smashed into the ground. Orifiel gouged his thumbs through Zherneboh's black orbs and the Arch Angel's electric light sizzled. Inside Zherneboh's eye sockets, his orbs melted and drained away, pooling down his face as if he were bleeding oil. Zherneboh writhed and, thrashing his talons, caught Orifiel's cheek. Zherneboh's claws farther jutted from his knuckles, and he pumped his fist, tearing through Orifiel's flesh and bone.

Orifiel's form might seem as though it were impenetrable, but Zherneboh's blades cut through him as though he were butter.

My stomach turned and, with my concentration broken, my gray smoke stalled.

Orifiel released Zherneboh as he fell backward with a pained wail.

Zherneboh retracted his arm only to then thrust his scissor-like blades through the Arch Angel's side.

Orifiel cried out again.

I looked away, bile rising in my throat at the sound of Orifiel's flesh tearing and his bones breaking. With my focus split, my smoke, which had been invading the Purebloods' insides, disappeared completely.

Zherneboh stretched his jaw, and a stream of hot dark matter dribbled down his lizardlike tongue, pouring out where it split in two. The black liquid wrapped around Orifiel's throat like a collar, and the Arch Angel's skin scorched and glowed red underneath it. Zherneboh tugged, leading away the once glorious Arch Angel as though he were a dog on a leash. Zherneboh's cloak lifted as he turned, and the Purebloods moved aside as Zherneboh strode back into the rain, back in the direction of the cliff.

A Pureblood at my back, I willed my light, and the Pureblood retracted an inch from my neck. His hissing spit sprayed against my skin before he took off.

The garden and the graveyard provided the setting for the spreading massacre. I picked out Phelan. He was deploying more of his men from behind the church in an attempt to flank the Second Generation Vampires, but there were too many of them.

Nearby Fergal was struggling to fend off a demon, but then Iona popped up out of nowhere and plunged a silver dagger in between the creature's shoulder blades.

The Purebloods filed out behind Zherneboh. As if they were royalty, the sea of soldiers parted, making way for their masters who glided along the aurora's red carpet. But down by my feet one Pureblood still remained, clutching his chest. He was the first that my gray smoke had invaded. Though the smoke had evaporated, for him, it did so too late. His insides were at war as he flashed from the image of who he was now to who he had been once upon a time.

It didn't take him long to burn.

As the Pureblood's ashes swirled and scattered, through the last of the flaming embers, Malachi appeared at my side. The scene around me was far worse than anything I could have created in my own imagination. Phelan was right. This was the apocalypse, and the Devil was winning.

I couldn't hear Malachi over the wounded's screams as the chaos unfolded. But then, climbing up and over the edge of the garden, which overhung the river below, Malachi's fallen Angels appeared. Fair-haired, with blue eyes and pale skin, they were unlike anything I had seen before. Their bare legs had a blue-green shimmer to them, and they weren't carrying any weapons. But then they began to hum harmoniously with one another, and I realized their weapon was within them.

The hymn was entrancing, and every single being, whether human or demon, halted. The fallen Angels formed lines, and they marched forward in rows of thirty as they switched up an octave. The change in note released Phelan and his men from the hypnotic sound, but continued to keep the Vampires caught within it. They couldn't take their eyes from the blond-haired beauties.

The male fallen Angels were naked save for a sliver of thin material strewn around their waists, held together by gold-and-crystal leaf pins, each one distinct and unique. The women wore the pins as charms hanging low on their necklaces, as earrings, or as hairpieces. They glowed in sync, flashing in a form of Morse code as the Angels came to a stop at the center of the garden. The fallen Angels' song grew louder, and Malachi flagged down Phelan, who pointed his arsenal toward the stationary Second Generation Vampires. The Vampire hunters with guns fired; the ones who favored blades cast from silver held them at the ready.

Zherneboh wavered, but only briefly. The song's effect

on him had lasted only a few moments, and he left his dazed Purebloods behind. Dragging Orifiel with him, he passed through the trees separating the garden from the hilltop, and I knew where he was going. He was headed for the fixed gateway to the third, but he didn't intend to simply kill Orifiel. No, that would be too kind. Zherneboh was instead about to bestow the same fate his brother had afforded him. If he succeeded, if his revenge against Orifiel was satisfied, what would he do, now that Styclar-Plena was destroyed? I didn't want to think about that too hard. I had to end him, and I had to do it now.

I rocked back on my heels and raced forward. As I swerved around the Sealgaire's bullets, a fallen Angel in the choir caught my attention; she was the only one not staring straight ahead. It was my mother, and as she had done throughout my entire existence, from afar she was watching my every move. The glow from the crystal hairpin of the fallen Angel to her right glinted, causing me to squint, and I recognized the ornate jewel.

"The hairpin," I said. It was the one I had borrowed along with Iona's clothing, the one Gabriel had returned to its "rightful owner"—and that rightful owner was a fallen Angel: Iona's mother.

She was still alive.

Iona was out in front, and I called her name. Her eyes met mine, and I turned my head, directing her toward the fallen Angels. I knew she'd seen her mother when her plump bottom lip hung low. And as she stumbled forward, a hand grabbed her wrist, a hand that belonged to Gabriel.

He saw me then. "Lailah."

Behind Gabriel, an archer laid down his bow and arrow at the sound of my name. It was Jonah. Brooke appeared next, ramming a knife below the ribs of a motionless Vampire to the right of Jonah.

My family.

They were all here.

Up ahead, Zherneboh was fast approaching the tomb that had concealed and contained the fixed gateway to the third. With the land pulled apart, the gateway was visible, dripping with black ink. A person was trying to get near it. Though he had his back to me, I recognized the retro glasses on top of his head.

What the hell was Darwin doing?

I kicked into a higher gear, but as I passed what I had thought to be Second Generation Vampires, I did a double take. Captivated by the fallen Angels' song, they were unmoving as the Sealgaire soldiers slayed them. But some of the faces were warming now with rosy cheeks; some of them were once again becoming human.

As I sped by them, the Purebloods were coming out of their trance, and they roared, clashing with the fallen Angels. The hypnotic hymn was interrupted. The Sealgaire waded through the mix of Second Generation Vampires and renewed humans in a bid to help defend the Angels against the Purebloods.

I reached Zherneboh, who had Orifiel slung over his back. The Arch Angel's expression was desperate, and it was agonized. But I knew that, for him, the physical pain he was experiencing now was still preferable to slipping into the void of the third and transforming into the creature Eden had become.

Zherneboh knew I was behind him, but he remained focused on his task. He emitted a supersonic squawk and from within Pandora's box the last reserve of his Second Generation Vampires leaped out. They paid no attention to Darwin, who was shaking as he tried to unpack his equipment beside the diminishing fixed gateway to the third. Instead, they darted toward me.

Instinctively, I jumped high in the air, managing to snatch a Vampire on my way back down. I grabbed the short and stocky demon by the arm and threw him as though performing a shot put. As he sailed and then collided with the border of trees, I caught sight of Gabriel and Jonah pushing through the shrubbery, making their way to me. Following Gabriel, Iona wasn't far behind. I cursed under my breath, conflicted. I was angry that they were here risking their lives, and yet the sight of their faces made me more determined.

I fought off the Second Generation Vampires as I pushed forward. Zherneboh was still ahead of me, arriving at the ledge of the broken tomb a second before me. He dropped down inside, and I came just shy of grasping Orifiel's robes.

Directly to my left, a demon darted, but with my impaired vision, I didn't see him in time. He knocked me down and yanked me back.

Clinging to the ledge of the tomb, I kicked the demon away. I tightened my grip around the edge of the rock, and using it as leverage, I catapulted my weight forward. Transitioning from a handstand, I propelled myself into a flip, landing on my tiptoes directly in front of Zherneboh. I stood between him and the shrinking gateway.

I expected to find Darwin, as this was where I had seen him last, but he was gone. The only sign he had even been here was the case that had contained his crystal syringes, which was lying empty beside the rift. My heart almost stopped with the thought that his attempt to withdraw dark matter from the gateway might have caused him to be sucked into the third.

Zherneboh was faster than me; as I willed my gray smoke, he howled, and swiping with his talons, he struck me through the shoulder. My smoke stalled, and a moan escaped my lips as I hit the cold, hard ground. As I lay on my side, I began to shiver, while Zherneboh swung his adversary in the direction of the black rippling gateway.

Held suspended by Zherneboh, Orifiel hung limply and he met my eye. There was nothing left for him to do now but accept his fate. In a last broken breath, again he repeated my words back to me, as if confirming that I had fulfilled the promise I had once made him. *"No mercy."*

And as his light rose to the surface of his skin, as it electrified down his form, burning him from the inside out, my words took on a whole new form. Suddenly they meant something entirely different than they had before.

They were not the words of a Savior or of a hero.

They made me the villain.

As my skin stitched back together, once again I willed my gray smoke. Orifiel's wails quieted, his body smoldering as Zherneboh allowed the gateway to gradually pull the Arch Angel through. Orifiel's head and shoulders disappeared first, and his robes turned from white, to gray, to coal black, and then he was swallowed whole.

The gateway swelled, and then along with Orifiel, it disappeared.

The fixed gateway was sealed. No matter what form Orifiel took, on the other side, he would be trapped in the darkness, and Zherneboh was towering before me free as a raven. He had spent his entire existence seeking his vengeance, but I could tell from the way his top lip quivered, rising up over his fang in a dissatisfied snarl, that it was a hollow victory.

Revenge didn't equal restitution.

Still on the ground, in my palms my gray smoke manifested, and I expelled it forcefully.

Zherneboh reacted immediately.

His cloak, now soaking wet from the rain, lifted as he spun on the spot. Zherneboh became a dark blur as he twisted like a hurricane, and my smoke stuck to his cloak, not even getting close to his skin. It was as though he were swinging a wet towel in a room filled with smoke as he cleared it away effortlessly.

He pulled the last plume into his makeshift shield.

The hurricane in front of me subsided as Zherneboh came to a halt.

I lay exhausted on the ground.

I stared into the soaking puddles of what remained of his dark orbs. I blinked trying to escape the sight, and an image flashed in a single still frame. It was a screen shot of the future, of a world where Zherneboh roamed free.

A world that burned.

I was overcome with fear, an emotion a creature such as Zherneboh had no comprehension of, for it was entirely human.

My blood ran cold.

Zherneboh's fangs cracked, and he scooped me from the ground, raising his clawed hand and curving his body over mine. Déjà vu hit; I recalled the frozen Pureblood in the third. Time stalled, affording me the opportunity to marry the feeling with the sight. I knew how to defeat Zherneboh.

With a short, sharp breath, I plunged my thumbs into the darkness of his eye sockets. With my fingers pressing against his temples, I transferred my freezing temperature, and in the same way I had turned the river in Styclar-Plena to ice, so too did I freeze Zherneboh's soul.

The hot dark matter that circulated through his form plummeted, transitioning from a liquid to a solid. Zherneboh swayed erratically, and his skin bulged, reddening and then purpling under my touch. He tried to shake me off but his limbs were too stiff.

His jaw unhinged, but his shriek was trapped in his throat, his lizardlike tongue freezing before it could escape. His huge and heinous body became cemented where he stood, and only when my fingertips burned, sticking to the dry ice of his skin, did I recoil.

Zherneboh's head twitched twice, and then he became a statue.

I stared blankly at his face, and I was able to see beneath the demon, to the Angel trapped inside. I moved to his ear. "Go now, Eden." The orange mist of the aurora fogged at our feet, rising around the two of us, and as I twisted the once Arch Angel's neck, his body cracked. He shattered to infinity, leaving this world twinkling like stardust.

I exhaled.

No more rocks.

No more rivers.

No more revenge.

TWENTY-SIX

I EMERGED FROM THE CRATER IN THE GROUND. As the mist dispersed, the rounds of shots being fired ceased, and as I looked down to the garden, the Purebloods who were tangled between the Sealgaire and the fallen Angels were dying.

Some of the Pureblood masters cracked like porcelain and shattered on the spot. Others ignited and then, flashing with white flame, melted into great big puddles. It was as if we'd struck oil as the Purebloods' remains spewed everywhere, painting the red and white roses that bordered the garden black.

The fallen Angels' hymn had stopped completely, and now able to move, the Second Generation Vampires that remained were tripping over themselves. The fallen Angels disbanded, diving from the garden's edge into the river below. Reemerging, they bobbed up and down, their legs, which had glistened with a blue-green shimmer, transformed into fins. Over the thousands of years spent hiding from Zherneboh and his Purebloods in Earth's waters, the fallen Angels had evolved into sea creatures mankind had been telling stories about for centuries—mermaids.

My attention veered as behind the oak tree Iona's scream pierced the air. I raced over to where Gabriel, Iona, and Jonah were all engaged in combat against the last of the Second Generation Vampires that Zherneboh's shriek had released.

Though Jonah was mortal, he still wore his trademark arrogant smirk as he fought off the demon circling him, only now he had learned how to handle a silver weapon. With a crossbow slung over his shoulder, he swiped a silver blade as though he was an expert in the art of demon slaying. I wondered if it had been Phelan who had taught him to wield his weapons; if in the year I had been gone, the two had buried the hatchet and become friends as well as allies.

As the demon attacking Gabriel brought him down, I recognized the black gloves of the Vampire who had repeatedly gunned for my Angel's life—Hanora's mate.

Jonah was to my right. Gabriel was to my left. Both in combat. Both of whom I could help. But I could only help one. I had to choose.

I sensed Gabriel's more immediate danger and headed for him just as, from the corner of my eye, I saw the Vampire that Jonah was fighting launch itself to his shoulders and press its hands around Jonah's neck.

I heard him choke, and instincts took over.

I plowed into the Vampire with such force that as he met the ground he broke through it as if he were a meteor striking the Earth.

On my left, Iona was lunging toward the Vampire attacking Gabriel, thrusting a sharpened stake forward. With one hand at Gabriel's collar, the Vampire anticipated her run, stretching and sweeping her legs out from under her before she could get near enough to do any damage. Iona landed with a thud, and Gabriel shouted her name as she rolled onto her back, blood pooling from behind her ear.

Jonah hunched over, hands on his knees, as he gasped for air. But when he looked up, I was already gone, charging back toward Gabriel.

The Vampire got hold of the stake before Gabriel could reach for it, and with nothing but murder on his mind, he didn't care that I was rocketing toward him. He rammed the stake into Gabriel's chest, and blood spurted from my Angel's lips as his body convulsed.

I think I screamed.

I landed on top of the Vampire and he spat at me as my fingers tightened around his throat. But as I squeezed, his skin warmed against mine, and I knew what was happening. Right then I couldn't have wanted anything less, because I couldn't have wanted anything more than to watch him die slowly.

It was as though my insides hollowed out, and the emptiness was growing, providing me with a dark place in which to hide from what I was about to do.

Why should he get to live when Gabriel would not?

My hesitation allowed the Vampire to blink away his red flaming eyes, and they simmered into a glowing green.

I wept angry, hateful tears as the Vampire below me became human once more. The black spots of my irises expanded, swelling so that the darkness was all I could see, but I could still feel his pulse held within my hand.

I wailed, and then I let him go.

I matched my breaths to the shallow, difficult ones Gabriel was fighting to take.

I didn't want to turn around.

I didn't want him to die.

But I did, because he would.

I stopped in my tracks. Iona had crawled to Gabriel's side, and leaning over his chest, she pleaded with him to stay. Gabriel brought his hand up, but then his eyes met mine over her shoulder, and he hesitated in placing his palm to her cheek.

Gabriel's gaze on mine, his final breath was taken in a whisper.

His arm became limp, but Iona caught his hand as it fell.

Where Gabriel lay, the fallen leaves lifted and then twirled on the breeze, scattering into the fading orange hue of the aurora.

My legs could barely hold me up as I passed by Jonah. Staggering over to the cliff's edge, I stared down at the river.

It was so quiet.

It was so still.

Iona stopped sobbing and she began to sing. I knew what she was doing then. She was trying to reach out to Gabriel, to the one she loved and had just lost.

I recognized the refrain. It was the melody to the song Gabriel and I had once shared—a song that had connected him to me.

Though the lyrics that left Iona's lips were to "Danny Boy" and had been rewritten for the modern day, the song was one and the same—a song that connected her to the ones she loved the most.

Gabriel believed in meant-to-be, and I had told him to stop looking for signs and start listening instead. And wherever Gabriel was, finally, he heard her.

Iona lifted her face from Gabriel's chest. Around her neck was my crystal, still set in the ring Gabriel had given me. Dangling low on the chain, it began to glow. Tiny, twinkling stars exuded, drifting toward Gabriel's nose and mouth. Merging with the twirl of the luminous ribbons of the fading aurora, the glittering crystals wrapped around Gabriel, repackaging my Angel and gifting him to Iona.

His faded blue eyes renewed back to his bright sapphires, and a gleam shone over them as if they were being polished. And though I was looking to him, he chose to look to Iona instead.

Gabriel sat up. His hand still in hers, he kissed Iona's fingers.

She had saved him, where I could not.

Gabriel was no longer fallen.

And he was no longer my Angel. He was Iona's.

The rain stopped, and the trees swayed as the remaining members of my family climbed up the hillside to meet us. Brooke, Fergal, and Phelan, who had his arm around the shoulders of Cameron.

Cameron.

As I scanned the scenery, every surviving Second Generation Vampire stood now human. I thought back to what Malachi had told me. He'd said that with Zherneboh's end his house of cards would fall, and fall they had.

My thoughts went first to Jonah.

I had ended his Pureblood Master, and consequently every Vampire in Emery's line would have been restored back to human. But minutes after Emery had burned, Jonah had fallen into the third; the time distortion must have interfered with the venom leaving his system. But it finally had. And when it left him, it left Brooke, a Vampire he had created. And when her humanity returned, the venom she had spread left Fergal, too.

Zherneboh's end had caused the venom he had infected the Arch Angels with to evaporate, but after existing in such darkness they mustn't have been able to go back to who they once were. Unlike human beings, who live in the spectrum of the gray, the Arch Angels' souls were created and existed in a state of pure light, and so every one of the Arch Angels had died Purebloods.

But with their deaths, they had set mankind free.

I dug my nails into my palms. Zherneboh's venom had infected me, too, and I had been created an Angel, but I was still standing; I was still alive.

I felt the sting then.

Ruby red seeped between my fingers.

I was bleeding.

My eyes crossed as one of the blue butterflies left my skin and landed on the tip of my nose. It stretched its wings and took flight.

The same as Jonah, all along I had made choices, even when there hadn't seemed like there were any. I had accepted and embraced my gray soul, and I'd considered myself superhuman. And now, I was simply human.

I finally allowed my gaze to meet Jonah's and our eyes locked.

I had survived.

Jonah and I were both mortal.

I had exchanged my existence to save Jonah's, but Emit had said the fabric of the universe was being torn apart, that I was to stitch it back together, and that would be my payment, not my life as I had first thought.

I had free will.

And Emit had left me signs, hidden messages. . . . Why would he have sent me warning if my death here on this cliff top were decided? *Action and reaction*, Emit had said, *the nature of free will.*

What happened now was up to me.

Maybe Jonah and I could have a fairy-tale future. Maybe now I had earned and deserved a three-worded ending.

Underneath the bowing branches of the half-uprooted oak tree, Jonah moved his foot to the top of the tombstone that had acted as the door down into the cave, and he watched me.

Wait.

I remembered this.

I scanned the area but all I found was my family, clustering together at the roots of the oak tree. As I began to step forward, from over my shoulder a voice sounded, calling out my name.

I took a breath, but as I turned to my right there was no killer robot; instead a battered-looking Darwin stumbled toward me clutching his balled fists tightly to his chest.

I exhaled.

I glanced between my family and Darwin.

Deciding my family could live without me a little longer, I went to Darwin.

Though Darwin was hurt, he was alive, and relief filled me, overtaking my fear. A pained smile stretched across his face as though he were thankful to see me. As he approached, in that familiar way of his, he brought his hands up and slid his fingers between mine.

But as he clamped down, something sharp pierced through my palms.

The needles slid through my skin easily.

My gaze dropped as he angled his thumb and pressed

down over the tip of the syringes poking out between his thumb and forefinger, injecting me with hot dark matter.

"*Darwin?*"

He pulled me into his chest by our entwined hands, so to my family, it appeared that he was embracing me. My body flush with his, he hissed in my ear, "*If you wrong us, shall we not revenge?*" His breathing became heavy. "All this time it was you. Disguising yourself as some sort of superhero . . ." He trailed off and then whispered, "But you couldn't disguise your markings."

Darwin was referring to the tattoos that had grown up my arms after Ruadhan had died, tattoos that must have resembled the ones he had seen in the CCTV footage of the Pureblood who had murdered his brother in France.

Darwin thought I had killed Elliot.

I swallowed. "*She*, I, did kill someone, but his name was Bradley."

A mournful snort left Darwin. "My father used to go on about it, the importance of the family name. . . ."

As he held me still, the veins in my wrist began to sizzle and I felt sick.

"Looking at my business card, you said, 'That's a whole lot of letters.' Evidently you missed the only ones that held any real meaning."

I tugged backward, and this time he let me go.

"Darwin B. B. Montmorency." He paused. "Elliot shared

the family name, of course. Elliot *Bradley*-Boulle Montmo-rency. He preferred to go by his middle name."

The world seemed to warp, and a vision reflected out at me from the glass of Darwin's specs.

"Where are you going, lad?" Ruadhan's voice sounded.

In the barn in Neylis, Jonah rummaged around Gabriel's office. He flipped through a Rolodex, and selected a card filed behind a tab labeled with Gabriel's business partner's name. "Albert Bradley-Boulle Montmorency." The card simply read "Le Baron, Limoux." He tapped the club name into his cell phone quickly and then shouted back through the door, "Out."

At the bar in le baron, Bradley took up a barstool and conversed with me. "I'm only passing, a fleeting visit; my dad owns this place," he said as he eyed the crystal around my neck.

In the dark, under the faint flicker of a dying bulb, Bradley pulled a knife from his pocket. The girl in the shadow mani-fested through my skin and, throwing Bradley around the building's side, pulled him apart limb by limb.

"Are you sure you want to watch?"

With his father's hand on his shoulder, Darwin nodded, taking the tablet. He sat squarely in an armchair beside a fire-place, his elbows on his knees, and pressed play. . . .

DARWIN WAS UNSTEADY on his feet as he watched me refuse Gabriel's comfort. And as the tattooed markings the girl in the shadow had worn inked up my arms and stained over my skin, Darwin's eyes grew wide.

THE WORLD SLOWED.

The dark matter traveled toward my heart. In the third dimension, Malachi's design had churned it clockwise, because he knew what Darwin did: that if the particles collided they would destroy one another.

I was dizzy.

Darwin stepped backward, and then I saw it.

The round-headed robot with the green triangular eyes and hands dressed in black gloves.

God's name was Emit, and apparently death had a name, too.

His name was Marvin.

The robot had always been a sign, a warning pointing to Darwin. Above a logo for *The Hitchhiker's Guide to the Galaxy*, the robot was stitched on Darwin's T-shirt.

Though Darwin was angry, his expression showed sadness and he hesitated before he slunk away. I brought my arms out to steady myself, and the last ribbons of the aurora spiraled around me as a new day began to dawn.

From the cliff top, I looked down upon my family, and despite the searing heat of the boiling dark matter as it surged through my veins, I was so cold.

The white-gold aura that surrounded Gabriel's form was luminous against the gray backdrop. I smiled at the sight, and as he realized what was happening, he couldn't bring his lips to curve at their corners. But for all the memories and the love we had once shared, with his eyes he smiled back at me.

His stare remained fixed on me as he wrapped his arm around Iona's back. He placed his chin to her temple and then finally he looked away.

My gaze wandered to Phelan and Cameron, who stood side by side, straightened their backs and bowed their heads— a mark of respect.

Brooke paced toward me, but Fergal snatched her hand and tugged her back. She buried her head in his chest and cried.

And then my eyes locked with Jonah's.

We had almost made it—*almost.*

For a fleeting second, I felt the beat of the drum sound in time with my heart.

"I'm sorry," I mouthed.

And I was. For the things I'd said to him and for leaving him now. And though I was more afraid than I had ever been before, I wouldn't take back loving Jonah for anything.

Emit appeared, his jacket dazzling as he came forward, and I realized I was no longer teetering at the edge of the end, I was falling from it. I said to him in a whisper, "I'm not ready."

And as I blinked, in the gray of twilight, I saw Ruadhan. He went unnoticed as he drifted behind my family, and then I heard his voice in my head. "No one ever is, sweetheart."

My knees buckled, and I closed my eyes. With my arms spread wide, I fell.

Firm hands caught me by my waist before I could meet the ground, and I opened my eyes to find Jonah.

The rush of the darkness surged underneath my skin, and I warned him away. "Go!"

Jonah was mortal now, no longer in the dark, and no longer alone.

He didn't need me.

Tucking my hair behind my ear, he said, "You were living for me. Now let me die for you."

I stifled a breath. He held me tight as tears splashed down my cheeks and he rubbed the tip of his nose against my skin, mopping them away.

I wheezed. *"Jonah—"*

Shaking his head, he said, "Don't be afraid." His lips stretched into a contented smile, and he kissed me.

The hot dark matter collided in my chest, but I didn't feel it. All I felt was Jonah's truth as he whispered it in my ear. Keeping his promise, he gave me the only three words that mattered. The three words the end of my story truly deserved.

And in that one perfect moment I had clarity.

I knew the meaning.

Here in twilight, finally I found my place.

A strobe of light beamed, and together we burst into a billion butterflies.

EPILOGUE

JONAH

IN HER EAR, I whispered, "I love you."